emily's new everything

Elizabeth Allison

Black Rose Writing | Texas

First printing

This is a work of fiction. Names, characters, businesses, places, events, and incidents are either the products of the author's imagination or used in a fictitious manner. Any resemblance to actual persons, living or dead, or actual events is purely coincidental.

ISBN: 978-1-68433-689-0
PUBLISHED BY BLACK ROSE WRITING
www.blackrosewriting.com

Printed in the United States of America
Suggested Retail Price (SRP) $20.95

Emily's New Everything is printed in Cardo

*As a planet-friendly publisher, Black Rose Writing does its best to eliminate unnecessary waste to reduce paper usage and energy costs, while never compromising the reading experience. As a result, the final word count vs. page count may not meet common expectations.

For my Opa, who lives on
in the smell of tomato plants.

emily's new everything

chapter 1

The small white pee-soaked stick teetered on the side of my bathtub. Instead of waiting the recommended five minutes, the timer on my phone was counting down from half-an-hour. During those excruciating thirty minutes, I distracted myself by maniacally vacuuming my small bungalow. I had purchased the most expensive kind of pregnancy test they had at the drug store as an anxious offering to the fertility gods, because I was desperate to be pregnant. My husband Tyler and I weren't in a good spot. We'd talked about counseling, and scheduled date nights that mostly got cancelled. The last time I had gotten pregnant, Tyler and I decided to get married. Being pregnant again *had* to be the boost our relationship needed. A new baby would put us back on track as a family.

My three-year-old son Dante was asleep on the couch in front of *Thomas the Tank Engine*. Dante's birth changed me from Emily the daughter, friend, sister, and wife, to overwhelmingly and irrevocably just *Mom*. Since Dante had been born, nothing else really mattered. Maybe if I had put 'wife' higher on my list of roles in life, the rest of that day would have been different.

My phone started making a sound like an air raid siren to let me know the timer was up. I swiped to stop the noise and saw two texts from my BFF Michelle which I ignored. Nobody knew about the pregnancy test or even that I was trying to get pregnant. With the stick upside-down in my hand, I scrunched my eyes shut and took a deep breath before looking. Only one line appeared in the window. My eyes blinked back prickly tears. I thought about throwing the test against the wall, or shoving it down the toilet to clog up the pipes. Then I pictured calling an overpaid plumber to pull it out and the look on his condescending face when he held up what was wedged inside my toilet. How many tables would I would have to wait to earn enough money to pay said plumber? The hours and dollars would be better spent on Dante's college fund. The pregnancy test made an unsatisfying, muted clunk when it landed in the bathroom trash, wrapped in layers of toilet paper and shoved into an empty shampoo bottle in a double disguise. I thought about calling Michelle, or my other best friend Grace-Ann just to chat about anything else, but they didn't know about my covert operation, and I didn't trust myself not to tell them now.

The rest of my efforts at housecleaning were half-hearted at best. Counters got wiped but the coffee maker was not moved. Dirty towels made it as far as the laundry basket but nothing actually saw the inside of the washing machine. No one could ever accuse me of caring more about a clean house than about Dante, whose nap would be over any time now. Tyler was late getting home from work, which gave me time to stop the intermittent sniffles I was indulging in, post-disappointment. His shift had ended more than an hour ago but it wasn't terribly unusual for him to go out for a few drinks with his work buddies. Nevertheless, I was looking forward to having him home more than usual today.

Once the house was clean-*ish* and a healthy, multi-colored snack waited for Dante in a Bento box on the kitchen table, I woke him up. His eyes fluttered and his little bottom lip made a sucking reflex, then slowly his wispy eyelashes opened up and his eyes focused on me.

"Snack time, little man. You're going Trick-or-Treating later." Gently, I picked him up and settled him on my lap. "You're going to be a T-Rex, remember?" I made a quiet roaring noise and rocked him in my arms as he woke up. Dante had already worn his costume once for a picture at the mall. Getting him to smile for the camera had required a ridiculous dog and pony show by me, but it was worth it for the one amazing picture I got. The photo shop attendant tried hard to sell me on the way-more-expensive digital version of the photo, but the online coupon only covered one printed picture, so that was what we got.

Reflexively, I touched the screen on my phone to check for a text from Tyler and was surprised to see that it was almost five p.m. It was just about time to take Dante out for Halloween, and Tyler was still not home.

The weary fog that would be waiting to overtake me at the end of this day was threatening to roll in, and the thought of going out Trick-or-Treating made my chest heavy. The lead up to taking the pregnancy test, the waiting and then the disappointing result would be less agonizing tomorrow. Things would look better after a good night's sleep. Tyler had a day off work tomorrow and I hoped he would get up early with Dante. Then we'd have a family day out to the zoo or a movie. The three of us were overdue for some together time, even if we had to settle for what was surely the one millionth viewing of *Thomas the Tank Engine* on the sofa.

Mercifully, Dante decided tonight that he very much wanted to be a dinosaur, and started roaring ferociously the moment he saw the costume. By five-thirty I had him ready for action. Just as Dante and I were getting ready to leave without an appearance by or any communication from Tyler, the doorbell rang. I grabbed my green plastic bowl of Kit Kat bars, popped two in the pocket of my hoodie for later, and opened the door.

There stood Tyler. For a minute I was puzzled. Why would he ring the doorbell? Was he pretending to Trick-or-Treat? His eyes looked down and his hands were jammed into his pockets. Why on earth was he was standing beside Amy Ballantyne? Amy and I attended high school together and still shared the same group of friends. She worked with Tyler at the garage as an administrative assistant. I stared blankly at them.

"Can we come in?" Tyler leaned awkwardly against the railing on the front porch.

I glanced behind me and saw Dante sprawled on the living room floor, watching TV in his dinosaur suit.

"You live here." I raised one eyebrow.

The pretend-candle in the pumpkin on the porch flickered for a moment while I waited for something to happen.

"Emily, let's go into the kitchen for a minute."

I didn't budge.

Amy stood with her chin jutting out slightly and her arms crossed.

"Em, the kitchen. Please." He looked up to face me and his eyes were glossy. I almost felt sorry for him in my struggle to understand what was going on.

We moved into the kitchen and sat down at the table, still covered in bits of Dante's abandoned snack. *Our* table. Where we ate meals together with little Dante. But this was a different type of meeting.

"Emily, things haven't been going well between us. I...We..." Tyler started to falter and looked at Amy.

"The thing is, Tyler and I," Amy started. My open hand shot up involuntarily like a crossing guard, almost colliding with Amy's face.

"Wait a second." I had to stop Amy's verbal advance. My voice remained cold and I whisper-yelled, even though I wanted to scream. "*You*," My eyes met her gaze above the hand I was extending, "Don't speak. *Do not speak.*" Tyler, who seemed to have lost his own power of speech, lowered my hand and I addressed Amy again. "In fact, I'd like you to leave." She didn't move, so I looked her straight in her unflinching, perfectly made-up eyes and repeated myself more loudly. "Please leave."

Inexplicably, Tyler also started to get to his feet. A thought flitted across my mind. Maybe none of this was actually happening. It might be part of a bad dream or some kind of alternate reality.

I put my face in my hands and rubbed my un-made-up and decidedly exhausted-looking eyes.

"Tyler stays." My voice wobbled involuntarily through my fingers. It was all I could manage.

Tyler found his voice. "You better go, Amy. I'll be out in a minute." She stood and pushed her chair in slowly before walking back to the front door.

I perched on the edge of my chair at the table with Tyler, suddenly very aware of the time. It was now five forty-five, and we needed to get Dante out to Trick-or-Treat. Thirty minutes ago it had been the only thing on my mind. Now it was the only thing that still seemed real.

"Trick-or-Treating. We have to take Dante out. We can talk after that." A new thought pinged in my brain like a text message popping up on my phone. Maybe all of this would come to nothing, and Tyler and I would just pick up and keep on as normal now that Amy had left the kitchen. We'd sort it out like we always had. "Let's get going. He's already dressed..."

"Emily." I looked up and my gaze met Tyler's. When did he get so many wrinkles around his eyes?

Tyler put his hand over mine. I wanted to shake it off, tell him to go to Hell, or at least demand to know what was going on, but I couldn't. Just like waiting for the pregnancy test, not knowing was better than whatever news was coming. My eyes began dropping tears that fell on Tyler's hand, still heavy on mine.

"Emily," he started again. I forced myself to look up. "This isn't a marriage anymore. What we have... it's not enough. It hasn't been enough for a long time. It's not..." His voice faltered.

"We could try harder. We could see a counsellor, you know – never mind about the cost. We could buy a new book about relationships. Or take a holiday. We could have another baby just like Dante. We were so happy when Dante was born, remember?"

"Babe. That wouldn't fix our problems." He paused for a lifetime that was really only five seconds. Five long seconds with the kitchen clock ticking and Dante's TV show in the background. Then, resigned, regretful even – "It's too late, Em."

Time snapped back into focus and my hand pulled away from his. A spike of anger began creeping up my spine. "It's too late because of *Amy*." Her name caught in my throat. My voice was sad and I willed myself to sound angry.

"Not only because of Amy. It's just time to move on. We don't love each other. We hardly even like each other." If I had considered what he was saying, I might have admitted he was right. The drips on the table were joining together into pools. Time to pull myself together.

With my eyes averted from Tyler's, I decided to focus, absurdly, on Trick-or-Treating. I stood up abruptly.

"I have to take Dante Trick-or-Treating. Are you coming or not?" I picked up the napkin that earlier had been used to wipe yogurt off of Dante's chin, opened it up and blew my nose. Deciding against smearing yoghurt onto my eyelashes, I brushed the tears out from under them with the cuff of my sweatshirt.

"Emily, do you understand what I'm saying? I'm not sure you're getting this..."

"Tyler, I'm not an idiot. You're leaving me for Amy Ballantyne. You think this isn't a marriage anymore. You don't want to try to fix it." My voice broke and I hoped it was inaudible. "Am I leaving anything out?" Momentarily back in control, I became hyper-focused on the task at hand. A Lysol wipe swept the crumbs and smears off the table, and my oversized mom-purse was soon on my shoulder.

"Anything else you need to tell me Tyler? Because Dante and I have to get going. You'll be staying with Amy Ballantyne, right?" I didn't look right at him but out of the corner of my eye, I saw him nod, confused. Maybe if he had known me better, he wouldn't be so surprised at how I was handling the worst news of my life.

"You can get your things together after we're gone."

Wordlessly, Tyler went into the living room and said good-bye to Dante. Without looking back, Tyler walked into our bedroom. I scooped up my miniature dinosaur, shoved his fall jacket into my bag and carried him out to my car.

Outside, in Tyler's car I was bizarrely surprised to see that bitch Amy Ballantyne in the front seat. Her eyes widened when they met mine. I stared straight at her until she turned away. She looked like she was crying. I hoped I looked like I was not.

chapter 2

Tyler was still in the house and the light was on in our bedroom as I buckled Dante into his car seat and got behind the wheel. I threw the manual transmission into first and squealed – way louder than necessary – out of the driveway.

Once we were driving and Dante's infernal *Wiggles* CD was playing, I started to think about my immediate next steps. The plan had been to start Trick-or-Treating on our street, but now it seemed like a better idea to drive to Mom and Dad's first. After several minutes circling the streets between my house and my parents', I pulled in to Dunkin Donuts and joined the line for the drive-through.

"Can I have a hot chocolate, mom?" Dante chirped from the back seat.

"Not today, buddy. Mommy just needs a coffee on the way to Grandma's house. You'll get a candy bar later." Mercifully, he accepted this treat-economy and didn't kick up a fuss.

As I accepted the large orange and white cup through my car window, I told myself that frozen coffee with extra whipped cream is still technically coffee, so I hadn't told a lie. Now it was just after six, and it was properly dark. My thoughts were cloudy and confused. I didn't know what to do with Tyler's bombshell, who to tell, or what to tell them.

I could tell my parents that Tyler had left me, which would accomplish exactly nothing. My mother would judge me silently, or out loud, depending on how much wine she'd had to drink. I could drive to Michelle or Grace-Ann's, skip Treat-or-Treat and buy Dante candy to eat while I cried on my friends' shoulders. That seemed like admitting Tyler had actually left, which *maybe* he had not.

An almost-happy thought occurred to me out of the blue – *maybe it wasn't even really true.* Tyler said he was leaving. But possibly he wasn't *really* leaving. Maybe he was just having some kind of fling and he was going to come right back. Maybe if I never mentioned Amy's name again tonight, the whole ordeal would turn out to be just a bad dream.

The more I thought about it, the more that seemed like the most likely scenario was this was all a bad dream. Tyler was having a mid-life crisis. Admittedly, at twenty-eight, a very early mid-life crisis. Most likely, he would soon be back home, with all his clothes hanging in the closet and his toothbrush put back on the sink. Amy would pout at work and gaze at me jealously when I dropped off lunch for Tyler at the dealership, because she would know that I had won and our marriage was for keeps.

And so, I decided, as I sucked sweet sugary caffeine through the orange straw, there was no point telling my parents anything. Because there wasn't even anything to tell. Tyler was having a sort of surreal break with reality, he had left for the night, and he would most probably be back tomorrow. Or the next day. Definitely by the weekend. We would put all this behind us without any more fuss or bother. And my mother would not get to say, "I told you so," verbally or non-verbally, or remind me that she had never liked Tyler anyway.

When the car stopped in Mom and Dad's driveway, I allowed myself a quick look in the visor mirror. After a wipe with a tissue, the bits of mascara under my eyes vanished. I practiced my big, fake waitress-smile and resolved to continue with the original plan for the evening. Dante would never even know anything had happened on Halloween when he was three. He would remember his childhood unblemished by this little spat between his father and me. It wasn't even a spat. We didn't even yell. It was practically over already.

Trick-or-Treating had to be carefully staged so that I could post all the the requisite pictures on Instagram and Facebook. I paraded Dante up onto the porch to the double front door that no one ever used, after texting my mother to put the outside light on. Dante stood on the front step and posed, by himself, roaring and with my mother. He wriggled out of her arms, pushed past them and into the house. I posted the pictures as I walked up to the side door, with the heading of, "Trick-or-Treat!" The social media posts would help to maintain the shaky reality I was still convincing myself I was living. Hopefully.

Inside, Dad settled into his armchair with the paper, and Mom and I moved into the kitchen. My younger sister Clara let Dante peel open and eat a peanut butter cup. Clara was a freshman at Michigan State, where I fully intended to one day finish my own English degree. She adored Dante and it was a good thing because I frequently needed her to babysit while I worked evenings and weekends.

"Em, can I take him Trick-or-Treating?" Clara called, already putting on her jacket. "Come on, buddy boy. Let's get you more candy."

A wave of guilty relief flooded over me. The dread of knocking on doors and smiling at all the neighbors I grew up with lifted.

"Don't let him eat too much candy." Clara was already out the door when I sank onto the plastic-covered couch, overwhelmed and exhausted. There was something about the smell of this room and this couch that took me back to a much earlier time, before there was so much to feel guilty about.

The blanket I was wrapped up in just barely kept me from sticking to the clear plastic sofa covering. My father's paper rustled in the background, mixed with the sound of my mother fussing in the kitchen. I closed my eyes and pretended to be asleep to avoid a conversation with either of my parents. I didn't trust myself not to tell them what happened.

Pretending to sleep drifted into sleeping. Waking up with my eyes still closed, I heard Clara come back with Dante.

"What's up with her?" she said to no one in particular.

"Looks like she's tired." My father's voice was steady. His calm was never affected by other people's level of excitement.

Small feet tapped across the floor and I opened my eyes just in time to see my son catapult himself up onto the couch and snuggle into me. I pulled him close and sat up. The memory of the evening's main event bled back into my waking thoughts. I rubbed my temples and squeezed Dante close for one more second before getting up.

I couldn't avoid at least a brief conversation with my mother before we left, especially since I had barely said anything to her before crashing into sleep on the couch. The secret to talking to my mother was to keep it light and breezy, so I started chatting with her about one of her friends who had come into the restaurant where I waited tables.

Mom peppered me with vaguely disapproving questions about my work, what Dante was eating, and whether I was keeping up any sort of exercise regime. I thought I had gotten away without mentioning Tyler until we got up to leave.

"Where's Tyler tonight?" my mother asked casually.

I took a shallow breath and didn't look at her.

"Working late," I lied, trying to sound casual. I quickly knelt beside Dante and took his hand. "Come on, kiddo. I'll race you to get your shoes on."

"Will you all be here for Sunday dinner? I need to decide what size roast to buy. Roasts are on sale this week, you know, Emily. You should pick up a couple for your freezer."

I was about as likely to cook a roast of beef as I was to roast a wild boar on a spit on the front lawn. I told her what she wanted to hear. "Yeah, we'll both be there." Lie number two.

"Will you bake me some of those shortbread cookies I like?" Clara called from my former spot on the couch, not looking up from her phone.

"Sure. No problem, sis." Lie Hat-Trick.

"Bye Gramps!" called Dante, as I let the screen door slam behind us on the way to the car.

chapter 3

On auto-pilot, I got home, stashed all the candy in the garage fridge, and kept it together until Dante was tucked into bed with his Peter Pan audiobook playing. I peeled away my clothes and got into the scalding shower, where I sat down, hugging my knees to my chest and started to cry. I allowed myself to consider, for the first time, the possibility that my marriage was over, that Tyler might not come back, and that I might be on my own forever. As the hot water pelted me, so did the realization of what my brain had miraculously spared me from until that moment: Tyler was having *sex* with Amy Ballantyne. Tyler and I had sex infrequently, but lots of married people had infrequent sex. All the magazines I read but didn't buy in the grocery store check-out line said so. It was normal when you were married with a small child.

When was the last time? Recently enough for me to purchase the failed pregnancy test. About two weeks ago. We were both quite drunk after a dinner party. There was a lot of fumbling and in retrospect, urgency. Before that...I couldn't remember. Months. But at the thought of Tyler having sex with someone else, the nausea twisted back into my stomach and I retched.

With my hands wedged against the wall of the shower and the top of the tub, I stood up. The hotter-than-usual water hit my face and stung my eyes. I stayed in the stream as long as I could stand it, and then turned the water off, forgetting to use soap or wash my hair. When I realized my mistake, my hand numbly turned the faucet back to the left and I lathered up. The tears started again when I noticed that Tyler's razor was gone, but he had left his shaving cream. Maybe he had nicer shaving cream at Amy's. Maybe Amy didn't only buy half-price shaving cream.

The water started to cool, a sign that our ancient water heater was emptying. I got out of the shower and put my pyjamas on. I looked at the messy, unmade bed Tyler and I had both woken up in that morning on what might be our last day of being a family. I started to lie down on my side of the bed but it was too much to bear. I couldn't stand the smell of Tyler on the sheets. I grabbed my headphones, a duvet, and my pillow and tiptoed to Dante's room to sleep on the floor. I'd passed out on Dante's floor more times than I could count waiting for him to fall asleep.

With my earbuds plugged into my phone, I scrolled through my limited music library. I moved past albums that reminded me of Tyler, and all the kids' music I kept for

Dante. With my eyes closed, my mind spun over and over around Tyler and his last words to me. "It's not a marriage anymore. Do you understand what I'm saying? I'm not sure you're getting this."

Finally, tossing and flipping my pillow to find a cool spot that wasn't wet with tears, I fell asleep listening to John Denver sing about saying goodbye.

chapter 4

The week after Tyler drove away with Amy Ballantyne closed around me like a muddy puddle soaks through running shoes. With every passing day, it seemed a little less certain he would be coming back through the door of our house and into my bed.

When I waited tables at Eugene's, Tyler sometimes came over and watched Dante. It was torture to have Tyler in the space we once shared, but he was Dante's father and I didn't know what else to do. More importantly, I hoped that being in our house would remind him of how much he needed me. I spelled out my expectations very clearly to him, whisper-shouting and including the punctuating pointing finger I had vowed never to copy from my mother.

"You are *not* (point) to have *that woman* (point, point) in OUR HOUSE." I used the word 'our' on purpose but if Tyler noticed, he didn't care.

I wanted to tell him to stay out of my bedroom but couldn't, because I still wanted him *in* our bedroom more than I had ever wanted anything in my entire life. I still mostly believed the 'he'll come back when he's good and ready' lie I repeated to myself over and over. I hadn't dared tell my parents, or anyone else, that Tyler was gone. Every evening I spent hours Googling 'how to get your husband back from another woman' but that was as close as I came to admitting that Tyler might actually be gone, to anyone, including myself.

Work was a good distraction. I had been waitressing at Eugene's for about almost two years, and it was a decent gig. Steady money and nice people. I knew my classmates who had finished college and gone on to get 'real jobs' looked down on me but I didn't care. Eugene's was a slightly upscale mom and pop place that almost overlooked the lake. The patio only opened four months of the year due both to the harshness of the Michigan winters and Eugene's reluctance to put heaters outside to extend the season. The clientele were the wannabe-classy elderly population of St. Clair Shores. In the back room we catered meetings and small parties. There was a salad bar on the weekends and we hand battered-our own fish on Fridays, which was a big draw.

Eugene, the owner, was from Greece and hired cooks who liked to yell obscenities at the waitresses in Greek, even though they all spoke English as well as I did. It was a right of passage to be screamed at in the height of a busy weekend lunch. After the first few times, it became easier to ignore. The odd time one of the kitchen staff threw a plate against the wall for effect and they all laughed uproariously, which at least temporarily stopped the yelling.

I worked mainly from noon to eight pm. Breakfast shifts were the best, and usually only the wives of Eugene and his old Greek buddies got to work them. People tipped more at breakfast than in the evening, and it took less effort to wait the tables and booths in the mornings because everyone only ordered one course. Drink refills just required walking through the dining room every ten minutes with a pot of coffee. The breakfast menu was cheap. People didn't mind throwing a few extra dollars on top of a thirty-dollar check. When the bill was already sixty or seventy bucks for a table of four, people tipped less.

The diner side of Eugene's had three rows of tables from the front doors back to the kitchen. The row of booths on the wall was called, 'wall,' appropriately. The center row was 'middle' and the one closest to the Formica covered counter we called 'front.' Behind the high counter were the soda fountain, coffee maker, and dessert cooler with sliding glass doors and little rows of Jell-O and gross rice pudding.

Technically the counter belonged with 'front' but no one ever ate there except Eugene's daughter Anastasia, who helped out pouring tea and soda when she wasn't at ballet lessons, or horseback riding lessons, or clarinet lessons. I also once heard her talking about scuba diving lessons. Eugene would have paid for her to scuba dive off Niagara Falls if she asked him. I tried to avoid Anastasia. If she got pissed off at me during a shift, she would pour my drinks wrong or pour the tea pots so full that I burnt my fingers on the way to the tables. Anastasia was a real gem.

The tips were best in the 'wall' section. The evening three days after Tyler left, I won the coin toss. The other girls at work weren't exactly my friends, but they were mostly friendly. All of us hated Eugene's wiry, hypercritical wife Bernadette equally, and that gave us something in common. Bernadette took all the best shifts, and would deliver an order to my table if I showed up an *instant* late picking up my food from the brightly lit window between the restaurant and the kitchen. The rule was that the waitress who delivered the food to the table got the tip. Bernadette used the technicality to scoop our tips whenever possible. All the waitresses knew to block her way 'by accident' when we saw her beelining to the pick-up window.

The money at Eugene's was okay, and Tyler made a pretty respectable salary with commissions at the dealership. My comparatively modest paycheck went toward the household expenses, and I saved my tips, splitting them between an education fund for Dante and my own spending money. Since Tyler had walked out I'd become a little less friendly and attentive to my customers, and I worried that I would see a corresponding difference in my tips.

Zoe was the closest thing I had to a friend at Eugene's. She had been working there a year longer than me. While Anastasia finished up the only table left from a busy lunch shift, we headed down the long narrow hallway to the back door to escape the smell of frying oil and singed toast for a fifteen-minute break.

Zoe was a smoker. During her break, she slipped out the back door to have a cigarette. I often spent my break in the staff booth drinking Dr. Pepper, but today I craved adult conversation. The flame of Zoe's lighter shook in the biting wind before catching on the end of her menthol cigarette. She inhaled deeply and breathed out, audibly relieved. I considered whether taking up cigarettes might help me get through my current crisis.

We stood in silence while Zoe smoked.

"What's the deal with you? You've had a face like a smacked ass for the last couple of days." Zoe was a little rough around the edges and never cared if her words were abrasive and blunt. She seemed more dangerous than me and it was at the same time scary and appealing.

"Nothing. I'm fine." I took a deep breath, accidentally inhaled a lungful of the smoke swirling around me, and coughed.

"It's none of my business. Just seems to me something's wrong with you is all." It would have been better if she had pried openly so I could get angry with her. Unbidden, tears hit the back of my eyes and were soon spilling down my face.

"Tyler left me." I blinked rapidly but kept control of my voice. The words sounded strange coming out of my mouth. "For someone else." I delicately wiped my eyes on the cuff of my uniform shirt and dug into my apron for a tissue or a napkin.

"He's an asshole, you know."

"What?" Her candor caught me off guard.

"Tyler. He's an asshole." She remained matter-of-fact. "He made a pass at me at the Christmas party last year."

"Zoe! He did *not*. Besides, you're supposed to be my friend! I've just given you the worst news of my life, which

I haven't even told anyone else and you're not making me feel better." This was not how I expected my reveal to go.

"I'm not really your friend. We just work together." She had me there. I'd never made any attempt to be more than collegial with Zoe "If you asked me last week or last month, I would have called him an asshole then too. You picked a strange person to confide in, and a weird time to do it. We have to be back inside in three minutes."

Without waiting for my reply, she turned around and held the door for me and crushed her cigarette butt under the heel of her black non-slip shoes. I went to the staff bathroom to splash cold water on my face and try to salvage my dignity.

I wasn't even mad at Zoe. Despite the harsh delivery, she told me the truth, and she wouldn't tell anyone else my news. The exchange made me realize that I needed to find someone better to share my situation with, preferably a listener who would give me a whole lot more sympathy and advice than Zoe.

chapter 5

I glanced up at the clock on the wall; it was three-thirty and my shift ended at eight. I grabbed a couple of contraband fries from the plate Dean the dishwasher always slid onto the soup station when it wasn't busy. We all kept it away from the prying eyes of Eugene and Bernadette. I picked up my phone from the stainless-steel counter of the waitress station and my thumbs started flying. There were only a few diners drinking coffee in the restaurant, but Eugene was a total hardass about using our phones while we worked. Within seconds of seeing me with my phone, he would tell me to refill all the ketchup bottles on the tables.

I sent the first text to Clara -

Can you pick up Dante pls from my house at 5 and take him back to Mom and Dads for the night? Something came up at work. I'll get him in the morning.

Then one to Tyler -

Clara is going to pick D up at 5. Don't talk 2 her. Pack D a bag plz. I paused, then erased 'plz' and hit send.

Now the text that would matter, a group text to Grace-Ann and Michelle -

Need to talk tonight. Working until 8. Meet up?

Just as I hit send on the last message, I saw Eugene beelining it for me. I grabbed a clean cloth and a spray bottle full of vinegar to wipe a row of tables before I ended up with ketchup all down the front of my shirt.

Before I had time to clean too many tables, the supper rush started. Zoe threw out what remained of the forbidden fries because we needed the space to fill soup bowls. So long as we stayed behind the screen at the waitress station, Eugene allowed us to drink soda from the fountain. We had Dr. Pepper on tap, which I considered a private victory, and I drank gallons of it during shifts. I figured all the walking I did burned off most of the calories.

When we were kids, my dad periodically took Clara and me to a greasy spoon called The Westside. It was just far enough away to be an exciting outing. The restaurant didn't mind if Dad parked in their lot for an extra hour in the middle of the afternoon, so after lunch, we always drove to a playground nearby with taller slides and better climbers than the ones near our house, as well as a fantastically dangerous roundabout. This restaurant had Dr. Pepper and it was during these trips that I fell in love with the stuff. My mother wasn't present to fuss over how much soda we were drinking, and my father let the waitresses refill our drinks while he leafed through the *Detroit Free Press*. I had a vivid memory of the cold blast of the air conditioning hitting my face when Dad pushed open the door of the restaurant in the heat of July. I wondered if the romanticized memory of The Westside was part of why I was happy waiting tables at Eugene's at twenty-five years of age, when most of my peers were starting their actual grown-up careers.

Mercifully, Eugene let us close up at right at eight that night. Sometimes people came in quarter to or ten to eight, and he insisted the cooks turn the grill back on and serve them. In those cases, the waitresses flipped a coin and the person who lost would be stuck at work until nine or nine thirty waiting for one table. Tonight, we were lucky.

At eight-oh-one I checked my phone while pulling on my coat.

From Clara -

Np.

From Tyler-

She picked him up. I took some more of my stuff from the house.

From Michelle –

My place. I have wine. Bring chips and dip. Not Doritos.

Michelle was practical and bossy, both of which I considered good qualities in a friend. I grinned at her predictability and quickly typed a text back on the way out to my car -

You are not the boss of me.

I started the car. Even for early November, the steering wheel was cold under my hands. I drove to Michelle's house, stopping at a 7-Eleven to get three kinds of chips, two dips, a large bottle of cheap vodka, a couple of two-liter bottles of Dr. Pepper, and for good measure, two bags of Cool Ranch Doritos. I paid mostly in ones and change, using all the tips I had made in what had been a relatively slow shift.

I got into the car with all my sugar, fat, alcohol and carcinogens shoved into flimsy plastic bags that would probably rip apart before I got to Michelle's. On the short drive to see my friends, I weighed up the pros and cons of telling them about Tyler, who had not returned home, as I had hoped he would, and instead moved more and more of his stuff into Amy's. It didn't bode well for my 'this is just a phase and he will be back soon' theory.

Telling Michelle and Grace-Ann would help. If Tyler did come back, it wouldn't be until he got this ridiculous phase out of his system. Part of me still feared that telling Michelle and Grace-Ann would make this nightmare real, but a bigger part of me knew it was already happening, and I needed support from the women who had been my two best friends since middle school. Maybe they would help me figure out what to tell my mother, because she was next on the list. I figured my mother would quite likely have a heart attack, die, and then find a way to blame me from beyond the grave.

Michelle and Grace-Ann greeted me together at the front door before I knocked. The comforting scent of Michelle's favorite candles burned in several rooms of the house. I left my shoes by the door, dropped the bags of food on the kitchen table, and headed to Michelle's bedroom to change into the leggings and sweatshirt in my backpack. Then I gave myself an all-over spritzing with the body spray on her dresser to cover up the smell of grease that always clung to my hair after a shift.

Both my friends were waiting in the living room, perched on the sofa expectantly.

"How are you *doing*?" Grace-Ann asked purposefully.

Shit. They already knew.

I sat down on the edge of the couch far enough away to avoid the physical contact I knew would set me off completely.

"Yeah, uh…fine. I'm okay." My gaze shifted from one of them to the other as they waited. "I take it you know about Tyler." I had every intention of being stoic and deadpan about the whole thing. There was nothing to be gained from blubbering now.

However, as I looked down to examine my bitten-past-the-quick nails, tears involuntarily tumbled down over my face, faster than I could blink them away. Before I knew it, my friends were on either side of me with their arms around my shoulders while I sobbed. Michelle pressed a tissue into my hands. I blew my nose repeatedly and tried to regain my composure.

After ten minutes of sniffling and blubbering, I could just about speak again. A glass of what I correctly assumed was vodka and Dr. Pepper appeared in front of me, along with three different bowls of chips, including the Doritos which Michelle had put front and center. A small laugh caught in my throat when I saw the bowl of chips none of us liked.

"I don't even like Cool Ranch Doritos. I just bought them to spite you." I managed a watery smile.

"I know," said Michelle. "That's why I opened them and threw away the bags so you would have to eat them all. To spite you back."

Grace-Ann spoke next, earnest. "Tell us all about it."

"What do you already know? How did you hear?" How stupid of me to think someone wouldn't have told them. St. Clair Shores was not a big enough town to keep secrets.

"I ran into Amy at the mall yesterday. She told me." Grace-Ann had been on the cheer squad with Amy in high school. Michelle and I were more the school newspaper types, but Grace-Ann excelled at athletics. She was invited to more and cooler parties than the two of us and brought Michelle and I, who were not invited, with her. When she pledged a sorority, she spent time with girls who didn't need part-time jobs to pay for school like Michelle and I did. We told ourselves we were mysterious and interesting when we tagged along to Frat parties we weren't invited to.

"There's not much to tell. Tyler left. He pulled me into the kitchen with that *bitch* Amy Ballantyne, had the nerve to bring her into our *house*..." my voice wobbled again but I got it back, "and told me he was leaving me for her. And I keep thinking..." I gasped for air, "I keep thinking he will come back..." For the first time since Tyler left, actual, ugly choking sobs overtook me. Grace-Ann pushed the drink into my hand and I gulped at it until the vodka started to fuel the anger rising up inside me.

"I keep hoping he'll change his mind, you know? Because what the actual hell is he thinking? How could he just leave like that? And why would he be leaving me for *her*?" I looked at them intently. "Is she better looking than I am? Is she smarter? She's not even younger. We're the same age! You're supposed to leave your wife for someone younger than you! She's not even *thinner* than me!" For some reason this seemed like the ultimate affront to my dignity. Sipping my vodka-Dr. Pepper emboldened me.

"Well," said Grace-Ann tentatively, "maybe he had other reasons. You know, maybe something else is going on? You never know why people do things."

"That is *not* the right answer," Michelle came back immediately. "The right answer is, 'He is an asshole. He doesn't deserve you.' And it's true, incidentally. He is an asshole and this is an asshole move. She's a bitch, like you said, and also a homewrecker." Michelle's eyes told me she believed what she was saying. "But more importantly, he probably *will* come back. And even if he does, *screw him.*" My eyebrows raised as I looked at her. "Seriously, Em, screw him. You're young, good-looking and smart and awesome." She hesitated, looked at me and saw I was unconvinced before adding, "Seriously. I just know there's someone out there for you."

"Yeah. Plenty of fish in the sea. I know." I picked up a chip and scooped up as much French onion dip as possible. "But this fish is Dante's dad." More tears rolled down my face. "What am I going to tell Dante?"

The rest of the evening blurred into vodka, Dr. Pepper, and my tears, all flowing in relatively equal measure. Michelle put *Dirty Dancing* on to try to improve my depressed state. We got as far as Baby and Johnny dancing in the off-limits cabin before I started blubbering all over again.

chapter 6

The next morning, I dragged my hungover, unshowered body to my parents' house to pick up Dante and face the music. If Grace-Ann and Michelle knew about Tyler and Amy, then chances were Clara also knew, and therefore so did my mother. I couldn't put off telling them any longer.

At 7-Eleven, the guy from last night still stood behind the counter. I bought the strongest gum they had to make up for the fact that I'd last brushed my teeth before my shift yesterday. Not the greatest start to the morning. I grabbed a few loose Twizzlers off the counter for Dante and a couple of packages of Starburst for Clara. This was going to be a terrible conversation and starting with gifts wouldn't hurt. In the car, I decided donuts and coffee would be good too, even though I knew buying food was just a tactic to delay facing my parents' disappointment.

Mom and Dad lived in a modest house on a cul-de-sac. They had moved there thirty years before and the neighborhood looked different from the one of my childhood. Many of the old neighbors had already sold their similar-sized houses to developers who built, not *McMansions* exactly but definitely *McBigHouses*. My parents were always very tight-lipped about money but Clara and I suspected they had been approached about selling and had declined. We weren't sure if they were maybe holding out for a better offer, or just digging in their heels on principle.

Walking into their kitchen door was like going through a time warp. Everything looked exactly like it had when I was a small child. In the summer, my mother worked in the kitchen, cooking and baking even in the hottest of weather. In the winter, she knitted and sewed. There was almost no room for grass in the back of the house because my father had filled all the space with vegetables, especially tomatoes and peppers. My parents had a tacit agreement: Dad grew the tomatoes, onions, peppers, and eggplants, and my mother made the sauces and pickled things, as applicable. They were as close to self-sustaining as possible in a city, and bought very little produce at the grocery store. If he could, my father would surely have kept cows and pigs, built a shed and then butchered them himself.

The house had four bedrooms. One was my parents', the door to which stayed closed. The second bedroom was Dante's. As their only grandchild, he had a room to himself complete with a loft bed my father designed and built with Dante's "help." The room had all the toys and games saved from mine and Clara's childhoods, and many new ones purchased just for Dante. Mom and Dad didn't believe in children watching TV. When Dante was at their house, he helped in the kitchen and the garden or played with the most beautiful wooden blocks and educational toys I had ever seen.

The basement bedroom was Clara's. She lived at home while she attended Michigan State. Clara worked part-time at Panera Bread and selflessly helped me out with babysitting while somehow keeping a 3.8 GPA.

The fourth and smallest bedroom served as a tiny sitting room. My parents watched *Jeopardy* and *Wheel of Fortune* most evenings while Dad peeled and sliced apples and oranges. They ate these between shouting the answers to the puzzles at the small TV screen. If they were still awake, they watched until the news at ten. I knew my mother also watched *Young and the Restless* when my father worked in the garden. She also made his doctor's or dentist's appointments during the time *Y&R* aired, or sent him out on errands and watched it in secret. Dad was completely aware of what was going on, but went along with the charade to humor her.

The rest of the house was covered in plastic, and freezing all winter, the thermostat turned up marginally only in the kitchen and living room. Knick-knacks were dusted daily, tables were waxed but never used. When Father Bob came over once a year to bless the house, Mom removed the plastic ceremoniously and put it in the basement. When he left, she cleaned both the couch and the plastic before she put it back on.

My father, Emilio Esposito, left the rural south of Italy to come to America and work in the auto industry in Detroit. He was promised opportunity and prosperity, one of many young Italian men who hoped to "trovare il suo America", or "find his America…" a popular phrase among his friends who longed for a new and better life across the pond. What he actually found was a job at Ford, working long hours until the bleakness of the Motor City landscape became too much for him. In his mind's eye, he still pictured his village in Calabria, where he could look down over olive groves to the sea beyond. After working every shift he could get for five years and saving every spare dollar, he quit and bought his first tiny house in St. Clair Shores. The then-small community had a sizeable Italian population and St. Lucy's Parish still celebrated mass in Italian every Sunday. He met my mother Franca at church, a dark-haired beauty from a village not far from his own. Franca sang in the choir every Sunday and bewitched my father, supposedly with her fierce wit and dancing skills, though I rarely saw the former and doubted the latter still existed.

Dad worked for anyone who would hire him in St. Clair Shores for two years, then landed an unofficial apprenticeship with a drywalling company. He bought our house soon afterward. Eight years later, he bought the drywalling company. He worked six days a week, covered in plaster until the day he turned sixty-five. The next day, he gave all his drywalling tools to a young man who reminded him of himself, headed to Home Depot, and bought the supplies he would use to build the garden he had been planning in his head since he left Detroit thirty years earlier.

While Dad pursued the American dream, Clara and I were born. We were brought up in an Italian-American culture surrounded by people who wanted to be more American than Italian but always found comfort in the things that reminded them of the old country. We were given decidedly American names echoing those of Italian family members. I was named after my father, and Clara after his mother, Chiara. Mom and Dad never returned to Italy even to visit, despite Clara and I offering to buy them tickets for Christmas several times. They had a standard reply when people asked why they wouldn't go: "There's nothing for us there. Our lives are here now."

Divorce was not something either of my parents believed in.

I fished a Tigers cap out of the back seat of my car, pulled it down over my greasy hair, and surveyed myself skeptically in the rear-view mirror. Ridiculously weighed down with a tray of drinks and a box of donuts, I eased myself out of the car and began the heavy walk up to my parents' side door. Before I made it up the steps into the kitchen, I heard the happy chatter of Dante and my dad. They were sitting at the ancient, spotless Formica table.

"Gramps, where does this go?" he held up a piece to a puzzle that looked too difficult for him.

"That one has a straight edge. It goes in that pile."

"With the edges," Dante said proudly.

"That's right. Now, what piece goes here?" The puzzle was in its early stages. My father had an amazing bond with Dante. When I was young he was always working. It thrilled him to be so important to his young grandson.

I stood in the door for a few minutes watching, before Dante heard me taking off my shoes and came running.

"Mommy!"

"Did you have fun with Gramps?" He nodded into my middle where he had buried his head. My father took the drinks and donuts so I could hug him back. "We're going to go in a few minutes. You play in your room for a little while and then you can have a donut."

Clara and my mother materialized and stood in the kitchen, watching me wordlessly. I sank down at the table, in the seat that had been mine at dinner time since I was old enough to sit up by myself.

"Have a seat. I have something to tell you."

"We know." Clara sounded devastated. She was absolutely bursting to talk about it. "We know all about it. How have you kept quiet? No one else has kept quiet I can tell you. That bitch Amy is all over town talking about how she and Tyler are *finally officially together*." The exaggerated air quotes she used made me smile weakly.

"*Language*, Clara." My mother broke her silence.

"It sounds like there's not much more to tell you. Tyler left me. For the aforementioned Amy Ballantyne. To be honest I'm sick of saying her name. I thought he would come back after a few days so I didn't say anything. It's, uh," my voice broke and there was silence while I regained my composure, "It's not seeming too likely at this point." I was determined not to cry again.

"Well," said my mother, "you look terrible." This was a typical reaction from her, but I was too defeated and exhausted to get into an argument about how inappropriate she was being.

For the rest of the short conversation, my mother inquired none-too-delicately about what I might have done to fix 'the situation.' The clear implication was that I had done something to cause said situation. Telling my parents felt like a huge step in the process of disentangling myself from Tyler, and trying to carve out some new kind of existence without him. There was no hiding from something once my mother knew about it. Once it was finished, I got up to leave.

Clara hugged me and promised to stop by my house later.

With Dante in the back of the car and the reclaimed donuts on the seat in the front "*We don't eat food like that, Emily. You might as well take them home*," I drove in the direction of home. Within the hour, I was once more crying under a too-hot shower while Dante dozed in front of *Bob the Builder* on the couch.

When I returned to the living room wrapped in my robe, Dante was on the couch with the box of donuts. The paper lid was flipped backwards and he was starting in on what looked like his second chocolate sprinkle. Instead of telling him off, I plopped myself down on the couch and grabbed a powdery jelly-filled, not caring about the crumbs and white sugar all over my robe and the couch.

"What are you watching?" I snuggled into him and breathed in the scent of his baby-shampooed hair.

"*Young and the Restless*." He was nonchalant.

"What?" I jerked my head up and saw Victor Newman in close frame on the screen. "Why are you watching that?"

"Grandma watches it," Dante spoke through a mouth full of donut. "He's Victor."

I weighed up my options in this bizarre situation, looked down at the contented Dante and decided that starting tomorrow, I would turn this around and start being the mother of the year. Definitely tomorrow. Maybe even today, because curled up on the couch eating donuts for lunch with a three-year-old while watching *Young and the Restless* was surely my parenting rock bottom.

chapter 7

Soon, Thanksgiving was approaching. It had been weeks since Tyler walked out, and his things were steadily disappearing out of the house. Although we had still not discussed finances, every month Tyler transferred money to our joint account to cover his half of the mortgage and the utilities. The fact that we couldn't continue like this indefinitely was something I repeatedly pushed out of my mind. Tyler saw Dante either by visiting him at my home or taking him out to Amy's house. *Tyler and Amy's house.* This was the new normal and I felt gradually less and less nauseous when I said the words in my head. A dwindling part of me still believed that if I played along quietly at this complicated game he had created, Tyler would see sense. Most of me was busy with all the things that still had to be done in the absence of Tyler, like working and raising our son.

In the meantime, I messed with Tyler's head in quietly passive-aggressive ways. He hadn't yet moved all of his clothes out of the closet in the master bedroom. Carefully, I removed all the collar stays from the dress shirts I had always lovingly maintained so he would look professional at work. Additionally, I snipped the top button off of several of them, picking the threads out one by one with a pair of tweezers so my work wasn't obvious.

I slipped the insole out of one of his beloved cowboy boots, poured just a dribble of juice from the can of tuna I was using to make Dante's lunch into the bottom and carefully replaced the liner, then put the boots in the garage, but neatly, as if they had been stored there all along. I typed Amy Ballantyne's name and address into the webpage of every questionable religious group, every product trial, and every company's 'contact me' page I could find with hands still sometimes shaking with anger.

These pranks kept me occupied for a while and fulfilled my need for revenge and vindication, but they didn't change the fact that a terrible post-Tyler reality was settling in and there was nothing capable of stopping it.

Thanksgiving dinner at my parents' house was tense, partly because Dante was eating with Tyler's family and partly because my mother and I weren't speaking. Afterwards, I went over to Michelle's for a girls' evening fueled by wine left over from Michelle's last birthday party. A tipsy Grace-Ann was insisting on painting my nails a bright teal color with the ring fingers canary yellow. Michelle splashed white wine into a clean glass for me as I splayed my fingers obediently over a towel on the coffee table.

"You're smudging it. Sit still," Grace-Ann was bent over my hand intently. "Do you want a pattern on the yellow one?"

"A pattern? What are you, an esthetician now? When did you learn how to do a pattern with nail polish?" The wine quickly started to lift my spirits and I surprised myself by feeling happy and even playful.

"I can't really. But I thought it sounded good and I hoped you would say no." She blew on the top coat. "There. Don't touch it."

Michelle surveyed her own nails and fanned her hands out in the air.

"We should do something." She sipped her wine, careful not to smudge her polish on the glass.

"It's Thanksgiving. What could we possibly do? Everything is closed. Except for Black Friday and I'm not doing Black Friday. Remember what happened the last time? That woman with the plasma TV almost killed you. I decided that day three years ago that whatever discounts were available were not worth the risk of mortal danger."

"No, I mean we should *plan* to do something," Michelle persisted. "We never do anything. Let's do something… *different*." With her toe, she nudged Grace-Ann who was glued to her phone, her thumb scrolling.

She looked up and gave Michelle about half her attention.

"Huh? Yeah. Ok. Let's do something. What do you want to do?"

"I just… can never do anything because of Dante. And work… we all work at different times. That's why we never do anything." Even almost-tipsy, I was leery of what

Michelle's 'something' might mean. My work schedule was erratic, and the nights I wasn't working belonged to Dante.

Michelle and Grace-Ann both had considerably more respectable nine-to-five type jobs. Michelle worked in a physiotherapy clinic as a receptionist, and Grace-Ann was a dental assistant.

Michelle disappeared into her iPad for long enough that I thought the matter was closed until she snapped her head back up and cried out triumphantly, "Painting with a Purpose!"

"Come again?" Grace-Ann looked up skeptically.

"This is what we should do. Painting with a Purpose. You go to this bar, and you eat and drink and everyone paints the same picture. Look."

She held her tablet up to display the picture - a gaggle of women each holding up a not-quite-the-same painting of a black cat with a full moon in the background.

"I don't know," started Grace-Ann. "That sounds kind of lame."

"Come on!" Michelle was instantly completely invested in the idea she had not even thought of five minutes earlier. "It's the perfect thing. We'll go, have a few drinks, and who knows? Maybe there will be men there. Maybe we will *meet* a man. *You* could meet a *man*, Emily! This might be the event where you start the rest of your life!"

She thrust the iPad in front of my face and I looked at it with a raised eyebrow.

"I see precisely zero men in that picture. That is a picture of fifteen women holding pictures of cats. Isn't exactly a 'meeting your soul mate' environment." The wine had clearly been an accelerant for this idiotic idea. I hoped Michelle would get over it just as quickly.

"There are lots of different paintings you can choose. I'm booking it right now. My treat. What are you doing next Monday night?" Michelle prodded Grace-Ann with her foot again. "Grace-Ann! Get off your phone and listen to me. What are you doing next Monday night?"

"Well, nothing actually. But I'm not sure I'm super into painting. You guys should go without me."

"Nope. We're all doing it. I'm buying the tickets right..." She paused and typed her memorized credit card number with lightning speed, "now. Done! Monday at eight. You'll both thank me later."

"Doubtful," I replied, suddenly and surprisingly thankful she had pulled the trigger without my consent. I made a mental note to ask Clara to watch Dante on Monday evening. "But I'm not doing a picture of a cat. Let me see what else they have."

"Actually, you have to choose the picture when you book," Michelle said cheerfully. "I signed us up to do Santa and the elves."

Hours later, on the drive home with the calming effects of the glass of wine long since worn off, I asked myself the same question over and over. How would I have Christmas without Tyler? Surely, he would return home before the holidays. Then Dante could give him my Santa painting as a Christmas present, and Tyler and I would ring in the New Year drinking champagne. That was definitely what was going to happen.

chapter 8

Painting with a Purpose turned out to be an evening activity that started at eight and ended at ten. Clara agreed to babysit at my house and I wore a slightly-better-than-casual top with a decent pair of jeans and put on mascara and lip gloss. It was the first time since Tyler left that I bothered with anything except soap, water, and, when I remembered, moisturizer.

We had agreed to meet at the studio at quarter to eight. Michelle's and Grace-Ann's cars were already in the parking lot when I arrived. At least I wouldn't be sitting around inside waiting for them like an idiot. Since Tyler left, I felt like people were staring at me, like they knew what a loser I was. It felt like an albatross with Amy Ballantyne's face was weighing down my neck.

The space was sparsely furnished and featured a lot of exposed pine. I glanced around the room, hoping a glass of wine would help my nerves, and quickly realized there was no food or drink sold on premises. *Great.* I spotted Grace-

Ann buried in her phone, and then found Michelle, who was talking conspiratorially to a man whose face I couldn't see. Had she managed to hook up before it even started?

"Hey, Michelle." I slapped her on the shoulder before I saw the drink in her hand. It spilled… onto the chest of the man she was talking to.

"Oh look. It's Clumsy LaRoo. Nice to see you, you moron." She grinned good-naturedly and I recognized the man Michelle was talking to as her older brother, James. A smile broke out over my face. James had been like a big brother to me since we were all in high school.

"James! How are you?" I moved forward to hug him and he hugged me back as he spoke.

"I hope you don't mind that I'm here. I'm back in town and I got roped into coming along by Michelle."

James was calm and confident, despite wearing most of a glass of wine, which was exactly how I remembered him. He was crazy smart, and so good looking it was almost obnoxious, but it was impossible for anyone not to like him because he was also so kind and sincere. James was a comfortable part of my past and my life now was anything but comfortable. Momentarily, my body stiffened as I realized James likely knew everything about my situation from Michelle. Just as quickly I decided it didn't matter. It was just James, after all. He was unlikely to judge me, and anything he knew he had been told by Michelle, who was my biggest ally. Before answering, I hugged him again, harder this time.

"I haven't seen you in ages. It will be good to catch up." The painting woman stood at the front of the area and waited not-very-patiently for us to take our seats.

"Except," declared Michelle, flexing her bossy muscle, "we are not talking about Tyler or that *bitch* Amy Ballantyne tonight." She shot a pointed stare in my direction. "At all."

"Sounds good to me," I said, to myself as much as anyone else.

"Welcome to Painting with a Purpose," the elderly woman at the front of the class raised her shrill voice over the chatter, "On Date Night! Please find your partner and choose a spot at a table."

"Date Night?" I shot a quizzical look at Michelle. "What's the deal with that? You didn't tell me it was Date Night."

"It was the only opening they had," she replied a little too quickly, pulling the still-texting Grace-Ann down into the stool beside hers. "Luckily, James was available to join us, so we have an even number."

There wasn't much time to talk during the first stages of the instructions. The lesson in watercolor technique was punctuated with pauses to eat and drink. Michelle brought enough snacks and drinks for us to share, including three cans of Dr. Pepper for me. Date Night, it turned out, meant each member of the twosome worked on one half of one picture.

"I'm going to have to arm-wrestle you for the other half of this painting," James joked as we worked away, trying to copy the instructor's brush strokes. As the night passed, we talked to each other more than we listened to the instructor.

"I don't think it's going to be a saleable piece of art. I can probably let you have it for the price of a burger and fries." I joked back, then babbled on, "I love fries, even though I spend so much time at Eugene's." I made a face, realizing I was talking too much but went on anyway. "I mean…it's a relief to be out of the house, and not smell the diner on my clothes. I can't tell you how much I appreciate a hot shower and the aroma of laundry detergent. It's almost impossible to get the grease smell out of my uniform. I have to wash it twice and once I tried bleach but it ruined it and they made me pay for a new one. That Eugene is a piece of work I tell you. One time he made me pay for a plate I dropped." Now I was just babbling on, and was glad about Michelle's rule regarding forbidden topics of conversation, without which Tyler and Amy would certainly have come up. "Anyway, it's nice to be out."

James waited for me to finish talking and seemed genuinely interested in everything I was saying, though I couldn't imagine why. Talking about how fervently I showered to eliminate the smell of restaurant grease from my hair and body didn't seem like polite conversation, even to me.

Once finished, our painting featured James' easily recognizable depiction of Jolly Old Saint Nick on one side, and my Picasso-esque version of Rudolph and the elves on the other. If they stood beside each other, presumably on a mantle over a roaring fire, the effect would be more Halloween than Christmas.

I glanced over at Michelle and Grace-Ann. They were deep in heated conversation about whether the colors matched in both halves of the picture. Grace-Ann even put her phone down, eating pita chips absentmindedly with her left hand as she swirled the paint with her right. James' and my art revealed that we clearly had not given it the same attention to detail. We looked at our work at the same time and laughed.

The evening was more fun than I anticipated, because of James' easy presence and the laughs we had talking about old times. I embraced Michelle and Grace-Ann in the parking lot.

"See you guys later. Call me. We should get together before Christmas."

"Before *Christmas*? What kind of social schedule are you keeping? That's weeks away." Grace-Ann released me from a hug.

"I know. But work is crazy this time of year. We've got a lot of banquets booked and I can't really afford to turn down shifts right now." Real life was settling back into my mind after a blissful evening of escape. I hugged Michelle and then turned to embrace James, who pulled me close into a hug that was maybe a beat longer than necessary. Had he always smelled so good? I suddenly wished I had reapplied my lip gloss before we left.

"So what else do you eat?" James fell into step with me, walking me to my car.

"I beg your pardon?"

"Aside from burgers and fries. I'm in possession of both these fine works of art, so it seems like I owe you a meal. What do you like to eat?"

"Since you asked, I'm quite partial to a shawarma at the moment, but I rarely eat there because Dante won't eat anything that exotic. Not that I think a shawarma is exotic...you know what I mean." I fumbled in the bottom of my purse looking for my car keys.

"We could go for a shawarma, just the two of us. Or you can pick somewhere else where Dante will eat and we'll take him with us. It would be fun to take him out." He paused, suddenly sounding hesitant. "Whatever you decide. Why don't you just shoot me a text when you want to cash in that meal." I was moved by his kindness but slightly worried it came from a place of pity.

"That sounds good. I'll call you." We separated, and James headed toward Michelle's SUV where she was waiting with the motor running, trying to heat up the interior.

"Hey, James," I called after him, seeing my breath hang cloudy in the cold air, "Thanks for being so normal tonight. I mean, you know, just like nothing is happening. It was nice."

"Don't worry about it." He smiled broadly and gave me a mock salute. "When I sell these to a gallery, you'll be wishing you hadn't sold out for a shawarma. Call me."

I rubbed my hands together, got into in my freezing car, and threw the transmission into first, considerably less unhappy than before my evening of Painting with a Purpose.

chapter 9

The following week, Eugene sent me home in the late afternoon of an extremely slow Monday, and Dante was scheduled to be with Tyler until my shift technically ended at eight. I was home and showered by four-thirty, and on the spur of the moment decided to call James and take him up on his offer of a meal out.

I pulled my favorite oversized white sweater out of the closet, ignoring the fact that there were an increasing number of empty hangers as Tyler's clothes disappeared incrementally. I selected a slightly better-than-average pair of leggings covered in brightly colored stripes, pulled them on and picked out matching socks, which wouldn't even be visible under my boots, all the while telling myself it didn't matter at all what I wore. This was just dinner with James, who was practically family and anyway, I was a married woman. Despite my emptying closet, I still wanted to believe Tyler might change his mind and come home. Besides, the temperature was in the twenties daily and down to zero overnight, so wearing a chunky woolen sweater was hardly an act of seduction.

James offered to pick me up after I texted him I was free for dinner. Soon we were on the way to the shawarma place. I chattered away like a monkey in a tree while he mostly just nodded and smiled, sometimes ahead out the windshield and at stop lights, sideways at me.

"Seat warmers. Very nice. My butt is toasty and warm."

"I aim to please. The temperature of your butt is of paramount importance to me always." I laughed easily and propped the toes of my Uggs up on the dashboard.

"Remember when you used to drive Michelle and me around because I didn't have my license yet and Michelle had crashed your mom's Trans Am and wasn't allowed to drive? She used to fight me for the front seat and you hated it when I put my feet on the dashboard."

"Yes, I remember. There weren't any seat warmers in that little VW Rabbit, that's for sure." The banter was comfortable. I decided to observe Michelle's rule from the painting evening about the topics that were off-limits while I was with James.

We pulled into Shawarma Shop, and I threaded my hand through James' arm, content and nostalgic as we walked toward the restaurant.

The bell chimed above us on the door as we entered, and I spotted Grace-Ann, laughing at a table in the corner. I began to call out a greeting, then felt my breath catch in my throat.

Grace-Ann was sitting with Amy Ballantyne.

My mouth fell open and the bottom dropped out of my stomach. I dug my fingers into James' arm and froze.

Suddenly, I was marching over to confront my old friend and my new enemy.

"What are you doing?" My words squeaked out through a quickly closing throat. I wanted to scream.

"Having supper," Amy smirked, daring me to speak again. Grace-Ann, unable to hold my gaze, looked down.

"What are you doing with *her*?" I pointed my words at Grace-Ann this time. The entire restaurant continued around us as if nothing was happening, as my worlds collided.

"Amy has always been my friend, Emily. So has Tyler." She paused. Her voice shook ever so slightly. "You can't ask me to give up those friendships. I just don't feel," she inhaled sharply, having obviously rehearsed the words she would use in this moment, "that it would be fair to Amy and Tyler."

My gaze moved back to Amy, who was still staring up at me with a face that could only be described as triumphant.

"Anyway, I thought you were *working* tonight," Amy quipped. I couldn't believe she had the nerve to speak to me. "It seems like Tyler's not the only one with secrets. You look pretty loved up yourself." Her steely eyes stretched into a sweet smile. "Hi, James," she called out and waved.

James watched me closely for a cue about how to respond.

My thoughts were incoherent. I thought about yelling, 'You're dead to me!' at Grace-Ann and stomping out, but that seemed too extreme. In the moment between staying and fleeing, I noticed a medium-sized diamond perched on the fourth finger of Amy's left hand. She saw me notice it, held up her hand, palm facing inward, and wiggled her fingers.

"Do you like my ring? Tyler and I are planning a short engagement – 180 days from when you get served with divorce papers. It's so impersonal to have the Sherriff drive them up to your house when I'd rather do it *myself*, but it's what our lawyer recommends."

Grace-Ann shifted awkwardly in the booth and said nothing.

That was the moment when I abandoned civility. I took two quick steps forward, picked up both Amy's and Grace-Ann's plastic cups of soda, poured them directly on their respective laps, and, just for good measure, threw the empty cups at their heads. Then I returned to James, gripped his arm and dragged him out of the restaurant, while the two women screamed and the other customers stared.

"Please take me home."

James drove to my house in silence and pulled into the driveway. I sat completely still and stared forward, not sure what to do next.

"What can I do to help you?" James tentatively put a hand on my forearm.

His small act of kindness was enough to break through the dam of my rage and tears poured through. The fresh wave of violent sadness instantly felt familiar.

"No." I didn't even bother to wipe the tears away. "No thank you. I'm fine. I'll call you." I blindly pushed through my front door and stumbled into the living room, kicking off my boots and shedding my coat backwards onto the floor. Splayed out on the sofa, sobs wracked my body, and I cried for all the old reasons and two new ones – Amy's engagement to my husband and Grace-Ann's betrayal. In the darkening living room the central heating hummed in the background, and music played on a radio that had been left on in another room of the house. I looked at my phone. Just half an hour until Tyler brought Dante back.

At the bathroom sink, I slapped freezing water up onto my face and forced a smile up to my eyes in the medicine cabinet mirror, determined not to let Tyler see me upset. I needed our interaction tonight to be as casual as possible, since he definitely already knew about my performance at Shawarma Shop. Amy probably texted him even before she grabbed for a fistful of napkins. I felt momentarily bad for the waitress who had to clean up the lake of soda on the table and floor, even though the blame lay squarely with Amy and Grace-Ann.

In the half-empty closet of what I now finally admitted to myself was only my bedroom, I took off my wedding ring and put it in my jewelry box. The lid closed with a thud.

chapter 10

Grace-Ann's betrayal was almost harder to stomach than Tyler's. Why was it easier to believe my husband was an asshole than to admit my best friend since grade school was a traitor? Even though Grace-Ann *was* being the most massive, horrible, traitorous bitch of all time. A bigger bitch than Amy Ballantyne even.

I waited to tell Michelle until she came over the next day.

"What?!" shock and rage exploded onto her face. "She said WHAT?! Not fair to Tyler and Amy? She actually said those words?"

"Yes, she did. She also said something about how Tyler was her friend too, and it wouldn't be fair to take sides. Something like that. Emotions were running pretty high, though. I don't remember it exactly." I dipped a chip into guacamole I purchased on sale because of its imminent best-before date, and which had to be eaten before tomorrow.

"I cannot believe what I am hearing. This is Grace-Ann we're talking about, right? The one you sat with on the bus to kindergarten? The person whose floor you slept on when she was afraid her stalker boyfriend would come through the window in the middle of the night? And she's worried about upsetting *Tyler*?"

It was true. Grace-Ann and I met on the first day of kindergarten when the bus driver made us sit together. We remained friends all the way up through elementary school and high school. When Grace-Ann moved away for a semester to Spain to study Spanish History, we sat in the park together for the whole summer before she left with one earphone each and a Berlitz CD. We learned Spanish for, 'The cathedral is on the left,' and 'Where is the pharmacy?' While she was gone I wrote her a letter every week and sent her the *State News*, the school paper from Michigan State, even though I had already dropped out, pregnant with Dante.

When Clara was hospitalized with fungal meningitis and we were afraid she would die, Grace-Ann sat with me in the hospital every afternoon for two weeks. She brought magazines she stole from the salon where her mother worked and candy I always suspected she swiped from the convenience store.

In our second year of college, she went out with this jerk Francois, who told her he only wore a wedding ring to fend off interested women at work, although it turned out he wore it because *he was married*. Francois came completely unhinged when she split up with him and wouldn't stop contacting her and coming to her apartment, even when she got a restraining order. I slept on the floor of her room every night to assuage her fear that he would climb up to the roof of the walk-up apartment building next door through the window where she lived over a pizza place. I thought we would be best friends forever, that we would, along with Michelle, live in the same retirement home, playing shuffleboard and bridge.

Grace-Ann taking Tyler's side signaled an onslaught of new changes I wasn't expecting. Surely my life should have gone on, just without Tyler, but my friend's betrayal was the first indication that other things would change too. Now, I found myself grieving Grace-Ann's friendship as well as my future with my husband.

"It seems ridiculous," I agreed. "But there it is. A lot of things that used to be ridiculous are happening to me at the moment, in case you didn't notice." I half-smiled, buoyed by Michelle's empathetic rage.

"Well, I will tell you one thing," she quipped, forcefully enough that bits of chip flew out of her mouth and hit the counter. "Sorry about that." She got a paper towel and wiped the crumbs into her hand before continuing. "She is *dead to me*. Dead."

"Right?" Relief washed over me. This was the reaction I had hoped for. "That's what I wanted to say in the restaurant. I thought it might be too dramatic, but it's totally true. Dead. And I'll tell you something else," now *I* was on a roll, "I hope she's ready to be disappointed in Tyler. Because if she thinks he's going to be the kind of friend to her that I have been, she's insane."

Michelle nodded her agreement. "Certifiable. She's made a very bad decision here. Apart from being a disloyal cow, it was a bad calculation." Michelle walked to the sink, rinsed the empty guacamole container and put it in the recycling box.

"Tyler doesn't even particularly like Grace-Ann," I surveyed the remaining chips at the bottom of the bag, decided there weren't enough to keep, and dropped them in the trash. "Tyler always thought I paid too much attention to her." A flurry of crumbs flew off my jeans when I stood up.

"And Amy Ballantyne! Ha! She'll turn on Grace-Ann just as quickly as she turned on Janet Harrison. Remember?" Michelle's eyebrow shot up at me.

Amy and Janet were friends all through high school and pledged the same sorority. Both of them inadvertently broke one of the plethora of pledge-week rules, and Grace-Ann threw Janet under the bus, feigning her own innocence. Janet was blackballed from pledging any sorority that year.

"Yeah. Like you said. She chose poorly. It just still pisses me off. All those years of friendship. You know, if she were in my position I would never have done that to her. I would have been loyal to her, always."

"I know you would. So would I." We headed into my family room.

"In fact," I continued for effect, straightening out the cushions on the couch and collecting up half a dozen DVD cases before we sat down. "If Grace-Ann had killed her entire family and burnt their house to the ground, I would have taken her side." I punched a cushion for effect. "I would have thrown shovels in the back of my car and helped her bury the bodies."

"That's quite drastic. But strangely, I actually believe you." Michelle put her feet up on the coffee table before offering, "Do you want to prank Grace-Ann somehow or leave it alone? I know how you like your weird revenge sequences." Michelle shared my penchant for revenge.

"It's okay. I don't really have the heart for any pranking."

"Good to hear. She'd probably know it was you anyway." Michelle reclined on the sofa, thumbing through an old copy of *People* magazine.

"Plus, tonight I'm going online to send her a big envelope full of glitter from one of those anonymous places." I shot a wicked grin at Michelle. "When she opens it there will be glitter all over everything in her house. The website promises it's almost impossible to clean up."

"Sounds perfect."

chapter 11

Soon Christmas trees sparkled in every front window and carols blasted from every radio station. I packed as many shifts as possible into the weeks leading up to the morning of the twenty-fourth of December. Maintaining a frenetic pace kept me from dwelling on how crappy and miserable Christmas was going to be that year. I spent my time between working and picking up Dante shopping for his presents, which were bigger and better than usual in direct proportion to my guilt. There was one especially teary conversation with Dante where I tried to explain to him why Mommy and Daddy wouldn't open presents together on Christmas morning, but overall, he seemed to be coping well. It broke my heart and inflated my already well-developed guilt to see the little guy saddled with grown-up problems.

Zoe became a close ally and almost a friend at work. Her initial observation about Tyler being an asshole had become proven beyond any doubt. Her honesty was as comforting as it was unsettling.

Christmas was strange because everything in my new life was strange. Tyler and I negotiated times, largely over text because I didn't want to speak directly to him, or God forbid, Amy. Dante and I hung stockings on Christmas Eve and opened our presents early the next morning. Then he toddled off happily with Tyler and Amy to spend Christmas Day with them. I spent the day sniffling through Hallmark movies, wiping my nose on the sleeve of my coziest pajamas when I ran out of tissues. The Christmas Tree lights blinked until they were the only bright spots in the dark living room. I ordered Chinese Food and ate it, mostly not crying. My parents put off their Christmas dinner until Boxing Day so Dante could join us.

The big and terrible changes in my life were blending into every day and creeping up to normal. It was becoming *normal* that this woman who I hated with the red-hot fire of a thousand burning suns spent a lot of time with my son. The worst part for me was Dante adored her, and I couldn't even complain without seeming like a big fat bitch.

Tyler served me with papers in the week between Christmas and New Year. I didn't see the point contesting a quick divorce. The only condition my lawyer named in the response was that Dante would continue to live with me, with liberal visitation alternate weekends, half of school holidays once he was old enough and 'other times to be determined by both parties.' Tyler afforded me six months to figure out how to buy his half of the home we both still legally owned. I imagined Amy and Tyler's house beautifully decorated in cream and beige, and visualized

Dante destroying a Pottery Barn love seat with finger paint and then spilling grape juice onto white carpet. My day-to-day life was a hundred kinds of horrible, and at the same time, it was becoming kind of okay. By the summer, the divorce would be finalized and we would be two separate families, legally, practically, and hopefully emotionally.

Tyler's stuff was almost gone from the house, including the shirts with fewer buttons, and jeans with white spots that looked suspiciously like splashes of Clorox. Several crumbles of blue cheese found their way into the bottom of his carry-on luggage which I hoped he discovered when he and Amy touched down on their first romantic vacation.

The devastation over how my life had turned out was fading gradually into acceptance. My lingering concern was Dante. Other than a few teary moments around Christmas, he seemed to be coping remarkably well. All the parenting books I bought and partly read, and the divorced-family websites open in browser windows on my laptop seemed to agree that he was young enough to normalize a situation such as this. As long as I refrained from badmouthing his father or soon-to-be-stepmother, Dante would come out of the divorce okay. 'Kids are resilient,' the books said, and I highlighted the words every time.

My own resilience was tested again when Eugene called a staff meeting, the same day the divorce papers from Tyler arrived. It was strange for Eugene to have such a meeting because everyone who came in to attend had to be paid for an hour. Usually, the only 'meeting' scheduled was the annual Christmas party when, at the stroke of eight, Eugene locked the doors, and appetizers and alcohol flowed freely until the small hours of the morning.

All the wait staff stood around awkwardly in the dining room of the restaurant at four in the afternoon. I kept one eye on my occupied tables because it was an hour into my shift.

"I have an announcement to make," my boss proclaimed in his thick Greek accent, "I've decided to retire." He smiled at the group of us in our maroon skirts and white shirts. "That's it. I wanted to tell you myself. You can go back to work."

There was stunned silence for a beat while we digested this shocking news. I always thought Eugene would work until he dropped dead, either sitting at the cash register or in the staff booth at the back of the restaurant.

"Hold on a minute," Zoe's voice pierced the shock. "What the hell do you mean, retiring? What's going to happen to the restaurant? Are you selling? Are we closing? What about our jobs, Eugene?" There were murmurs of agreement from the rest of us.

"The restaurant will be on the market. If it sells, it sells. If not, we close and sell the building. Or the lot. Whichever happens first. For your jobs..." he looked around, "You are all good girls. You will find other jobs if we close."

Only in the restaurant business can the boss still call the employees 'good girls.'

"This is all I know," he continued. "You might as well go back to work."

"Not so fast," Zoe's voice rose again, "How long are you going to try to sell the business before you close and sell the building?" Now the silence was palpable. No one exhaled.

"End of January," said Eugene peacefully, "Then we close. Everyone who came to the meeting gets paid for the hour."

He put his hands in his pockets, sauntered back to the cash register, and sat on his stool. So ended the meeting.

I walked back to the waitress station in a daze. The off-duty staff sat down together at a booth, subdued. I brought them fries and Diet Cokes and 'forgot' to write up a check. Since there were almost no customers around, I went back to talk to Dean and Mario.

"Mario, Dean-o, did you know about this or what?" my voice was raised over the noise of the kitchen.

Mario was cleaning the grill in smooth, measured motions, the grill brick beating out a steady rhythm back and forth across the black surface.

"Yeah. He mentioned it. Offered me the chance to buy him out, didn't he, Dean?" Mario asked, without interrupting his cleaning.

"And so? Are you going to buy the place?" He was a good cook. Probably Mario had a decent shot at making a go of the place if he wanted.

"Nah. Ownership isn't for me. I like to cook, that's it. Besides, I likely can't afford to buy him out. You have to have credit, get a business loan…I just like to cook and drive my Camaro." He finished scraping the grill and started to wipe down the adjacent stainless-steel work surfaces, then tossed a couple of empty plastic bowls through the air to Dean.

"Why don't you ask Eugene to hold the mortgage? I bet he would. You should think about it. You'd be great to work for." The first part of this might have been true but the second part was a desperate lie. Mario was a bigger prick than Eugene. He was the one who liked to scream at me in Greek, words Anastasia used to translate for me before she became such an uppity cow. They weren't nice words.

Back at the waitress station, Zoe stood behind me as we waited for the full dinner rush. She had her back to Eugene, head bent over her phone. I side-stepped, grabbed the now-cold plate of fries Dean had smuggled to us earlier and dumped them in the garbage. I didn't have a clue what the hell I would do for employment if Eugene's closed, and even less idea who would want to buy the place. There was no shortage of greasy spoons in town. Eugene's was a decent restaurant, but nothing special. If Mario didn't want it… a new part of my future seemed suddenly uncertain. I felt my head start to hurt and fished a couple of Tylenol out of my purse, washing them down with flat Dr. Pepper.

Within ten minutes, there was no time to worry about Eugene's bombshell of the day. The tables filled up with customers and Zoe and I were rushed off our feet. Our conversation during that shift was sparse and strained. Both of us were clearly weighed down by what Eugene had told us, and weighing up our respective options.

"What are you going to do?" I questioned Zoe as we paused together at the window, waiting for our orders.

"I've been thinking about getting out of this place for a while. But I don't know..."

I bit my lip and considered my own options as I ferried the toasted Club, and BLT with extra bacon to the couple in 'middle three.' My downcast mood continued until closing. After all the tables were clean and the salts, sugars and pepper had been filled up, I headed for the door. Dean looked up at me while he pushed a wet mop under the tables.

"What about you, Dean? What will you do if this place closes?"

"Well, I have a few options. But there are a few different factors at play... I've been thinking about what to do for a week already. Eugene told the kitchen staff early, like Mario said." He looked down and concentrated while he pushed the mop head back and forth over a stubborn spot on the dull-gray tile.

"You'll get something. You're a good guy, Dean. I appreciate you looking out for us in the front. I probably haven't told you that before." I turned to go. "Take it easy."

He glanced up again from the mop. "You're not so bad yourself, Emily. You're a great waitress, you know, but you could do whatever you put your mind to." A warmth that was probably a hot shade of pink rose up over my face. "Hold on a second. Emily?"

I turned back around, expecting Dean to ask me to prop the door open so he could take the kitchen trash to the green metal bin at the side of the building.

"What's up? You want me to leave the door open?"

"Yeah, that would be great, actually. But what I was going to ask you is if you might want to go out with me one weekend."

This caught me completely off guard. Not only did I not think about Dean that way, I also hadn't thought about *any* man that way for years. In a very real way, it hadn't even occurred to me that I was actually single.

"I don't know, Dean-o. I don't usually date people from work..." this was absurd and we both knew it because I didn't usually date anyone at all.

"Come on, Emily. It'll be fun. There's this new axe-throwing place in Detroit a buddy of mine has a share in...no strings attached, I promise. Just a fun night out. You seem like you might need one. Just as friends. What do you say?"

He had hit on a good point. I answered quickly before I had a chance to change my mind.

"Alright. That would be fun. Sure." This was another turning point between my Tyler life and my post-Tyler life. It was difficult to keep up with the outwardly insignificant but inwardly earth-shattering events that kept happening.

"A week from Friday?" It surprised me slightly to hear him mention a time so soon. In seconds we had gone from talking about a hypothetical to a time and place to a real date. Like a cloud of water vapor that changed into an ice sculpture right in front of my nose. Bang.

"That would be great." This whole song and dance was likely mostly pity on the part of Dean. I had been miserable for the past several months behind my waitress smile, and he had already said no strings attached. Now I had just over a week to either get used to the idea, or cancel.

Before putting the car into first, I touched Michelle's name on my phone in the dashboard mount, anxious to hear her say it was okay for me to go out with Dean, but her phone was either dead or turned off. At the house number, James answered.

"Hey!" I smiled to hear his voice come over the Bluetooth speaker in my car. "How's it going? I thought you would be gone back to Atlanta by now."

"I had a change of plans. I've given up on Atlanta and decided to stay around here for a while. I'm going to take some time to think about it and then maybe find a position in Detroit, or Cleveland." He was happy and laid-back, just like always.

"Wow. Is everything okay? With your job I mean?" I was pretty sure James was a high-powered executive type. It seemed unlikely he would leave a job in Atlanta for unemployment in his parents' basement in suburban Michigan.

"They restructured my office and offered me a pretty good package, so I took it. It was just after our uh, shawarma date." He hesitated slightly. "How did that all turn out, anyway? You made quite an exit."

"I imagine Michelle filled you in. It was a disaster but eventually it will probably be mostly okay."

"If it's any consolation, I thought the beverage dump was inspired. They do say revenge is best served cold."

I surprised myself by laughing at the situation. "It felt pretty good. I would have regretted letting the opportunity pass. I can laugh about it now I guess."

"Michelle isn't home I'm afraid. She went to the gym."

"The gym? Michelle? Are you sure about that?"

"I know. It defies explanation. I'll tell her you called though."

I hung up shaking my head. Michelle did not go to the gym. She must have a crush on one of the personal trainers. I drove the long way to my mother's house to get Dante. If Michelle had joined a gym then pretty much anything was possible. Maybe Eugene would be able to sell the restaurant after all.

chapter 12

Within days, almost all the waitresses at Eugene's quit to find work somewhere that wasn't closing. I suddenly had all the tables I wanted to wait and more besides. Finally having a modicum of professional waitress-leverage, I plucked up my courage and told Eugene if he didn't give me regular breakfast shifts, I would quit too. It was a bluff but he bought it. More work meant more tips, and breakfast shifts meant a few more evenings free to work on my mother of the year nomination with Dante.

The nights Dante slept over at Tyler's, my heart ached but I didn't worry about picking Dante up, putting him to bed before crashing myself, and dropping him off before a morning breakfast shift, either back at Tyler's or at my parents'. The more I worked, the less time I had to worry about the *rest of my life*. I spent so many hours busting my ass in that damn restaurant that there was not time left to spend my paycheck on anything except very frequent pizza delivery. Dante and I ate on the couch and watched TV like zombies. The pizza boxes in the garage were piled up taller than Dante, as he pointed out to me one day, because every week I was too embarrassed to put so many boxes out on garbage day.

Instead of months or weeks, it was only eight days until Eugene called another meeting. Two days before my planned and as-yet-uncancelled evening out with Dean. It was a short meeting with fewer staff in attendance, because there were fewer staff left. I waited somberly, hoping desperately Eugene wasn't going to announce the restaurant was closing.

"Dean. Dean is buying the restaurant." Eugene's words broke the quiet of the nervous assembly. "That's all." He ambled slowly back to the cash register.

"Uh, Eugene, hold on please." Without Zoe, it fell to me to break the shocked silence. "Do we still have our jobs?"

Eugene turned around briefly and smiled the wan smile of a man about to retire.

"Not up to me," he replied. "Ask Dean." He then calmly continued his walk to the cash register.

I didn't dare to verbalize what we all had to be thinking. How was a *dishwasher* going to buy Eugene's?

"Ask him," whispered a young part-time waitress named Juanita. "He likes you best. Go ask Dean what's going on." I was thankful none of them knew about my upcoming date, which even though it *wasn't* a date, now seemed inappropriate.

"Yeah, maybe," I poured myself a large Dr. Pepper, shoved a plastic straw down in it and took a sip so the straw wouldn't bob back out on the walk back to the waitress station. My feet trudged back to the kitchen where Mario was mincing onions and Dean was loading plates into the dishwasher.

"Uh, Dean," I began, trying to sound casual. He looked up and smiled. "Eugene just told us you're buying the restaurant."

"It's great, isn't it? I haven't really wrapped my head around it completely, but I'm pretty pumped about it." He seemed pleased with himself. I probably would be too if I'd just bought a restaurant.

"I can't believe you kept it a secret!"

"I'm a man of mystery. Lots of secrets tucked away." There was a moment of silence before I plucked up the courage to continue.

"I guess we're all wondering…will we still have our jobs?" Heat from the eyeballs of the other staff behind me seared the back of my head while they all waited for him to answer the question.

"I can't very well run it without you all…" He continued, still grinning at me. "For now, everyone who is good at their job can count on keeping their job. So you have nothing to worry about. In fact," he pulled the sprayer down and rinsed off the plates before pushing the sturdy, pale green tray into the dishwashing machine, "I'm going to need a new head waitress. It's a buck more an hour but you'd have to manage the schedule. You'd get your pick of shifts though." He spoke casually. Was he avoiding making eye contact?

"Are you... offering it to me?"

"If you want it. I understand if you don't. Not effective until we get the changeover sorted out... think about it."

"Thank you, Dean," was all I managed to say before heading back to my tables to clear dirty dishes, momentarily forgetting the gaggle of waitresses desperately waiting for the answer to the question they wanted me to ask Dean.

Head waitress pay was, as Dean said, a buck more per hour, plus events in the banquet room and pretty much all the breakfasts I wanted to work. It would mean more evenings at home and maybe I would even have a social life again. Over the next hour, one nagging worry spun in my head, one I had to put to rest before seriously considering Dean's offer.

I returned to the door of the kitchen.

"Uh, Dean, I'm not sure if maybe we should give that date next week a miss now if you're going to be my boss? I don't want to put you in an awkward position."

Which more truthfully meant, I don't want to put *myself* in an awkward position. Like the position of being let go in a 'restructuring' if our date went badly. There were rules about how employers were allowed to treat staff but there were also harsh realities about what *never actually happened* if employers broke those rules.

"Listen, Emily, like I told you. No strings attached on the night out. We've worked together here for ages. Consider it an evening out with a friend, and the job offer is just that: a job offer. You're the best waitress we have and you should be recognized for it. I'm going to need good leadership out there on the floor to run this place." He paused. His eyes were calm and sincere. And very blue, now that I noticed. "But it's totally up to you."

"Okay." I decided to allow myself to be cautiously optimistic. It was possible, though not particularly *probable*, that things were looking up.

I picked up Dante from my parents' house in a sunnier mood than I had been in for a long time. Their raised eyebrows seemed to indicate they noticed, but they knew better than to comment. Dante's eyes were dinner-plate sized when we made an unannounced stop at Toys R Us. He enthusiastically chose two Thomas engines and a new DVD, spending all the tips I'd made that day. We hit the drive-thru at McDonald's and ate our burgers and chicken nuggets cuddled up on the couch, dipping fries into my chocolate shake. Dante fell asleep and I carried him to his bed, alarmed that he seemed heavier - that he had grown without me noticing.

chapter 13

I didn't tell anyone but Michelle about my plans for the evening with Dean. 'Outing' was the word I settled on in my overthinking head. Using 'date' threatened to propel me into a time of my life I wasn't ready for. It was one thing to wrap my head around my husband getting married to Amy McBitchface-Ballantyne. It was something else to start dating other people myself.

I told myself getting a haircut and a manicure had nothing to do with Dean. Even though my feelings for him were collegial, even bordering on fraternal, putting on makeup, and clothes that weren't leggings and a hoodie gave me a small, quiet happiness.

At the last minute, I convinced Clara to come to the nail salon with me. She was always helping out with Dante and she never let me give her any money. I sometimes treated her to little luxuries she couldn't afford as a college student.

I lingered in front of the wall of nail polish bottles, trying to decide on a good color for a casual evening out that wasn't a date.

"You want Shellac?"

The Korean women's voices at the nail place were *shrill*, which probably wasn't politically correct to say, even in my head. They mostly spoke Korean to each other. Their sentences in English was sharp and percussive.

"No, thanks. Just regular polish for us."

"Shellac is better!" Christine owned the salon and when I didn't stand firm from the beginning, she talked me into a full spa manicure and pedicure, or just gave me one without my permission and then charged me. I fell for that twice, not wanting to insult Christine by refusing the manicure she had already started giving me.

"No thanks. Just polish." Once she had me hooked on the shellac I would have to keep coming back every two weeks to have it changed or peel it off myself, which would destroy my nails.

"What about your sister?" Was it strictly necessary to speak so *loudly*?

"Just polish for her too."

"Last two chairs." We moved down to the chairs at the end of the long table. Clara picked a bright purple and I chose a more muted rose I hoped would look confident and low-key.

"Who is this guy you're going out with?" Clara never minced words.

"What? How do you even know about that? I didn't tell anyone but Michelle!"

"Come on. You got your hair colored and you're getting your nails done. You've looked like hell since Tyler left. No offense."

"None taken." She was right.

"Suddenly you're acting like you're getting ready to get 'Glamor Shots' at the mall."

"They don't do those anymore, you dummy. But if you must know, it's just an evening out with a friend from work. We're going axe throwing." It was anyone's guess how much of our conversation Christine and her squad of nail artists were listening to. I vaguely intended to record them on my phone and find a translation app to figure out if they were talking about me but it seemed like a lot of work.

"You should bring a picture of Tyler and ask them to put it on the bullseye for you." Her nails reminded me of Ursula from *The Little Mermaid*. She regarded the right hand approvingly as Christine's daughter started on her left. "I thought all the waitresses were women at your restaurant. Isn't that kind of in the name? Wait-*ress*? Who are you going out with?" Clara positioned all her now-purple nails in front of the small white fan on the counter in front of her.

"You are seriously such a dimwit. First of all, we are called *servers*, not waitresses." Clara rolled her eyes dramatically and made a gagging noise. "Secondly, if you must know, I'm going out with one of the dishwashers." I decided not to tell her he had recently bought the place. It seemed like less of a big deal without that piece of information. "I have known him forever. It's just an *outing*." I emphasized the word, and heard how stupid it sounded.

"Yeah, whatever. It's a date. A woman and a man going out on Friday night is a date. I didn't realize you were dating."

"Again," I articulated slowly, "I am not dating. I am going on an outing with my friend Dean to throw some axes. And likely dinner. Most likely also dinner."

"That's a date. But we can agree to disagree. I'll tell you this for free - you know who I think you should date?"

"Do tell." I valued my sister's opinion about my love life about as much as I respected Dante's opinion about movies.

"James."

"James?" I almost spit out the soda I was drinking very gingerly with my still-wet-nails. "What are you talking about? James is practically my brother. Have you lost it completely?"

"Well, he has a thing for you. He's always had a thing for you, since high school. Do you really think it's a coincidence he moved back to Michigan after you and Tyler split up?"

"Yes, actually, I think the fact that his company restructured at the same time as my marriage destructed is a complete and utter coincidence."

"Well, agree to disagree…again."

It was time to go to the cash register and pay for the surprise manicures Christine and her daughter had given us while I was distracted talking about Dean. 'Just polish,' I had said. I tipped better when they just did the polish but if they noticed they didn't seem to care.

"It's not a date." The chimes on the door made a cheery noise as we left into the cold air and snow hit our faces.

"Do you need me to babysit Dante?"

"No, he'll be with his father on Friday."

"Want me to come over and do your make-up for you before you go out?"

"Yeah, that would be great, actually. And can you bring that MAC foundation with you and that grey sparkly eye shadow?" Clara had always been better than me at make-up.

"Only if you admit it's a date. Otherwise, you're on your own with your Maybelline mascara and your shaky eyeliner hand." Clara grinned at me over the top of my car with her hand on the door handle. I exhaled a huge flying white cloud of breath into the freezing air.

"Fine. It's a date. Okay? Happy now?"

"Extremely." The doors closed, the key turned in the ignition and we pulled out of the mini-mall parking lot. I instantly scuffed a fingernail on the gear stick. "Shit!" I muttered through teeth clenched against the cold.

"You should've gotten shellac."

chapter 14

Often, I worried my life was accelerating out of control, that I was on a collision course with a future as yet unknown. In such moments I reminded myself that the worst crash of my entire life had already happened and whatever was ahead had to be better. It was an only-okay consolation.

The radio said the winter weather was 'unseasonably cold,' whatever that was supposed to mean. For me winter always meant being freezing cold, except when I was in bed under an ancient electric blanket which would probably end up burning my house down. Why my father could not have settled in, say, Florida or Arizona was beyond me. Before Tyler tanked our marriage, I always had secret hopes we would move someday, and start over in a warmer climate. Maybe in a small town near the ocean. All that was gone now. I couldn't, legally or ethically, move across state lines with Dante, and the Michigan winters now felt like a life sentence.

Scraping and brushing the car off every morning was a job I hated, and that Tyler had usually done for me when he left for work, and now it was left to me. I developed a routine. First I traipsed outside to start the car while Dante ate breakfast, so it had time to warm up. Then I got Dante dressed to go out in his winter coat, snow pants, hat, and mittens. I then left him at the front door, rushed out to scrape the windshield, on which the defroster had now loosened the ice, and brush off the snow. Then I shot back into the house to get Dante and back out to put him in the car. The car seat was a nightmare in the winter because it always required tightening and loosening depending on which coat Dante was wearing.

Once Dante was secure in his seat with a CD playing, I went back, locked the door, checked that my straightening iron was unplugged and made my way out into the biting air one last time. None of this began until I checked whether there was snow that had to be shoveled first. A few times I chanced not shoveling the drive before leaving, and got stuck at the end of the driveway. I then spun my wheels feverishly, rocking the car from first gear to reverse and back before lurching into the road and starting on my way.

Sometimes, the kindly older neighbor next door blew the snow out of my driveway with his snowblower before I got outside. I almost cried the first time I trudged outside after a heavy snowfall, with a shovel in hand, and saw the driveway was clean. It was on my to-do list to bake him a dozen cookies or buy him a plant. Or maybe a puppy.

On the evening of my outing with Dean, I packed Dante's overnight bag especially carefully. Sometimes Tyler or I would forget a toy or a book that Dante wanted at bedtime, and there were many trips back and forth to ferry the missed stuffed animal or the favorite pajamas to wherever Dante was. I didn't want that to happen tonight. Into the bag went his top three stuffed animals, as well as his favorite pajamas with the scratchy tag cut out. I packed *Good Night Moon, Curious George Goes to the Hospital* and three *Thomas the Tank Engine* books, even though he had lots of books at Tyler's. It was a bigger than usual bag, and Amy looked at it with an arched eyebrow. I had learned, in those dreaded hand-offs, to smile and greet either of the people I hated most in the world politely, give Dante a hug and a kiss and watch him run into the house. The books said it was a good thing he was happy to go into his father's house and happy to come home to mine and it meant I was doing a good job that he wanted to be with his father. I clung to affirmations like this.

I considered turning my phone off but decided to leave it on, 'just in case.' As I was about to silence my phone and tuck it into my purse, a text chimed, from Michelle:

Good luck. Remember – just because he's your boss doesn't mean you owe him anything.

I was surprised to hear myself smirk out loud. She was even bossy over text.

chapter 15

On Friday morning, Dean told me his car was in the shop.

"I hate to ask you but…could you drive tonight? I had to take my car in yesterday. Something's up with the muffler."

"Oh, sure... no problem. Don't worry about it, Dean." My smile felt strained. Braving the winter roads on the way to and from Detroit was not my idea of a good time. I hoped the heavy snowfall that made me late for my shift would be plowed by late afternoon.

After work, I considered the inside of my car. It was a disaster and I didn't have time to clean it up to any standard acceptable to people without preschool-aged children. The backseat was littered with food wrappers and empty juice boxes. The books that were supposed to stay in the bin beside Dante's car seat spilled out onto the floor. I briefly considered having the car valeted inside and out, considered the cost, and settled for the 'value wash' at the gas station. "Lou's Service Center" was the only full-service gas station in town and I was religious about getting my gas there.

Clara routinely rolled her eyes whenever I asserted that the disappearance of the full-service gas station was a sure sign of the decline of modern civilization. As a woman who worked for tips, it made me happy to tip Lou, the kindly almost-elderly man who pumped my gas every week, and often washed my windshield for free in the summer. Lou's wife Meryl sat behind the counter inside the service station, where I occasionally treated myself to a gossip magazine or an ice cream bar. When Dante was with me, she always gave him a lollipop.

"You need oil?" Lou wore thick gloves and a plaid quilted hat folded down over his ears. His breath billowed in the air when he spoke. His smile never faded.

"No, I think I'm okay today. But I'm going to get a car wash. Just the basic."

"There's a lot of salt on the road. You want the under wash too?" From most people, this would have constituted a pesky upsell, but Lou's face was kind and genuine.

"Sure, actually that's a good idea. This car has got to last me until retirement you know, Lou." I was keenly aware that my words were only partly spoken in jest.

"You got a lot of years left, a young lady like you. I tell you what," his eyes crinkled at the sides, and he tapped the top of my car with his gloved hand. "Today, I'll throw in the under wash for free."

Lately, any kindness like this brought with it the threat of tears, and I turned away momentarily to avoid showing emotion to Lou.

"Thanks, Lou. I appreciate it. You're a good guy, you know."

"Ah, yes, a good guy. Tell that to my wife in there." He gestured to Meryl, who was bent over a book of crossword puzzles. I thanked Lou, put the car in gear and headed toward the car wash.

Once back at home, I decided to vacuum the inside of my car until the battery died on the handheld dust buster, or until I got too cold, whichever came first. Because the vacuum had not been charged after the last time I cleaned up Cheerios in the living room, there was only ten minutes' charge in the unit, but it would have to do. By the time most of the crumbs in the passenger seat were brushed away by hand, I could barely feel my fingers.

Clara showed up right on time to do my make-up. After half an hour in her capable hands, I saw my reflection in the mirror, and I remembered what it felt like to have an occasion to dress up for. I hugged Clara longer and more tightly than normal, and she hurried off leaving just enough time for me not to be late.

I typed Dean's address into my GPS and started the drive to pick him up. What was the etiquette? Should I go and knock on the door or wait for him to come out? It had been a very long time since I dated anyone, and none of those dates had started like this.

I retrieved my silenced phone from my purse and texted Dean that I was waiting outside, worried about whether that was rude, but it was freezing and we weren't supposed to be on a *date* anyway. I was still on the fence about whether the evening was a good idea, and hoped Dean would at least pay for dinner and the axe throwing, though I knew I would have to offer to split the bill. The Brazilian steakhouse, BrazilMeat, had been his choice and it wasn't going to be cheap.

Dean texted me back quickly, and soon he was in the car, sitting on the almost-clean passenger seat. Because I had stayed in the warmth of the car, there was no awkwardness about the kiss hello or the hug hello or any of that. I just said 'Hi,' and waited for the click of his seatbelt before I pulled away.

The conversation was uneasy at first but soon became work-related which, while boring, was at least familiar and more comfortable than sitting in silence.

"Have you and Eugene worked out the details of the switchover yet? Not that it's any of my business...I mean, I'm not trying to pry, or whatever." I hoped this question wouldn't change the conversation from semi-normal to *awkward*, and that whatever happened tonight wouldn't impact my coming promotion.

"We're still going back and forth about the numbers. He's holding out for more than he would get from anyone else. But honestly, even if he doesn't budge, I can stretch to what he's asking. I just want to give him a run for his money. He's not always been the easiest guy to work for, as you know."

I surprised myself by laughing out loud.

"You think?" I rolled my eyes sarcastically but kept them on the still-snowy road. "He's been a total disaster most of the time. Remember when Anastasia accused Andrea of stealing her tips and he yelled at Andrea just before his precious daughter discovered them tucked behind the coffee maker where she had hidden them?"

"You know, Andrea's parents called him up on that. Eugene paid her for the rest of the weekend and apologized."

"Jeez, I wasn't sure an apology was even in his vocabulary. I've never heard that story before. Do you have any idea about the timeline for the changeover? I'm wondering when I should start to think about making up the schedule, you know..." I hesitated. "Is this too much work talk for you?"

"Nah. I haven't thought about anything else lately. My family is sick of hearing about it. I've been talking about nothing but buying the place for weeks."

“Do you have a big family?” Driving down the middle lane of the highway, I realized that I knew essentially nothing about Dean, despite having been friendly with him at work for several years.

“My dad died a year ago from a stroke. My mom died of breast cancer when I was sixteen.” My face flashed a guilty glance over at Dean. I vaguely remembered him being off work for a family emergency just over a year ago, before last Christmas.

“Oh Dean, I’m so sorry. I remember when you took time off but I didn’t realize what had happened.” A tenderness for him rose in my chest. It was obvious from the tone of his voice, which had almost imperceptibly cracked as he spoke about his parents, that it was still difficult for him to talk about. “Did anyone at work know?”

“I had to tell Eugene to get the time off. He was okay with it. Even came to my dad’s funeral. But I didn’t tell anyone else. I wanted to come to work and *not* talk about it, you know?”

I knew that feeling all too well. For me, work was a respite from constantly dwelling on the Tyler situation.

We drove along in fairly easy silence and Dean turned the radio on. He hadn’t answered my question about the timing of acquiring Eugene’s. I wasn’t sure if that was deliberate, and decided to let it go. There was construction once we got to the city which my GPS hadn’t accounted for. Eventually, half an hour late for our reservation, we arrived at the restaurant.

chapter 16

When Dean and I walked through the door of BrazilMeat, my mouth involuntarily fell open. Servers circulated, impeccable in their whites. Watching them weave between the tables was mesmerizing. I wondered how they kept their uniforms so spotless while they handled all that food. Brianne, our hostess, showed us to our table. Working in the restaurant industry made me very critical of other restaurants. I always noticed things that weren't perfectly clean. Servers annoyed me when they didn't refill my drink fast enough or when they didn't notice I needed more napkins or fresh cutlery.

This was not a problem here. It occurred to me that, of course, Dean would have the same predilections, and he had chosen the restaurant accordingly.

We worked our way through the meat of cows, pigs, chickens and crawlers of the ocean floor. I stopped worrying about Dante, work, and even Tyler, and laughed genuinely with Dean. It became obvious, to my great relief, that Dean and I were genuinely enjoying an evening between friends, and any concerns about Dean's *expectations* faded away.

"How...How are you doing?" Dean asked, draining his water glass. "I know you don't talk about your home life at work, but are things going kind of ok? I mean, tell me if it's none of my business."

"Well..." I paused, not sure how much to share. "It's been tough, you know? I guess every breakup is tough. And then with little Dante...I just never know if I'm doing the right thing." I hoped my face was neutral but suspected it betrayed my sudden sadness at the question. "Nothing prepares you for this. It's like I was on this path to what I thought was the rest of my life and suddenly the road just ends and I'm falling off this cliff I didn't see coming."

Dean was listening intently. I paused as the server filled both our water glasses and replaced dirty plates with clean ones.

"For what it's worth, it seems to me that you're doing a great job." Dean's tone was refreshingly matter-of-fact with no trace of pity, which was liberating. "You never miss a shift at work. Lots of people call in sick for less." He was right. I showed up at work the next day. No one else knew Tyler had left, and I hadn't even acknowledged he *had* left, which made it slightly easier for me to put on a brave face professionally.

"I just keep trying to show up, I guess. Who was it who said that eighty percent of success is just showing up? I show up for work, and for Dante. I try to do the next right thing. Some days are harder." I paused to bite a shrimp after dipping it into a spicy peanut sauce. "But then," with my mouth still partly full, "that's life, I guess. Some things are going to be harder..." It felt a lame thing to say and I spent a few moments chewing slowly to avoid saying anything else stupid.

"I'd say you're doing a pretty decent job. I think anyone who had gone through what you did would still be having a tough time. Is it getting better, at least?"

It was incredibly freeing to talk openly with someone who was a little bit removed from the situation and genuinely concerned about me.

"You know, it is. Little milestones happen that move the process along in tiny increments, and each one is a little easier to get over. I'll go home and Tyler has taken his golf clubs and his high school football trophies out of the house, and I sort of think, well, a little more of him is gone. At the beginning that was tough because I still wanted him to come back so badly. For a long time, I thought he *would* come back, actually. Like, for weeks I thought it was just a phase he was going through. It made it easier, being in that level of denial."

"It was a coping mechanism," the last of our plates were cleared away and Dean changed the indicator on our table to let the wait staff know we were finished with our main course. "That's understandable."

"Exactly. I can see that now. And it worked, partly. I spread the grief out over a longer time. That's what the books say anyway."

"Books?" Dean raised an eyebrow in interest.

"Oh yeah. You would be surprised at the secondary market of marital break-ups. There are books about how to get him back, books about how to heal from him, books about how not to screw your kids up after the divorce – I've read just about every one of those, I can tell you. I've read pretty much *all* of the books you can read. I'm trying really hard to do the right thing."

I reached into my oversized mom bag and pulled out a copy of *Mom But Not Wife – Losing Your Husband Without Losing Your Children.*

"Impressive," Dean took the book and flipped through the dog-eared pages.

"I thought it would make me feel less guilty if I did a lot of research about how not to screw up getting divorced. So, I bought every book I could find. I'm working my way through them. I usually have one or two in my purse."

"Does it?" Dean handed back the book.

"Does it what?"

"Make you feel less guilty? Reading the books."

I put the book back in my purse. "Oh. No, it doesn't usually. Not even a little."

A tall, spotless chef-type of individual arrived at the table brandishing a dessert with layers of brownie and ice cream, chocolate syrup and shaved chocolate.

"Oh we didn't order…" I started. Then Dean stood up.

"Victor. Good to see you." He shook the man's hand. "This is my friend Emily. Victor is the owner; we used to work together. Thanks so much for getting us a table at such short notice."

"My pleasure. Nice to meet you, Emily. Dean is an old friend of mine. I understand he's about to become a proprietor in his own right."

"Well, it's nothing like this. But I'm still excited about it." Dean's face reddened. It was obvious how proud he was about owning his own restaurant.

"Don't listen to him, Victor. Dean's going to be a great boss. I'm looking forward to him taking over."

"She's just saying that because I promoted her to head waitress. Which she will be great at too."

"Then consider this dessert a congratulations present to both of you, and enjoy it. Thanks for coming to see me, Dean. Anytime you want to visit, just let me know." Victor leaned in conspiratorially, "You two have a good night. Looks like you're having fun."

I leaned over the table and looked at Dean. "I am having fun. I was a little worried about going out with you tonight."

"I knew you were. But I told you – two friends going out. That's it. We're going to need to work more closely together very soon. I'm glad we get along so well."

"I was worried there would be weirdness. Especially since you're my boss now. I didn't want to get into all that. But it's totally fine. I should have trusted you." I was aggressively digging into the ice cream with a ferocity I would not have displayed on an actual date.

The amount Dean left for a tip was more than the cost of a meal for two at Eugene's. We thanked our server on the way out and pulled our coats together as we left BrazilMeat and headed back into the winter night.

chapter 17

Dean and I were in great spirits after our meal, and the axe throwing turned out to be a lot more fun than I expected. It also turned out to be considerably harder to do. It took absolutely all the muscles I could muster to hurl the axe at the ring around the bullseye, and even make it to the target board. In addition to superhuman strength, the axe had to rotate exactly once through the air on the way to its destination. The man who explained it to us was named Guy.

"Who wants to go first?" Guy held the axe out to me.

"Emily, you go ahead. Let's see what you can do." I remembered Michelle's advice, pictured a headshot of Tyler on the bullseye and let the axe fly with everything I had, missing the target completely. The axe lodged itself in the wall.

"Oh crap. Sorry about that. Did I wreck the wall?" Guy smiled and clapped his hand on my shoulder.

"You're not the first person to lodge an axe in that wall and I doubt you'll be the last. Dean, your turn."

Right in front of my non-believing eyes, Dean raised the axe – one handed if you will – and I watched it glide through the air, rotate once, and hit the middle yellow ring on the target.

"You've done this before!" My voice was a mixture of accusation and admiration.

He chuckled. "Once or twice. I told you my buddy owns part of this place, right? We used to throw in a league together. But when I started," he continued as he guided me to hold the axe properly with his hands over mine, "I found that it was very useful in relieving stress, which is why I thought it might be a good choice of activity for you." I threw again, slightly less disastrously, my axe managing to touch the outer ring on the target. "There you go. You're getting the hang of it already."

We threw for almost an hour, punctuated by a lot of laughing and talking. Guy assured me I would 'feel it in the morning' and advised a bath with Epsom salts to get over the muscle pain that was coming my way.

Dean and I headed back to my car. We were still joking around and genuinely enjoying each other's company. I pulled my phone out of my purse for the first time that evening and looked down at the screen.

Instantly, my contentment disappeared and my stomach clenched. Five missed calls from Tyler and one text –

Call me. 911.

This was the old code Tyler and I used only when something was wrong with Dante. My feet froze to the ground where I was standing and Dean stopped beside me.

"Is everything okay?" His eyes widened curiously.

"No. I'm not sure... I think something's wrong with Dante. I have to call Tyler." I started walking quickly toward the car. Dean caught up and was soon beside me again.

"Why don't you let me drive? Then you can focus on talking. Toss me the keys."

"It's a standard. Can you drive a standard?"

"Yup." Dean caught the keys, unlocked the doors and opened the door to the passenger side before he circled around to the driver's side and got in. I forced myself to sit down and fasten my seatbelt before moving my now-freezing fingers across the screen of my phone. We were about thirty minutes from home if Dean avoided the construction. The frustration of the past several months was instantly pushed back into my mind in full force, and the happiness of the evening was a distant memory. I was pissed off Tyler couldn't handle one single evening with Dante so that I might have just one night to myself. I prayed Dante was okay, and inwardly swore that if something wasn't actually wrong I would kill Tyler for making me come back.

The first time I called the number it went straight to voicemail. Tyler had left no messages when he called me, so all I had was his text, which told me nothing.

"Try not to think the worst," Dean said, as he deftly maneuvered the car in and out of traffic in considerable excess of the posted speed limit.

"I know," I attempted to say, but my ability to make conversation was gone. I called Tyler incessantly. Finally, he answered.

"Emily. Hi. How are you?"

"What's wrong? What's wrong with Dante?"

"Emily, he's going to be fine. Try to calm down."

"Calm down? Are you fucking kidding me right now? What is *wrong*?" My voice rose in pitch and in volume with every word.

"Listen." He paused and waited for me to stop yelling. "Listen. We went swimming tonight at the Y. Dante hit his head." I felt all the blood drain from my face. Suddenly my voice was barely a whisper.

"Is he…is he okay?" I felt the first tears spill over onto my face. Dean looked around in the front seat of the car, found a Dunkin Donuts napkin wedged between the seats and handed it to me.

"He's going to be fine. He's got five stitches. They're keeping him in overnight. Emily, listen to me. He's going to be fine. But I knew you would want to come."

"Okay." I managed, before a sob escaped my lips. "I'll be there in half an hour. I'm staying with him overnight. I'm staying." I was now almost unable to speak. "Tyler I have to go. Half an hour. Make sure Amy isn't there. I do not want to see her tonight." I hung up before he had a chance to answer, put my head in my hands and cried.

Dean was quiet for several minutes while I cried before he said softly, "Hey. Take a deep breath. It's going to be okay you know." He had obviously heard Tyler's voice audibly coming through the phone. "Really. Take a deep breath."

I tried to do what he suggested. I tried several times before finally, I stopped sobbing long enough to talk to Dean again and he spoke.

"Do you want me to go to the hospital with you? I can come with you if you want and maybe stay with you for a while?" I tried to straighten everything out in my head as he spoke. I needed to pull myself together.

"No, Dean, that's very kind. I appreciate it. I'm going to be there all night. I'll go on my own. And you're right – Kids get stitches all the time." I knew I was trying to convince myself, not Dean.

We pulled up to Dean's house and this time, Dean hugged me tightly as we switched places.

"You sure you're okay to drive? You're pretty upset."

"I'm sure. Thanks, Dean. You're a good friend. It was a fun night. I needed that."

"I'm just sorry you're coming home to this."

"Me too. But thanks. I'll see you Sunday. I'm working twelve to eight."

"Do you want to maybe call in sick?"

"I'll see how Dante's doing tomorrow. Thanks again, Dean."

And then, without another thought to the delightful evening I had just spent, I drove away a little too fast towards the hospital. Onto the next problem in this new life that never seemed to pause between one catastrophe and the next.

chapter 18

The trip to the hospital was a blur. I navigated the familiar streets on auto-pilot, thinking only about Dante. I prepared myself for the worst, picturing him with bandages and black eyes, or with his head shaved. I resolved not to show my shock no matter what he looked like. The guilt for being out having a good time when he hurt himself was all-consuming.

At the hospital, I quickly parked and ran inside the Emergency Room door. At the reception desk, I wiped away tears and gave my name and Dante's to the nurse. She was an older woman, matronly, and took my shaking hand in hers.

"Dear," she said, "Your boy is just fine. And we can't have him see you crying, it will only upset him. Take these," she pressed several tissues into my hand, "and go in there and clean up just a little bit. I promise you I will take you right to him after that, and I *guarantee* you he is going to be okay." I hesitated, and she squeezed my hand. "Go on now, dear. It will just take a minute."

Mechanically, I walked into the restroom and looked in the mirror. The nurse was right - I looked an absolute mess. Dante should not see me like this or he would assume something was really wrong. I put a dab of hand cream on a tissue and wiped the makeup from under my eyes, fished out a sample tube of mascara from my purse and applied it to my teary eyelashes. Better.

The nurse, whose nametag read 'Cheri,' beamed at me.

"There you go. That's lots better." She took my elbow and began to walk with me. "Your boy has a few stitches over his left eye and he's going to have a good shiner tomorrow to brag about. Other than that, he's okay. He's awake and he's not in any pain. In fact, I think he's watching cartoons on his iPad. We're going to keep him overnight and make sure he doesn't get any swelling."

As she finished speaking, she pulled back a curtain and there was Dante. Sweet, lovely, perfect Dante with just a tiny row of neat blue knots above his eyebrow. He was smiling as he watched the iPad. Tyler was sitting by the bed in a green armchair. He looked very stressed and I felt glad. *Serves you right, asshole.*

"Dante, I have someone here to see you." She squeezed my elbow and retreated from his bedside.

"Mommy!" Dante's face lit up and I forced a smile and rushed to grab him up. He smelled like antiseptic and chlorine. I held him tight, probably *too* tight, and fought back tears for the millionth time that day. Fighting back tears was becoming my default emotional state.

"Mommy, we went swimming. And I JUMPED! I jumped so high and then when I was getting out of the pool I slipped and hit my head. And I got these," he pointed proudly to his stitches. "Daddy said I was brave. I was *brave* Mommy."

I sat down and kissed his forehead ever-so-gently. "I'm sure you were buddy. I'm sure you were. I'm just going to talk to Daddy for a minute."

Tyler and I moved just outside the curtain and spoke in hushed voices.

"How could you let this happen to him? You were supposed to be watching him. How are we even going to pay for this?" My voice was quiet and seething.

"Emily, he's a little kid. Kids get hurt. And besides, you heard him in there...he's totally fine." A beat. "And my insurance will cover it. You're overreacting, honestly."

I fought every instinct to throat-punch, or in some other way seriously injure Tyler. *Keep it together for Dante.* I tried to remember the advice in all the divorce and parenting books on my bookshelf.

"Tyler, I want you to leave. Just go." Infuriatingly, he said nothing, turned, and walked back toward Dante's bed.

After Tyler left, Dante and I cuddled in and watched *Paw Patrol* on Netflix. Eventually, we both fell asleep.

The first thing I saw when my eyes opened the next morning was Dante's chubby hand, still wrapped around his iPad. Instinctively, I looked up at his head to check the status of the wound. There was nothing there except the neat stitches and the start of the black eye Cheri promised he would have.

I pulled myself up from my uncomfortable sleeping position and felt every muscle in my shoulders and arms protesting. Guy wasn't kidding about feeling it in the morning. On the walk from Dante's bed to the bathroom I noticed what a hive of activity the Emergency ward was. People were coming in by ambulance, and many in the too-small waiting room were brutally injured or seriously ill. People coughed violently behind masks. No wonder the nurse was able to assure me so confidently; Dante was probably the least injured person she saw yesterday. I made a mental note to send her a thank you card. Her kindness had made the disaster a little more bearable.

I got back from the bathroom, thinking about how glorious it was going to be to have a good hot shower. Dante was awake and chattering away to a nurse while she took his blood pressure.

"There's your mom. I told you she wouldn't go too far." She turned to me and continued, "Now, everything here seems good and we are confident that this little man is going to be just fine. I'll get you the discharge papers and we'll wave goodbye. Dante just asked me something about McDonald's for breakfast...I told him brave boys sometimes get treats and he should ask his mom really nicely." She winked at me and I surprised myself by smiling.

"Sure, buddy. Let's get you checked out and in the car and we can drive through McDonald's." I picked up his iPad and looked around the cramped space for the rest of his things.

"Can I have ice cream? Dad said we could get ice cream last night but then we came here instead."

"Ice cream for breakfast?" I hesitated only briefly "Why not, I guess. If they have ice cream at breakfast time, you can have ice cream. I might even have some too."

The nurse smiled and handed me a clipboard with paperwork to sign and places to initial.

"There you go, kids, you're good to go. You be careful, Dante. I don't want to see you in here again anytime soon."

Dante's big eyes looked very seriously at the nurse. "I'll do my best." His voice sounded wiser than his three years. It was my fault he had a seriousness a three-year-old shouldn't have. Another stab of guilt.

After the nurse left, I glanced around again, searching for the rest of Dante's stuff.

"Where's your coat, buddy?"

"Dunno, mom."

I pulled out my almost-dead phone and texted Tyler quickly –

Where is Dante's coat and bag

Quickly the reply came back.

Sorry. Came straight from the pool. No coat. I have bag.

What an idiot. How was I supposed to put the child in a freezing cold car with no coat? Not to mention all the favorite stuffed animals and DVD's were in his bag, thanks to my careful overpacking. I quickly texted him back -

Bring both to my house.

I assessed the situation and decided to go and get the car, crank up the heat and leave it momentarily running outside the Emergency room doors. Then I would dash back in and grab the underdressed Dante and strap him into the warm car.

"You stay here for just a minute, Dante. I'm going to get the car and then I'll come back and grab you." He accepted his iPad from my outstretched hand. "Here you go. Watch Thomas for just a minute and do not leave this bed." I hated leaving him alone, but didn't see another option. Once again, a problem created by Tyler and left for me to solve.

With my winter coat wrapped around me, I set out to retrieve my car. The snow was swirling again. Thankfully, the half wall outside the hospital entrance had only about three fluffy inches of new snow; not enough to stop me from getting my car into the driveway. I arrived at the spot I had parked the car and looked around, first casually and then with increasing urgency. My car was nowhere in sight. Panic began to creep in. I grabbed my key fob out of my purse and hit first the LOCK button and then the PANIC button. Still nothing. The only sound was the wind whipping the snow.

chapter 19

This was not happening. I put my hand on a metal sign post to steady myself and regroup. In that exact moment, I saw the red lettering on the sign: PICK UP AND DROP OFF ONLY. NO PARKING. The sign had been covered in snow the previous evening. Affixed to the pole was the name and number of a towing company; presumably, my car was in their possession. Towed away. Burning rage at Tyler kept me from crying, but only just. I resolved to take the cost of retrieving my car from the Mortgage account and strode purposefully back to the hospital to weigh up my options.

The nurses hung expectantly around Dante's bed, which they obviously needed for other patients. I plastered on my waitress smile and held Dante's hand as we walked out to the entrance of the hospital and sat down on two of what must have been the most disease-ridden chairs in all of Michigan. I tried not to think about the germs and focus on the task at hand.

I had sent several angry texts the night before. There were replies from Michelle and Clara, empathizing and asking me to keep them informed about Dante. I decided to call Michelle to ask her for a ride. I scrolled through the recently dialed numbers on my phone and touched her name while still forcing a happy face for Dante. Her number rang, though I had no idea what Michelle's phone number was anymore, because I just touched her name on my phone. Dante would likely never have to memorize an actual phone number. It was a good thing I didn't have to call Michelle from a pay phone because cell phone numbers weren't even listed.

"Hello," The male voice on the other end of the line threw me off kilter.

"Uh, sorry. I think I have the wrong number."

"Emily, is that you? It's James. You called my parents' landline."

"Oh, sorry, James. This is the most recent number I dialed for Michelle. Is she around?"

"No, she's at work. How's Dante? She told me last night he had stitches and was in the hospital. Is everything alright?"

"Dante's okay. But my car got towed because I parked it in a stupid no parking zone. And Dante has no winter coat because stupid Tyler didn't bring it to the hospital. So now we are stuck at the stupid hospital with no money, no car and a kid who I have *stupidly* promised ice cream from McDonald's for breakfast." Every time I said the word 'stupid' I hit it with more emphasis and my voice raised slightly. People nearby were glancing sideways at me.

"Tell you what," said James, "I'll pick you up and take you to McDonald's, my treat. All the ice cream you can eat. And then I'll drive you home."

It didn't occur to me as I spoke that I was suggesting James come and get us by complaining to him about the situation. My brain was exhausted and foggy. Even though it wasn't my intention, when James offered me a ride, a wave of relief washed over me. I glanced down at Dante and knew I couldn't turn down James' offer, pride be damned.

"Oh, James, that would be, uh, great. But I didn't mean to suggest, I mean, I wasn't trying to ask you to pick us up." My voice sounded lame, even to me.

"I know. But I'm happy to do it. If you can't count on your friends, who can you count on? Or in this case, your friend's big brother… I'll be there in fifteen minutes." He laughed, (awkwardly?), hung up and left me to sit down and pull Dante closer on my lap. The sliding emergency door let the freezing wind in every time it banged open and closed. On the plus side, Dante was fascinated watching ambulances come and go outside the window, many with sirens screeching.

The time slipped by quickly until James arrived, in a toasty warm car. Soon we were driving away from McDonald's with ice cream cones, and breakfast in brown paper bags. My eyelids started drooping. It was heaven in the warm passenger seat with someone else driving. I didn't even care that I looked like a total disaster.

"Oh, crap, James, how am I going to get my car back? I didn't write down the towing information. I can't even imagine how much money that's going to cost." The thought shattered the momentary drowsy contentment the ice cream and heated seats had tricked me into.

"I'll drive by, take a picture of it and text it to you. It's no problem." It struck me how *competent* James was. He just always seemed to know what to do and he wasn't full of himself about it either. I remembered a few sticky situations he bailed Michelle and me out of in high school, but was quickly jolted out of my reverie when we pulled up to my house.

"I'd invite you in, but the house is a mess and honestly, I just really want to get in the shower." I opened the back door and unbuckled Dante, who was strapped into James' back seat without a car seat, secured only by the lap belt. I knew this made me the worst mother on earth but I was too tired to care, and Dante had survived worse, and very recently.

"Sure. Get some rest okay? I'll catch up with you soon. I still owe you a shawarma, don't forget." His smile was warm and genuine.

I did my best to smile back.

"We'd better give the shawarma place we went to last time a miss. I wouldn't be surprised if my picture is up on their wall. See you, James. Thanks for the ride." I felt pain rip through my shoulder as the back door of the car closed, and trudged up the driveway.

Dante and I watched out the window as the fat snowflakes continue to fall while we ate our Egg McMuffins. Dante had a quick bath and then curled up on the couch with a blanket. He hadn't gotten a great night's sleep last night, and I certainly hadn't either. My plan was to join him on the couch after a very hot shower. I rummaged around under the bathroom sink for a bottle of body wash without cartoon characters on it, then cranked the water up as hot as I could stand it, letting the heat soothe my sore shoulders and neck. Soon I was wrapped in my robe, unplugging my phone from its charger on the kitchen counter. There was a text from Tyler -

Dantes stuff is on the side step

I opened the door, grabbed the bag, and shook the newly fallen snow off of it before lugging it inside. If it kept snowing I was going to have to shovel. Everything from Dante's bag went immediately into the washing machine. Amy used a flowery, obnoxious fabric softener and I couldn't stand having the smell in my house. I threw two Tide pods into the drum, selected 'extra rinse' and closed the washing machine door slightly harder than necessary.

chapter 20

Time continued to roll by. Some days were easier than others. The official date when Tyler and I would be divorced was drawing ever closer but I didn't know how to feel about it. I read about people who had 'divorce parties' to celebrate their freedom, but partying didn't ring true for me. No matter how much better things were slowly getting for me, and no matter how much I hated Tyler, the fact that we had failed and left Dante stuck in the middle of our failure didn't make me feel like partying.

I was working my way through a new book called *D is For Divorce- Not For Disaster* on my breaks at work when it wasn't too noisy, but I kept losing my place and ended up reading the first chapter five times before the book got lost under the passenger seat of my car.

It took about six weeks for Eugene and Dean to finalize the sale of Eugene's. To celebrate, the two men hosted a party similar to the yearly Christmas party. With my help, Dean was slowly hiring people to fill the gaps left by the staff who had left when the sale was announced. Dean was reluctant to rehire Zoe because she had jumped ship so quickly after Eugene's announcement. In the end, I convinced him she was a great waitress and worth having on staff, and I had my ally back at work.

At the party, Dean unveiled a huge poster of the new sign that would hang on the outside of the restaurant. He had the poster printed on thick cardstock and propped it up on the staff table under a sheet. Once everyone had a glass of soda or juice to drink, Dean stood up at the front of the group.

"I'm not someone who likes to talk much. But I'm excited to show you this."

He pulled the sheet off and we all read the words, 'New Dean's.' After the reveal, he announced that he had promoted me to head waitress, which only Zoe already knew. I convinced her to come back partly by telling her she would get whatever shifts she wanted.

After much cheering and applause, the party continued. Lots of people congratulated me. I soaked up the admiration of the younger waitresses and enjoyed the begrudging congratulations from the older ones. More than one of them thought they should have had the job of the head waitress. Too bad for them.

To celebrate my promotion, Michelle insisted on taking me on a girls' day out. We were both sitting in her kitchen when she informed me, after I had already agreed to go, that Grace-Ann was coming as well.

"Are you kidding me? No way. *No way* am I going anywhere with her. Forget it. I thought you said she was dead to you? This is the dumbest idea I've ever heard." A small muscle in my left eye threatened to twitch.

"Hold on. It's not dumb. We have a ton of mutual friends and you're always going to see Grace-Ann in town. The three of us have been friends forever... Can't you try to, you know, forgive and forget?" I stared at Michelle in disbelief and shook my head.

Michelle gazed up at me and tilted her head slightly like a puppy.

"Do it for me?"

I forced my breath in and out slowly two times before I answered. The muscle in my eye relaxed a little.

Michelle had always been there for me, most especially since Tyler left. She'd spent time watching me cry, and even more time trying to make me laugh. She never asked for anything in return. My eyes squeezed shut and my fingers massaged my temples.

"Okay. For you. Only for you, you understand. Not for her because she doesn't deserve it. And I'll tell you this for nothing – this is her *last chance*. I'm telling you right now, Michelle, this is it. If she's a jerk, then I'm done."

"Fair enough," Michelle pushed a fresh cup of coffee across the kitchen table to me. "If she screws this up, we're both done with her and Tyler can have her."

"I'd quite like Tyler to have her actually," I mused as I watched hazelnut-flavored cream swirl in my coffee. "I can't picture anything that would make me happier than if Tyler slept with Grace-Ann. Today preferably."

"Emily, behave." Michelle spooned Splenda into her cup and made a disapproving face.

Michelle and Grace-Ann were already in the front seat of Michelle's car when they picked me up to go to the Once Upon a Spring craft show and sale.

"*Spring* is a stretch, don't you think? It's forty degrees." I hoped Grace-Ann wasn't going to continue to complain for the entire day. As for myself, I was not speaking to her any more than required by the strictest rules of civility.

"When was the last time you remember having Spring in March?" asked Michelle both to Grace-Ann and me. "We get Winter and Summer. That's it. By Thanksgiving, we're freezing and by the Fourth of July, the heat is insufferable. Why the Pilgrims left Europe to come here will always be a mystery to me."

"It's supposed to a Spring-*themed* craft show or something," I replied. "Easter and Spring and rebirth. All that crap."

We drove on mostly in silence. Grace-Ann played with the radio and Michelle made more comments about the weather, or the scenery, or tidbits of gossip she heard in town about someone or other from high school. The conversation was occasionally natural but mostly forced. I grudgingly mused to myself how long the three of us had been friends.

We pulled in to the craft show, paid to park, and picked our way through the slushy gravel parking lot to the front door of the event building.

As soon as we were inside, my spirits lifted a little. Michelle, of course, knew I loved big craft shows, the kitchier the better. For me, they were mostly about looking look at how beautiful it all was, more than buying the lovely things I could never afford. Wistfully, I wished I knew how to *make* things for a living, instead of just delivering things to tables for people to eat.

Michelle threaded one arm through my elbow and one through Grace-Ann's, and pulled us close, slightly more dramatically than necessary.

"Listen. Both of you. I'm serious. We are celebrating today. Emily, our dear friend," I pursed my lips slightly, "Has gotten a promotion. And so we three *friends*, are celebrating. Now let's celebrate. Okay?" She didn't let go until we both stiffly said 'okay.'

"It is my mother's birthday on Sunday," continued Michelle, "And I am still pissed off at her for forgetting that I turned vegan and serving roast beef for my own birthday dinner last year. Our mission here today, ladies, is to find her the most hideous present possible for under fifty bucks."

"Didn't you give up being vegan, like a week after your birthday?" Grace-Ann quipped as we entered the throngs of craft shoppers.

"Yes of course. Being a vegan was *horrible*. I don't know how people do it. I hated every minute of it and I didn't even lose any weight. But the point is, she was told I was a vegan and did not prepare me a meal I wanted to eat on my own birthday!"

"In that case, isn't fifty dollars is a bit on the high side? We should find something hideous for ten bucks, tops." I moved toward a table of anatomically correct felt puppets and began to look through them very gingerly.

"No. It's got to be fifty. She gave me fifty bucks for my birthday, the miserly cow, so I'm spending it on her in protest. But she has to hate the present."

"I'm truly in awe of your capacity for spite." It was a sincere compliment.

"I know. It's a gift." Michelle joined me at the table.

I held up one of the puppets with especially saggy breasts for her to see.

"That's not bad. How much is it?"

I searched for the price tag.

"Sixty-two dollars and ninety-nine cents." I was taken aback.

"Get *out*," gasped Grace-Ann. "You cannot be serious." She picked up one of the puppets herself and read the back of the tag out loud, quietly enough not to disrespect the puppet-maker who sat nearby. "Each Body by Dee puppet is handcrafted and infused with the correct chakra energy for each part of its body. The proud genitals of the felt creatures cry out in celebration of the sexual joy available to us all."

We carefully and silently walked away from the table. About fifty feet away from the puppets, we dissolved into fits of laughter. Grace-Ann had tears running down her face. I found myself in the middle of my two oldest friends again and this time it was my turn to grab both their arms as we continued into the craft fair.

"I tell you what, Michelle. If we don't find anything better, I'll give you the extra twelve ninety-nine to get that puppet. But you have to invite me to your mom's birthday party."

"Done. But we'll have to find the one with the most pubic hair." She was happy but completely serious.

"I can just imagine her opening it. Oh Michelle, she'd never speak to you again!" The thought of Mrs. O'Connor opening an anatomically correct puppet at Sunday birthday dinner was enough to make Grace-Ann and I dissolve again into fits of giggles.

chapter 21

For the rest of the day, both Grace-Ann and I were careful to avoid the topic of Tyler and Amy, and Michelle didn't bring it up either. There were moments when I forgot it was hanging between us. In those moments, it was like old times.

It was unclear whether Michelle had made up the quest for her mother's terrible present to get us to spend time together, but if she had, it was a smart move. Grace-Ann and I were united with her in the search. Walking through the arena-turned-market, I deeply coveted many lovely things I couldn't afford. At one modest stand sat an Amish woman selling the most beautiful quilts I had ever seen. I hesitantly touched the rich, thick cotton fabric; each stitch was uniform and perfect. There were dozens of bright colors and complex patterns and the lady behind the table smiled openly at me from under her black bonnet.

"You can go ahead and touch them, dear, they won't break." Her voice had what sounded like a thick German accent.

"Did you make all of these? They're so beautiful."

"We make them together. My name is Rachael." She offered me her hand, and shook mine firmly, clearly touched by my reverence for her work. "You could learn, you know."

"Me? Oh no. Really. I couldn't do anything like this. I wouldn't know where to start. But I'd love to own one…someday."

"Would you like to know more about these quilts?"

For the next few minutes, Rachael showed me the differences between the patterns, told me their names and explained what separated the Nine Patch Quilt from the Double Wedding Ring. My favorite was the Royal Star. Each fabric square had an eight-pointed star, with variations in a different color. The quilt looked like a cross between a rainbow and a kaleidoscope. I lingered over it and wondered if I would ever own something so grown-up and beautiful.

Michelle came over and joined me.

"Rachael, this is my friend Michelle. Michelle, check out these quilts. Aren't they amazing? Rachael and her friends make them by hand."

"Wow." Michelle ran her hand gently over the quilt I was looking at. "How much are they?" I hadn't even dared to ask. It seemed rude to attach a price to such a magnificent thing.

"The one your friend likes," Rachael smiled up at us, "Is eight hundred and seventy dollars. Some are less and a few are quite a lot more."

"Wow. Eight hundred dollars is a lot," I said out loud before realizing I was probably being rude to Rachael. "Totally worth it, though, I mean, I wish I could afford one."

"Maybe one day," said Rachael, "Here, take our card." The delicate script on the card read 'Amish Home Quilts.' Michelle and I both took a card. I tucked mine in my purse, and we thanked Rachael before continuing our walk through the craft fair.

We bought paper bags of kettle corn and walked around eating it for the next hour, working our way past handmade items of varying in degrees of amazingness, ranging from the Amish quilts to what we were calling the genital puppets, until we had walked all the way around the building and seen all the vendors. It seemed like a pretty natural place to end our time at Once Upon a Spring. Michelle found a bowl for her mother that was made on a pottery wheel by an ultra-left-wing feminist group, something that was sure to offend Mrs. O'Connor almost as much as the puppet would have. Michelle named the color of the plate piss-yellow. It was truly hideous, and at forty-four dollars, came in right on budget.

The drive home was a lot easier because the three of us had gotten most of our old groove back. Every time the thought of Grace-Ann at Shawarma Shop crossed my mind, I felt a flicker of anger but tried to let it go. For her part, Grace-Ann didn't bring up the fact that I had poured sixteen ounces of Coke on her lap, so I guess we were both on our best behavior.

Michelle's phone rang at a stop sign and she picked it up and hit speakerphone.

"Hello? You're on speaker."

"Oh hi, Michelle. It's James. Are you on your way home?"

"Yeah, we're about forty minutes away. What's up?"

"I was just going to ask if you wanted to go for dinner. Mom and Dad are at The Bingo."

Some things didn't change and for that, I was thankful. My parents and the O'Connors had been going to 'The Bingo' as they called it, for as long as I could remember. My mother said it was the best day of her life when they banned smoking at 'The Bingo.' Before they went non-smoking, my parents came home every week reeking of cigarettes. When we were teenagers, we spent a few Saturday nights at 'The Bingo' to raise money for the school marching band. It was a lucrative fundraiser, but the smell afterward was terrible. I washed and washed my hair and I could still smell the smoke in it the next day.

"I'm with Grace-Ann and Emily."

"Hi, James," we called in chorus.

"Oh, hi there. Why don't you two come with? I'm thinking maybe Ruby Tuesday's."

Michelle poked Grace-Ann and smirked at her.

"Because you got those coupons in your email, right?"

"You know it. I'm a sucker for coupons in my email. You guys in?"

"Girls? You want to go to dinner with me and my dorky, penny-pinching big brother?" Michelle and James' banter was comforting, the same way it was when they talked about 'The Bingo.'

"I'm in," said Grace-Ann.

"Yeah, me too." This was turning out to be a good day. I decided I was looking forward to seeing James... then asked myself just how much was I looking forward to it? Was it because Clara brought up dating James? I pushed the thought away. This was just dinner with friends. The important thing today was Grace-Ann and I were getting back on track. *Probably.*

Still, when Michelle offered to drive us all to her house to hang out until dinner, I asked her to drop me at home instead to quickly shower and change. I told myself it didn't mean anything at all. After my shower, I did my best to accent my mostly plain features with what Clara rightfully referred to as my shaky-eyeliner-hand, and found a clean pair of jeans and a slightly fitted sweater to wear over top. The sweater had a neckline that wasn't exactly plunging but definitely wasn't a turtleneck either. I sprayed a cloud of my favorite body spray into the air and walked through it, wondering whether I was trying too hard. I grabbed my favorite lip gloss from the vanity, chose a bling-y denim jacket, despite the frigid temperatures, and dashed out the door.

chapter 22

The parking lot at Ruby Tuesday's was packed. Inside, my friends already had a booth by the window, because I was fifteen minutes late, owing to the level of vanity involved in my getting ready.

"Nice of you to join us," remarked Michelle, peering over me at the menu.

The only seat left in the booth was beside James, and a soda water with a twist waited for me on the table. I sipped it while I perused the menu.

"What are you guys having?" I asked.

"Why do you always want to know what other people are having? Every time we go to a restaurant, it is the first thing you say." I kept my head in my menu and answered Michelle.

"It's not the first thing I say. The first thing I say is 'Do you have Dr. Pepper on tap?' and the *second* thing I want to know is what you guys are having. If everyone is having a burger I'm hardly going to order a steak, am I? They wouldn't come out at the same time and my steak would end up overcooked or your burgers would sit under the lights. Or vice versa." I turned the menu over to read the 'lighter options.'

"This is the fun of going out to eat with a waitress," remarked Grace-Ann dryly.

"You guys should thank me for offering my expertise at no charge, is what I think." I set my drink down on a paper coaster and folded my menu.

"I'm having a bacon cheeseburger," said James, "and the salad bar."

"The salad bar goes without saying," said Michelle, "why would you come here otherwise?"

"I'll have a burger too then," agreed Grace-Ann.

"Me too," ended Michelle. "There. We're all having burgers. What are you going to have, Em?"

Right on time, the waitress arrived at the table.

"Hi, I'm Susie and I'll be serving you guys tonight. Are your drinks still okay? What can I get you?" She beamed and I felt a waitress-kinship with her.

Michelle, James, and Grace-Ann all ordered burgers of various descriptions.

"What about you, hon? What would you like?"

"What do you recommend tonight?" This was the third question I always asked at a restaurant. The servers always knew what was good in the kitchen. If they were smart, they told you their actual opinion instead of what the chef was trying to push, because happy customers always tipped better.

"The eight-ounce sirloin is good tonight."

"Great. I'll have that. Medium rare with a baked potato and the garden bar."

She took our menus and walked away, telling us to help ourselves to salad. My three friends stared at me incredulously.

"You're quite something, you know that?" said James, as we got up out of the booth. "I thought you said it was better to all order the same?"

"I know. It *is* better, but I always order what the waitress suggests and that rule trumps the rule about ordering all the same." This made perfect sense to me.

"Again, welcome to the fun of eating at a restaurant with Emily," said Michelle to James as she heaped sunflower seeds on the top of her mixed greens and blue cheese.

The rest of the meal passed without incident. We ordered coffee, and two desserts to share between the four of us. Just after Susie brought dessert to the table, Grace-Ann's phone rang and she glanced down at it.

"Oh crap. It's my little brother. Hold on a sec. Sorry." She answered the phone and then mostly listened to whatever he was saying.

"No, it's okay. Don't go anywhere. I'll be there in – oh crap. I don't have my car. Hold on," she hit the mute button on her phone. "Michelle, I hate to do this but how think it will be until we leave? My brother is stuck at the train station and my parents are at 'The Bingo' and they're not answering their phone. Would you drop me home when we're done here so I can pick him up?"

"Sure. Let's just go now. I'm not really into dessert. James will pay for dinner, right James? And then Emily, you can you just run James home?" James nodded his ascent. "Tell Edward we'll be there in ten."

Amid a flurry of promises to get together again soon, Grace-Ann and Michelle disappeared, and James and I were sitting on the same side of the booth with two desserts in front of us and four coffees. I waited just a moment. I didn't want to seem like a pig but I was staring longingly at the chocolate cake and ice cream sitting in front of James, and less lovingly at the apple pie sitting in front of me.

"Don't hold back on my account," said James. "Now we have one each." He smiled at me and picked up his fork.

"Uh, James, a question for you. Do you actually like chocolate cake, like a lot? Or do you maybe like apple pie better? Just a question."

"You'd like the chocolate cake, is that what you're saying?" I stifled a laugh which came out anyway and then spread to James as well. He switched the plates.

"Only if you don't mind," I pulled the cake toward myself.

"What if I did mind? What should I have said then?" James poured cream into my coffee.

"Well then, you would have to be a gentleman and still give me the cake." I picked up my fork and put what I hoped was at least a moderately delicate amount of cake into my mouth. "Or arm wrestle me for it," I said with my mouth full, taking a drink of coffee to wash down the cake. "I'm freakishly strong. I would have kicked your ass in an arm wrestle, just for that piece of cake."

"Then I'm certainly glad I offered. The last thing my fragile male ego needs is to be beaten by a girl, in public, at an arm wrestle over a piece of cake. There are a lot of things wrong with that, I'm sure you'll agree." James gave me a look of mock seriousness.

"I'll agree to no such thing. It all sounds perfectly reasonable." I paused briefly. "I can't help noticing you're not eating the pie either. Are you just not a dessert guy, or are you taking your time with it? Just wondering."

James looked over at me, raised his eyebrows and then pushed the pie over to occupy the space the cake had previously occupied.

"Food makes me happy," I said by way of explanation. "It's one of the reasons I'm a waitress. Also, I got pregnant and dropped out of college. That's another big reason." It was supposed to sound like a joke, but it definitely didn't. "Oh my gosh. This is likely too much information. I'm cake drunk."

"You're quite an interesting woman, Emily. I'm enjoying getting to know you better."

Hot color rushed up my neck and into my face.

"I'm just going to pop out to the ladies' room. I'll be right back." I took the opportunity to be alone in the restroom to stare myself in the face and have a harsh talk with myself.

"James is your friend." I said to the mirror, "and you need all the friends you can get." Then, forcefully - "Pull yourself together, woman!"

I finished my self-pep talk and started to wash my hands before returning to the table when I heard a flush, and Susie the waitress popped out of a stall.

"I'm going to have to disagree with you on that one. He's totally into you, and you can always make more friends. Good luck!" She finished washing her hands next to me and disappeared back into the restaurant.

chapter 23

I returned to the table, slightly more composed, but also a little rattled by Susie's unsolicited opinion.

"All ready to go?" James sipped the coffee Susie had managed to refill between leaving the restroom and my return to the table. Admirable.

"Sure." I grabbed my purse and we headed out to my car, me in my not-warm-enough coat, trying not to let my teeth chatter.

"Thanks for the ride," James offered as he closed the passenger side door and I rubbed my hands together before putting them on the freezing steering wheel.

"It's a no-frills experience, I'm afraid. No seat warmers here. Your butt will have to brave the cold." It was a little surprising how comfortable I felt with James. Something to do with him being my best friend's brother, and our history of good-natured teasing when we were younger, probably.

"I appreciate your concern for my butt. So far tonight I have learned that you are an arm-wrestler and a butt-nurturer."

"You know your sister got your mother *quite* the birthday present today." I hoped my changing the subject wasn't too clunky and obvious.

"Is she still mad about the vegan thing?" He asked, sighing.

"Yes! How did you know? She said she had to spend..."

"The same amount of money my mother gave her," he joined me and we finished the sentence in unison. "I know. She's been talking about it since last April. She doesn't let things go."

"When is your mother's birthday?" I asked, slowing down for a yellow light we could probably have made. I was enjoying James' company, and not looking forward to going back to my empty house and the three loads of Dante's laundry that needed to be folded and put away before he came back tomorrow.

"What's today? Thursday?" James asked in response to my question.

"I think you'll find it's Friday. You really need to find a job to go to. You're losing touch." The left-hand turn signal clicked as I turned the wheel.

"I'm starting to think that myself...if it's Friday then my mom's birthday is tomorrow. Would you mind stopping for a second at the bookstore so I can run in and grab her a card?"

"Sure." Best not to wonder whether I was glad to be spending an extra half hour with James. I knew full well Barnes and Noble was closed at eight-thirty on a Friday evening but drove there anyway. And just like that, I was officially making excuses to spend more time with James. Clearly it wasn't only about not wanting to go home to an empty house.

We drove up to the bookstore door and when James realized it was closed, I suggested we drive to Target. We got a parking spot close to the door because of the odd hour and walked in.

"I won't be more than a couple of minutes. I just need to zip over there and grab the closest greeting card and then we can go," said James as we moved over to free one of the giant red plastic shopping carts.

"I, uh, actually have a system at Target. So, I'll just do my thing for five minutes here and meet you back."

"What do you mean, a system? I literally just need one birthday card." I would have understood if he were annoyed, but his face was only bemused.

"When I come to Target, I like to go through the store in a certain order. It's a system. Not in an OCD way." I paused. "Kind of in an OCD way, actually."

"Go on," said James, falling into step with me beside the cart.

"I get the cart, and then I go to this part here, which is where you get things for one or two or three dollars. Sometimes I find cute things for Dante in here. Or post-it notes for me. I like post-it notes." I dropped in an educational board book for Dante and a package of pens with *My Little Pony* on them for the waitress station.

"Then I go clockwise through the store, through the women's section, and around past the toys and housewares and menswear. At the back corner is the seasonal stuff." We walked on until we were beside the beginnings of a display with BBQ tools and lawn darts.

"It's the middle of winter. Why are these things out?" James asked.

"This is when they put them out. Anyway, it's March. Almost Spring." We continued through the store. "Then, after a hard right at seasonal, I dip back into the homewares and have a look at coffee mugs and blankets. And candles. I like candles." He joined me in sniffing a bunch of different candles and watched while I held up various serving platter and cake stands before putting them all back carefully on the display.

"Then we keep going past electronics which doesn't really interest me, to be honest. But sometimes I'll buy a DVD for Dante here if they're on sale or I see a *Thomas* one he doesn't have."

"You seem to know a lot about Target. And yet our cart remains almost-empty," he mused.

"I know. I sometimes would rather admire stuff than buy stuff. Admiring is cheaper as well." We did another ninety-degree turn with the cart. "This is the pharmacy. This stuff is cheaper at Meijer. But here," I gestured grandly to my left, "is the hair and make-up. And they have more Suave products here than anywhere else. And Suave is my favorite. You will also find," I continued, "if you turn your head to your right, that you are in the middle of the paperware and more importantly, the greeting card section. I will leave you there while I choose several hair care products I may or may not actually need."

"Deal," James said as he veered off into the tall rows of pre-written paper sentiments.

In the check-out line, James looked at the five things I was buying. The pens, the board book, a brightly colored tube of *Bob the Builder* bubble bath, and two gold-colored bottles of leave-in conditioner.

"You're buying surprisingly little, considering how thoroughly you covered the store."

"I have to follow the system." I paused and then added, "There are very few things in my life I can control. I like my Target system."

Once we had checked out and returned the cart to its resting place, I drove James home. How could it be ten-forty-five pm? We had spent more time at Target than I intended.

Back in the house, I started folding Dante's laundry and made a pile of things that needed to be put through a refresh cycle on the dryer to get the wrinkles out. The odd time I got a whiff of Amy's fabric softener that hadn't washed out. It was an accurate representation of how my life was now. No matter how I tried to separate my life from Tyler and Amy, or make my way forward without them, there was always a faint Tyler-ness surrounding me. I wondered what Dante would look like when he grew older and admitted to myself that there was a real possibility my own son's face would be a constant reminder of his father. These were things I only thought about for a few minutes at a time before dismissing them. It was the deal I had struck with myself - frequent short wallowing, then move on.

Once all Dante's clothes were neatly tucked into his drawers, I did a quick tidy and headed to bed, satisfied with how the day had played out, but mostly looking forward to greeting Dante in the morning.

chapter 24

Gradually, the brutal cold lifted a little and the crocuses and daffodils pushed their head up between bouts of snow and freezing rain, eventually outlasting the cold until Spring broke. I always found hope in the victory of the crocuses, this year more than ever. Dante's wet snow boots gave way to muddy rain boots, and people in the neighborhood took their Christmas lights down as soon as they were sure their ladders wouldn't slip on the ice.

I allowed Dante an occasional package of the Mini Eggs that were everywhere at the grocery store. He loved pulling egg decorating kits off the shelf and into the shopping cart from his seat at the front. Easter would be another first - the first Easter without Tyler. Just like Christmas had been a first, and Valentine's Day and soon the summer. I looked forward to the day after Halloween, when nothing on the calendar would be the 'first' of anything.

We put four dozen eggs in the cart and three 'Dudley's Eggceptional Decorating Kits,' one each of tie-dyed, sparkly, and some set-up with stickers you were supposed to melt around the eggs with a hair-dryer. That one would probably get 'lost' in the back of the cupboard. It looked like it would be a nightmare to execute.

"Do you think that's enough eggs, Mom?" Dante looked over his shoulder from his seat in the front of the shopping cart.

"Yes. I think you will have more eggs than the White House lawn if we decorate all these eggs." I smiled down at him and patted his chubby hand.

"Can Dad and Amy come over and help us do them? Amy is really good at stuff like this." The casual innocence of his question stopped me momentarily dead in my tracks. Dante was focused on the sugar cereals, and which ones he could reach from where he was sitting. His request was totally innocent and offhand. I tried to focus on being thankful. He was so well-adjusted to his new situation.

"Maybe not this time. But do you want to get a box to take to their house? Why don't you take this amazing sticker one to Dad and Amy's?"

"Yeah," he replied, trying, from his perch in the front of the cart to score a box of Lucky Charms. "Amy would like that one. But we better send her eggs too. Just in case."

"Sounds good. It's nice of you to remember Dad and Amy. You're a good kid." I liberated the biggest 'family-size' box of Lucky Charms from the shelf and put them in the cart.

My contribution to Easter dinner at my parents' house on Sunday was dessert. There were a lot of variables involved in choosing what to bring. It had to be something nicer than anything I could make myself, but also had to have a price point my mother would not be able to place. Otherwise, she would subtly shame me for spending too much money, clucking her tongue. "I could have made that for much less than you paid, Emily." Unless it was something mom didn't like. Then she would say, 'Oh I would have made dessert if you didn't have time to make something, Emily.' There was no pleasing her. After deliberating in the Meijer bakery department, I drove to the 'CakeSmith' and bought a dozen hand-decorated cupcakes in four flavors I hoped would please at least almost everyone.

Nevertheless, when the cupcakes came out at dessert, my mother considered them skeptically. "In my day, cupcakes were usually more for children." She wrinkled up her nose. "Of course, these are lovely, Emily. But I could have made a cake if you couldn't find one you thought we would all like."

"I like cupcakes, Mom," Clara came immediately to my defense.

"Me too!" called Dante, reaching for a chocolate one.

"Dante, let me see your cupcake." I took it from his hand and looked at it. "It doesn't smell good to me. Does it smell okay to you?"

He looked seriously at me and bent down to smell the cupcake. I pushed it up gently until he had icing on his nose, and we all laughed.

Dante wrinkled his nose, touched the frosting and yelled, "Selfie! Do a selfie!"

I took out my phone, which earned another withering look from my mother, and opened the camera, leaning into Dante for the photo. Clara joined from the other side and we took several selfies.

"Let me see! Let me see!" Dante always wanted to see the pictures of him instantly and I loved how pleased he was with himself.

After he looked at the pictures, he turned to Clara, "Auntie, let me see your cupcake." It was immediately obvious to everyone what he was going to do and Clara played along. "It doesn't smell good. You smell it, Auntie."

When Clara bent her head slightly toward him, Dante smashed the cupcake with full force on her face, until she was completely covered with lemon frosting.

"Ha!" Dante said.

There was the briefest pause before everyone, even my mother, burst out laughing.

"Selfie!" yelled Dante, and this time Clara's phone came out.

The time after dinner at my parents' house had a predictable, comfortable rhythm. My mother cleared the table and then retired to the little living room to put her game shows on. Her job was done. Dad took Dante for a walk to the park if the weather was good, or got a puzzle or game to play with him if it wasn't. Clara and I met up in the kitchen behind the sink, on the right and left respectively. I methodically washed the dishes in my side of the double sink and passed them to Clara to be dried and put away. My mother had never owned a dishwasher.

Once when we were children, Clara whispered to me, "Drop one and break it. Then we won't be allowed to wash and dry anymore. I'll do it too. You go first."

Gamely, I dropped the gravy boat and it smashed into shards on the floor. When Clara heard and then saw the carnage she instantly lost her nerve, and my mother was immediately upon us. "What have you *done*? That is your grandmother's china! They don't make that pattern anymore!" Mom was livid. It didn't get me out of washing dishes, and my mother still glared at me pointedly whenever she set the plain replacement gravy boat down on the table.

Now as adults, Clara and I enjoyed doing the dishes. Out of the earshot of the other members of the family, we talked about what had been said at dinner and what we were planning for the week. Clara, with a little bit of prodding, would tell me about her courses at Michigan State, and which profs she liked and didn't like. She was usually hesitant discussing anything she was enjoying at college because she knew I wanted to go back and finish my own degree. 'As soon as Dante's a little older.' It was a reverse mantra – the more I said it, the less I believed it.

We also generally avoided the topic of Tyler at these dish-washing sessions, but occasionally the conversation naturally moved its way to include him, especially when we talked about Dante.

"Have you decided where you're going to enroll Dante for pre-kindergarten?"

"I'd like him to go to St. Isaac's. I've got to make an appointment to go there and talk to them." It was on my list of things to do. I was putting it off because it involved talking to Tyler and I didn't want to talk to Tyler.

"Will you be able to swing the tuition? I mean, will Tyler split it with you?" Clara worried about my finances, probably because she saw that I constantly did too.

"I think so. I'm not entirely sure if he technically has to or not. It's not too much money until Dante's older. About thirty-five hundred dollars a year, so if they let me spread the payments out over all twelve months and Tyler pays half, it's pretty doable at least for the time being. I'd really like him to go there." Clara passed me back a plate that wasn't completely clean and I plunged it into the soapy water.

"I wonder if Sister Mary-Francis is still there. Remember how we snuck into her classroom at lunch and crazy-glued all her pens to her desk?"

"Yeah. They stayed like that all year, remember? She completely refused to acknowledge that anything had happened." The now-cleaner dish was passed back to Clara to be rinsed and dried.

"It took all the fun out of it, not seeing her upset, so I guess she was smarter than us in the end." All that remained to wash were the serving plates. I started draining the sink to refill it with cleaner water. Clara used the time to put the stack of dried dishes in the cupboards.

"Have you gone on any more dates since your outing with Dean?" Clara was trying to sound casual.

"No. I just haven't had the heart for it to be honest. And anyway, who am I going to date? I don't even go out enough to *meet* someone to date, let alone date anyone. Dating would take time and effort. I don't have a lot of either of those things to spare."

"What about a guy from work? You need to start putting yourself out there."

"Clara, that's such a cliché. Give me a break." The sink was now half-full of water again and I squeezed dish soap out over the sponge and picked up the second-rate gravy boat to clean it. We continued washing and drying in familiar and comfortable silence.

"Do you want to know what I think?" My mother was standing behind us. I had no idea how long she had been there.

"Oh, hi Mom," Clara said over her shoulder.

I ignored the question and kept washing. I decidedly did *not* want to know what my mother thought, but that didn't matter because we would hear it anyway.

"I think you should be spending all your free time with Dante. He seems to spend a lot of time here, and that's before you factor in how much time he's away from you when he's at *his father's*." She had a certain acidic tone she used to refer to all things relating to my separation and impending divorce.

"Well, Mom, I don't know what to tell you. I work a lot. I'm doing my best with the situation I have." I tried to keep my voice steady, but my hands started to shake in the water. I closed them over a serving platter and concentrated on breathing slowly. Clara looked sideways at me cautiously. Maybe my mother had gotten her vitriol out of her system, and was finished.

She was not.

"It seems to me," she went on, "that this whole mess you find yourself in right now is just par for the course with you, Emily. It was only about four years ago when you stood here in this kitchen and told us you were dropping out of college because you were pregnant and getting married to Tyler. And we all know how that's turned out." She paused. "I told your father at the time, I said, 'Emilio, we're going to end up raising that child.' And now, it looks like I was right."

My anger was bubbling over but I was determined not to let my mother see how upset she had made me. I remembered Sister not reacting to the pens stuck to her desk, took a deep breath and then turned around, still holding the slippery gravy boat in my wet hands.

"I tell you what, Mom. I'm going to do you a favor today. I'll take looking after Dante completely off your plate for you. In fact, I'll take seeing him at all off your plate. As well as seeing me. Or talking to me," I continued. I hoped my voice sounded resolute and not shaky.

"Emily…" Clara started softly, touching my shoulder.

"No, I'm serious, Clara. This is ridiculous." To my mother, "I'm sick of you judging me. I'm sick of you sneering at me like I'm a failure. And if you're talking like this when I'm here, I hate to think what sorts of things you're saying about me to anyone else who will listen when I'm not here, or to Dante, for that matter." I should have stopped to take a cleansing breath but I didn't. "So as of now, don't worry about looking after Dante. And *you* can explain to Dad why he's not coming here anymore. Because I'm sure as hell not going to." On the word *hell*, the soapy gravy boat slipped out of my hands. Clara grabbed for it and missed. It shattered on the floor and my mother's face became even more pale and strained.

Ignoring the mess, I walked into the living room, grabbed Dante's bag and set it by the door, ready to go when he came back with my father.

My mother stood rooted to her spot on the kitchen floor, staring at the shards of porcelain Clara was picking up.

"Fine. If that's the way you want to play it. We'll just see who comes crawling back to who first."

"It's *whom*, actually. I learned some grammar in the first half of the English degree you refused to help me pay for. And yes. We sure will." I put my own shoes on, ready for an exit.

chapter 25

I was tying the laces of my sneakers when the door to the garage flew open. Dante was standing in the frame, on his own.

"Mom, it's Gramps. He fell. Come quick. Come!" he grabbed my hand and pulled me out the door.

My father had slipped on a patch of ice at the end of the sidewalk and now sat on the ground holding his ankle with a grimace on his face. "I'm fine, Emily… I'm sure it's fine. Just help me up for a second here." I gripped my father's forearm while he put his other hand on my shoulder and he tried to rise to his feet. He was okay on his left foot but when he tried to put weight on his right foot, he yelped in pain and had to sit back down on the driveway.

I knelt down beside him. "What happened? Did you land on your hip?" A broken hip in a man my father's age might result in a long convalescence.

"No, I slipped on the ice and kind of fell over on my ankle. I'm sure I just twisted it. It's probably a sprain. Let's try again."

Reluctantly, I tried a second time to help my father into a standing position. No dice. "Dad, you need to stay there while we figure out what to do. Don't try to put weight on it. Maybe you just need to rest for a minute." I was not being truthful. It was obvious that he had done at least relatively serious harm to his ankle.

Back in the house, I pointedly ignored my mother. She pushed past me out the door and began walking to where Dad was sitting on the pavement.

"Clara, I think he's busted his ankle. Can you take him to the hospital? I'm supposed to have Dante to Tyler's house for seven-thirty and I still have to stop home to get some of his stuff." Including the loathsome hair-dryer Easter Egg kit.

"Should we call an ambulance?" Clara wondered out loud, "Or can we get him in the car?"

I thought about it for a second. There was no way Dad could stand up. Could he hop to the car and stretch his leg across the back seat?

"Do they have coverage for an ambulance? How much does it even cost to take an ambulance? I'm worried it will be a lot."

"Yeah," Clara was chewing her lower lip. We watched my mother try unsuccessfully to get Dad to stand up and walk back to the house.

"Does Gramps need an ambulance? Is he going to *die*?" Dante appeared behind me, his eyes big.

"No, no, sweetie. He's not going to die. He hurt his ankle. He needs to go to the hospital, just like you did when you banged your head."

He nodded seriously, taking the news in.

"They're nice there. Gramps should go there if he hurt himself." He seemed satisfied with his conclusion. "Can we go now? I want to get to Dad and Amy's so we can do eggs before bed. Dad said we can do some tonight and some tomorrow." He pulled on the sleeve of my jacket.

"We'll go in a minute." I reached down and swung Dante up to rest on my right hip.

"Clara, you're going to have to take them to the Emergency. Take mom's car and for God's sake be careful where you park. They tow. Spread him out in the back seat and don't let mom guilt you into waiting there all night. They're perfectly capable of taking care of themselves."

"Except Dad's ankle is likely broken and mom will be a puddle on the floor when the doctor tells her." Clara followed me out the door to where my father still sat on the ground and my mother was now fretting over him.

"Dad, Clara and I have been talking. She's going to drive you, in mom's car, to the hospital. You stretch out in the back seat and when you get there," I addressed Clara now, "put him in a wheelchair and wheel him in." I turned back to Dad. "Don't try to walk on it. I have to take Dante to Tyler's house."

Dante slid down my side and stood on the ground beside my parents.

"Say goodbye to Gramps and Grandma, Dante." I shot a cold glance at my mother on the word 'goodbye.' White-hot rage was still simmering beneath the situation with my father. Dante hugged them both. I hugged my father and ignored my mother completely.

Clara hugged me harder than usual and whispered in my ear, "Try not to let it bother you. You're doing a great job."

It would have meant more if she had said it in front of my mother, but she hadn't really had the opportunity. It all happened pretty fast.

When we pulled out onto the road, the clock on the dashboard read seven-seventeen. I hated being late to Tyler's because it was harder to assert the moral high ground when Tyler was late if I had also recently been late. Hopefully everything would not always be such a negotiation of guilt and obligation.

The encounter with Tyler was thankfully without incident. Now it was a countdown to being home in my pyjamas. Seven forty-seven. Not sure what fast food was open on Easter Sunday evening, I beelined hopefully to Dairy Queen and drove up at seven fifty-five. Admittedly, it was a jerk move since they closed in five minutes. By eight-oh-two there was a large Cappuccino Skor Blizzard in the cup holder. By eight-twelve, I was home, on the couch, with the television on. The Blizzard got me way through two episodes of *The Office* on Netflix. The sugar rush gave me a drowsy almost-contentment. At nine-ten, I stared into the empty paper cup with the tall red spoon leaning inside it and told myself it was time to go to bed.

"The thing is, Emily," I mused out loud to myself while walking to my bedroom, "Your mother is an idiot. She's totally in the wrong here." Moments later, wrapped in my comfiest pyjamas and slippers, I texted Clara to see how Dad was doing. The answer came back quickly -

They xrayd. He has a low energy open ankle fracture. They are casting it now. 628 weeks until it can come off.

Six hundred and twenty-eight weeks? Was she joking? My fingers flew over the calculator on my phone before texting back -

How can it be 628 weeks??? That's 13 years!

The phone quickly buzzed in my hand.

Six to eight weeks moron.

I smiled – slightly – in spite of myself.

Ok. Call me tmw. Going to bed.

I fell asleep, reading, *Not the Mom You Could Be – The Mom You Already Are!!!*

chapter 26

Waking up without Dante in the house was always strange. I constantly misjudged how little time it would take me to get out the door without him. I often had time before my shift to sit at the staff table, drink coffee and look over the schedule for the day. Early into the head waitress gig all the wait staff were given my personal cell number and told to text me if they weren't going to be at work. This was less work than checking messages when I got to the restaurant and trying to cover missed shifts then. It also made it easier to pick up a few of the extra shifts myself. All the waitresses joined a group chat and messaged out when a shift was available. Usually, it was filled right away. This was way better than the days of Eugene and Bernadette phoning around frantically, or telling some poor girl she had to stay late.

Today, there was a text from Gracie, a waitress and high school senior. Her mother's car had broken down in Pittsburgh after Easter dinner and she couldn't make it back for her shift from four to eight. I was working seven to one, a good shift because both the breakfast and lunch rushes were included. Dante was at Tyler's, and the Tuesday after a long weekend was always slow at the restaurant. I penciled myself into the four to eight shift. I could get two or three jobs done in the dining room during the shift and Zoe could take most of the tables. Content with the schedule for the day, I walked to the coffee maker, opened a package of coffee grounds and started a second pot of coffee.

Pat and Sue were working the morning shift with me. The ladies were in their late fifties to early sixties and had the matronly diner waitress vibe down pat. Both of them were pretty blunt about the fact that they thought one of them should have gotten the head waitress gig, but they became more okay with it as time wore on. I worked hard at winning their loyalty and in turn, they were decent, if not enthusiastic, about helping out when we were stuck.

We settled into the breakfast rush. Three things weighed on my mind. My mother, finding a sitter for Dante, and going on a real a date. 'Putting myself out there,' as Clara had put it. Both the second and the third thing were related to the first. The sitter was required because I was so pissed off at my mother that I wasn't letting her watch Dante. Finding a date was urgent, mostly because my mother said I shouldn't be dating. In order to think about the sitter and the date without thinking about my mother, I used a little trick from one of my self-help books about divorce. In my head, I shoved a shrunken down, teeny tiny version of my mother into a mason jar, closed it up tight and then pictured myself walking out onto the middle of the Ambassador bridge and hurling it off into the river below. The book didn't actually specify where you should hurl the mason jar. I liked to visualize the Ambassador bridge because there was a chance my miniature mother would end up, in the mason jar, washing up onto the Canadian coastline without her passport. It would serve her right. I had given it a good deal of thought.

The book said, rightly, that it didn't always work the first time but if you kept at it, you could take the person in question out of your head and focus on more important things. All morning, every time I poured a coffee refill, the mason jar flew over the bridge in my mind's eye. By the end of the breakfast rush, my miniature mother was definitely running from a moose or a polar bear in the Canadian wilderness.

This freed me to reflect on the second two things: the babysitter and the date. Between the breakfast rush and the lunch rush, I thought mainly about the babysitter. It had to be someone dependable and not too expensive, who would come to the house and work weird times that weren't consistent.

I was so hyper-focused, first on throwing my mother over a bridge and then on finding a babysitter that I didn't bring my 'A-Game' to work that morning. Pat and Sue seemed keenly aware of this.

"You okay, honey?" asked Sue. She seemed concerned but she was also annoyed because I had delivered her Denver omelet to my table and left my mushroom omelet at the window.

"Yeah, I'm okay," My face felt sheepish, even to me. "I'm a bit distracted."

"Mmm-hmmm. We noticed. You wanna talk about it?"

I glanced around briefly. Almost all the tables were empty and only a few needed cleaning. Pat motioned to a nearby newly vacated table and helped me remove the dirty dishes.

"I need to find a babysitter for Dante." The topic of my mother seemed best avoided. "I'm not sure where to start looking. It's not like it will be regular work, and I need someone reliable who I can trust." My fingers clutched four dirty juice glasses in my right hand from the top and held them together.

"What about sending him to a sitter? Or a daycare? Might give you time to yourself sometimes." Her voice was kind.

"I thought about that. But I don't really want more time to myself...and I don't want him to have to adjust to another new setting. I just need a girl who will come to the house and watch him when I'm working and he's not at his dad's."

I finished scraping two plates into the garbage, and Pat left to take an order.

"What about you, Dean?" I called into the kitchen. "You know anyone who might want to babysit Dante when I'm at work sometimes?" Dean still helped out in the back when it wasn't busy in the front.

"Not really. I could ask my little sister. She's a high school senior."

"That would be great." He was trying to help, but a high school student wouldn't be very useful unless she was willing to skip a lot of class to cover my morning shifts.

It wasn't long before lunch was in full swing. Zoe was working twelve to eight and we started transitioning my remaining tables over to her at twelve-thirty.

"How's it going?" she asked me when we were both at the soda fountain.

"Pretty good. I need to find a babysitter." The machine spit out a burst of carbonation and the glass in my hand overflowed. "And a date. And Dean needs to change the *freaking* CO2. What is the matter with him?" I wiped the soda from my hand onto my apron and set the glass down more forcefully than necessary.

"Well, I don't like kids, and you're not my type, so I can't really help with either." She handed me the Coke she had just poured as a gesture of goodwill, put the overflowing glass in the sink and wiped the counter with a deft move of her left hand. "I'll tell Dean about the tank. You need to take it down a notch."

She was right. There was five minutes left in my shift, so I delivered the drink refills to the last of my tables, let them know Zoe would be taking care of them, returned to the soda fountain and wiped it down absently with a fresh cloth, hoping my luck would change.

chapter 27

By one-oh-five, I had changed into sweats in the back room of the restaurant and bid goodbye to the staff, with three glorious, empty hours all to myself. I decided to hit the grocery store before Dante came home, get a couple loads of towels and sheets through the washer and dryer, and put the groceries away. I needed to visit my father, and made a mental note to go to the hospital when *Young and the Restless* was on TV so there was no chance my mother would be at the hospital.

Walking through the automatic doors into Meijer, I thought fondly about my time at Target with James. That was a fun trip; this was a necessary grocery store run that was necessary, and pretty lonely.

Mostly healthy food went into the cart, with a few exceptions, like another box of Lucky Charms. A bowl of the magically delicious cereal was my new go-to for a very quick breakfast, lunch, or dinner on my own. Lucky Charms for One. It sounded like the name of an album by

Morrisey. In dropped the family-size box, and the irony was not lost on me.

At home, when the groceries were put away and pink hearts and green clovers floated in the milk of my cereal bowl, I realized there wasn't time to visit Dad before my afternoon shift started. With only a half hour to kill before I had to drive back to the New Dean's, I grabbed my iPad, googled, 'how to find someone to date' and started scrolling. I clicked on a link called, 'Eleven Best Ways to Find Someone in Real Life' and started reading. Among the suggestions were: get a dog, take a class, volunteer your time, agree to be set up. I shook my head and bit my lip. All these suggestions would take too long. I needed to find a date *today*...or at least tomorrow... sometime soon. The idea was tumbling forward in my brain with an urgency that felt increasingly uneasy. I pushed the feeling aside. It was full speed ahead.

My evening shift went pretty much as planned. I wiped down and filled the ketchup bottles as well as the salt, pepper and sugar containers that sat on every table. Next, I cleaned the silver napkin dispensers with a vinegar and water-infused cloth, and stuffed them with white, one-ply napkins. Everything came off the waitress station and I cleaned it right back to the wall, which obviously hadn't been done in a while. Several spots of unidentified gummy residue required scraping with the edge of a pie lifter. The way the restaurant looked and felt was more of a reflection on me now that I was head waitress. All of these jobs had annoyed me back when I felt less appreciated.

Zoe waited most of the tables and I helped her out for an hour or so when it was too busy for one person. Our

"Yeah. I'm going out with the deli clerk from Meijer later tonight as it happens. What do you think, you dummy? I don't even know *how* to find a date, and I need to do it quickly before I lose my nerve and my mother gets back in my head about it."

"You need Tinder. Or Match.com. Match.com is less creepy in my experience. Tinder can be overwhelming."

"I am not doing online dating. And that's my last word on the subject. Can't we talk about your boring life for once? Why are we only talking about my problems today?"

"I don't have any problems. My life is awesome." I knew very little about Zoe's life outside the restaurant, so it was possible she was telling the truth.

"How do you meet men? Are you volunteering? Walking dogs? Taking courses? Attending friends' birthday parties?" Some of the list I read online had stuck with me.

"I meet plenty of men, don't you worry," Zoe assured me. "And when I haven't met anyone for a while I use Match.com. I've met a couple of not-terrible people that way." She scraped spaghetti off a dinner plate into the garbage with a saucer, and put both dishes into the dirty bin. "There's also a lot of assholes, so be warned."

"Has it led to a serious thing for you? Don't you want to get married and all of that?" It was the most personal thing I had ever asked Zoe.

"Oh yeah. I can't *wait* to get married. I've seen how well that turns out. My parents are divorced, my brother's wife left him, and he went bankrupt because he had to sell everything to give her half the equity in their house. And oh, let's see, there's your situation to consider as well.

Marriage turned out super well for you. I can't wait to open that can of heartbreak." Her words stung and surprised me. "No thanks, I'll stick with what I can find online."

"Touché," I muttered under my breath, and grabbed the broom to sweep under the booths. It was seven forty-five and all the tables were empty and wiped down. I would be on time to pick up Dante at Tyler's house.

"When are you working tomorrow?" Zoe put her coat on and popped a fresh stick of gum into her mouth.

"I'm off tomorrow. Spending the day with Dante. Also I have to go and visit my dad in the hospital."

"Your dad's in the hospital? You've been talking about your life to me non-stop all day and you didn't think to mention that? You're really weird."

Zoe wasn't wrong about me being weird, but I just wasn't overly worried about Dad.

"He just broke his ankle. It's not a big deal. I should likely have visited him today I guess."

"You think?" Zoe's tone was dry. "If it's no big deal why is he still in the hospital? Why didn't they just cast it and send him home?"

"How should I know? I'm not speaking to my mother so I can't ask her. I'll go tomorrow and see what's up, I guess."

"Good luck with all that. I'm going home to my apartment to do whatever the hell I want. You should come in tomorrow and talk to Mario though. If you haven't found a babysitter before then, like, at the hospital or whatever." She unwrapped the second stick of gum. "Hey, maybe you'll pick up a *doctor* to date. Or a nurse." She paused for a moment as we headed to our cars. Zoe and I did not hug hello or goodbye. "A *murse!* You could find a murse. A male nurse, you know?" Her car door shut and the engine roared to life.

However curt and annoying Zoe often was, she was also probably right about talking to Mario's sister, whose name I did not even know. I knew even less about Mario than about Zoe and that usually suited me just fine.

The changeover routine came off without a hitch – arrive at Tyler and Amy's, smile and say hello, and squeeze Dante's hand on the way down the sidewalk to the car. Then, ten minutes later, lift him sleeping from his car seat, carry him inside and lay him down into his bed.

chapter 28

The next morning, it took me about thirty seconds after I regained consciousness to remember all the things that had been weighing on my mind the night before. I rubbed my eyes with my hands and realized yesterday's makeup was still, mostly, on my face. Oh well. Dante never judged me. I picked up my phone and reflexively checked Instagram, Facebook and my email, in that order, as my I.Q. slowly climbed out of the single digits.

The bed I once shared with Tyler was now firmly only my own. The fingers on my right hand counted the months since he'd slept there - November, December, January, February, March. Almost five months. Tyler's side of the bed, or more accurately what *had been* Tyler's side of the bed, was now perennially covered with clean laundry in various stages of being folded. I was aware of the probable psychological implications of my choice to fill my ex-husband's sleeping space with an annoying chore that remained constantly unfinished. Every time I planned to catch up on the laundry, something happened and any clothes that had been put away were replaced by unfolded clean clothes added to the heap.

Was the laundry a placeholder for someone else who would one day sleep there? One thing it did was keep Dante from sleeping in my bed. When he couldn't sleep, I snuggled up with him in the bottom bunk of his IKEA bunkbed. I used to hope that someday Dante and a little brother would have sleepovers, arguing about who got the top bunk, and using sheets and towels to make a fort in the space between the beds. If Dante slept in my room, it reminded me too much that our family used to have three people. If I slept in Dante's room for more than one night, the laundry threatened to take over my entire sleeping space.

Mindlessly, I brushed my teeth and squinted at myself in the bathroom mirror. Except for the raccoon mascara and eyeliner disaster under my eyes, my face didn't look too bad. How might I stack up against the other twenty-five-year-old women in the dating game? They were women who were fresh out of college and partied at clubs on the weekend. I was mostly worried about making my half of the mortgage payment, and spending enough time with my three-year-old son. It didn't seem likely that I was going to do too well in that equation.

Out of the pile of unfolded clothes I selected a wrinkled outfit for me and one for Dante, threw them in the 'refresh' cycle on the dryer and headed for the shower. Once clean and wrapped in a towel, I dumped my towel in the washing machine, quickly dressed in the now warm and relatively wrinkle-free clothes from the dryer, and carried Dante's favorite overalls up to his room.

While he slept, I sat down on his bed and gazed down at him. Agonizing over every decision about Dante had started when I was pregnant. I fretted about genetic testing, and what to eat, or not eat. Then it was choosing a midwife or an OB/GYN and researching doulas, water births, home births and elective C-Sections. It was exhausting. To make matter worse, almost the moment the second line had materialized on the pregnancy test, I started vomiting. It wasn't only in the morning, and not just for the first trimester. I threw up *everywhere*: in the trash can in the mall, out the driver's side door of my car at a red light, and out the window of the passenger side of Tyler's car on the freeway. The worst was when I barfed at my aunt's house. She had blue cleaning stuff in her toilet. The smell of that stuff made me barf even more.

Whenever I wasn't working or obsessively reading pregnancy and parenting books, I slept – parked at a service station, in bed, and on the couch. Once I was so happy to have eaten a bowl of yogurt without being sick that I rested my head on the kitchen table 'for just a minute' and woke up two hours later. The whole pregnancy was completely mentally and physically exhausting.

Everything was about waiting for 'the baby' to be born. I told myself things would get easier when 'the baby' finally came. I was wrong. Having Dante was joyful in many ways, but also turned me inside out emotionally and exhausted me every day. Six weeks wasn't even close to being enough time off, so I quit my waitressing job.

The decisions about pregnancy seemed difficult, but once I had Dante they were like a pleasant daydream. Every choice now seemed crucial to Dante's development, and his future. Each one carried an insurmountable burden of guilt if I got it wrong. At every stage, there were too many opinions. I tried to ignore other people's input, but still heard their voices in my head during moments of doubt. I worried about whether to use cloth or disposable diapers, when to start solid food, and whether to pick Dante up when he cried.

To make matters more complicated, Dante turned out to be what my mother called a 'difficult' but I preferred to call a 'needy' baby. He cried whenever he wasn't held. After reading everything on both sides of the 'sleep-training' issue, I decided never to let him cry if I could help it. There were enough things to cry about later in life which couldn't be solved with a cuddle.

Coming back to the present, I watched Dante sleep for a few minutes, then brushed the hair off of his face and rubbed his back until he stirred and opened his eyes. A smile came over his face.

"Hi, Mommy." My hand stayed on his warm back while he rubbed the sleep out of his eyes.

"Good morning buddy. Did you have a good sleep?" He nodded. "Do you want breakfast?" I pulled him up out of bed and held him close. "How's your pull-up? Dry?" I put my hand on his tiny bottom and felt the sagging overnight diaper. "Better luck next time buddy. Off you go to do a pee."

When his feet hit the floor, he beelined it for the bathroom and his toddler-sized potty, abandoning his pyjamas and pull-up on the bathroom floor. I suppressed the urge to tell him to put his pull-up in the garbage and his pyjamas in the hamper in the linen closet beside the shower, instead, picking them up and doing it myself. He wouldn't be little for long. Soon he wouldn't need a pull up, even overnight.

Dante ate his breakfast dressed in his overalls and his favorite yellow t-shirt. For the first time since waking up, my mind moved forward to the tasks of the day. I needed to visit my father, speak to Mario at work about his sister, clean the house, finish the laundry, and take Dante out for an hour of meaningful mother-son time. I vaguely remembered talking to Michelle about getting together this week. Maybe my life would seem more normal if any of my friends were in a similar situation to mine or if they had kids to take on playdates together. A little voice in my head reminded me that in addition to everything else, I had to find a date. Unfortunately, the little voice did not offer any actual ideas about how to go about arranging said date. Maybe Michelle would have some ideas on that, if I remembered to call her.

chapter 29

Every book I read directed me over and over, to 'put your best face forward!' 'Be the best version of yourself!' and my personal favorite, most recently echoed by Clara, 'Put yourself out there!' Oprah always said something about luck being preparation meeting opportunity. The opportunity wasn't up to me, but a glance at my puffy, un-made-up face in the window above the sink made me realize that I wasn't living up to my side of the bargain. More preparation was definitely in order.

"Hold on, Dante. I'll be ready to go in ten minutes. You play Legos." He looked wistfully at the TV. "We can watch *Thomas* after we get back from seeing Gramps." Dante sat down cross-legged on the carpet, dumped the entire green bin of chunky Duplo pieces out onto the floor and got busy sorting them by size and color.

Back in the bathroom, I surveyed the mostly empty jars and eyeshadow pans on the vanity. Since Tyler left my make-up routine had slipped into the realm of quite pathetic. It was past time for a visit to the mall with Clara to stock up on better brushes and a decent foundation…whatever would make me look slightly more…if not glamorous, then at least female. I plugged in the designer brand straightening iron Michelle had convinced me to buy at TK Maxx and waited for it to heat up.

With the limited resources available, I did my best to even out my skin tone and highlight my best features. My straightened hair was tucked behind my ear, secured with a fancy bobby pin and coaxed into obedience with hair spray. A quick check in the mirror left me almost-confident about my appearance, for the first time since my outing with Dean. It felt good to look good and I surprised myself by smiling at my reflection.

The old guilty voice sounded in my mind: Would Tyler still be here if I had made an effort like this more often? I clenched my fists briefly and shook my head. Self-defeating thoughts weren't helpful. Aside from these momentary lapses, this fact was getting a little easier to remember.

I decided to make visiting my father the first order of the day. We left Dante's toys on the floor and headed to the hospital. On the way there, I gave myself the following ground rules:

1. No engaging with Mom. I will only say, "Hello Mom," or at the absolute most, "How is Dad doing?"
2. No letting Dad realize that I am mad at Mom.
3. If Mom starts in on me with her passive-aggressive bullshit, or references, see rule one.

Those rules seemed simple enough to follow. Impulsively I added a fourth:

4. I will find a doctor to date. Or a murse. Or an intern. Or a janitor. Or a parking attendant.

The consequences of screwing up my rules could have lasting implications on our family dynamics, which was why rules were essential to success. I parked my car carefully in an appropriate spot at the hospital and retained my parking slip, ready to pay at the exit.

"The last time we were here, you had those stitches in your head. You remember that?" Dante put his chubby finger on the spot above his eyebrow and felt his scar.

"I remember. I was brave. Then your friend came and drove us home. Remember, mom? It was *cold* that day." It was funny which details he remembered and which ones he forgot. We never talked about it, but he didn't seem to have any memories of his father and I living together. I wasn't sure whether that made me happy or sad.

"That was my friend James who came to pick us up. He took us to McDonald's, do you remember?" I pushed the button for the elevator with the cuff of my sweatshirt. Germs. Clara had texted me the floor and room number the day before. She let me know she wouldn't be able to get in to see Dad today because she had a midterm. I felt guilty for not asking her about school at all lately. The elevator doors closed and we lurched upward.

"Up we go!" called Dante with his fist in the air, just like he did every time we were in an elevator. Hopefully, his happy mood would cheer my father up.

We navigated the maze of hallways and nurses' stations, and found my father. He was in a semi-private room, in the bed next to the window. Both my mother and a doctor were present in the room and it became a very crowded space when we joined their number. I picked Dante up, balanced him on my hip, and we squeezed in between the window and the bed to make the space more manageable given the number of people in the room.

"How's it going, Dad? Are they letting you out today?"

The atmosphere in the room was not happy.

"I don't think so, Emily. Dr. Iger, this is my daughter, Emily." My father was pale and tired. I glanced at his ankle. It was in a cast and there was an IV line running from a tall pole into his hand.

Dr. Iger extended his hand to me and I shook it.

"Nice to meet you. Are you taking good care of my dad? When can he come home?" I was struggling to understand the mood in the room. My mother remained silent, a small mercy, but also not a good sign.

"I was just telling your mother, Emily. We're not sure why, but your dad's condition is not significantly improving. His ankle surgery went very well but he's developed flu-like symptoms. We suspect he may have developed an infection at some point and we're treating him with pretty strong antibiotics, so we're going to keep him in here for a few days to monitor how he's doing." Despite myself, my eyes flitted to Dr. Iger's left hand and noted his wedding ring. Too bad.

"But it's all under control, right? He's going to be fine." It was feeling more likely that something was going on, and that Dad might *not* be fine at all.

"Dante, come with Grandma and we'll see if we can find you a package of M&Ms in the vending machine." I put Dante down and he happily took my mother's hand. I heard them chattering away to each other as they left the room.

"Emily, your father has developed the early stages of sepsis." Dr. Iger was speaking with the calm demeanor of a professional whose job it was to keep people like me from freaking out. "We're monitoring it closely. We have caught the infection very early and there is every reason to believe that your father will be fine. But he does need to stay here for the time being so we can keep an eye on the situation and make sure it doesn't accelerate."

"But he's going to be fine, right?" I repeated again, stuck on the word *fine*. He's not going to…I mean he's going to be fine." I felt a slight wobble slip into my voice.

"As I said, we caught this very early. We have him on the right antibiotics. But it is serious. In rare cases, sepsis can develop into a condition called septic shock which can be fatal. But this usually only happens when the situation goes undiagnosed and the patient isn't in the hospital."

I looked over at my father. He smiled wanly and spoke for the first time since my arrival.

"I'm a tough old goat, Emily. I'm going to be fine. I'm one of the lucky ones. They don't always catch it. Lucky for me your mother watches a lot of Dr. Oz."

Dr. Iger cleared his throat. "Yes, uh, we wouldn't normally have checked for this situation so early. But your mother was quite insistent and in fact, she was right."

I took a deep breath.

"Okay. So what can we do? Is there anything we can do to make him better faster?" As soon as I had accepted the problem, my attention turned to finding a solution.

"Just spend time with him. His biggest problem is likely to be boredom at this point."

"Boredom. Right. Well, can we hook his TV up or something? Can he go for a walk down to the parking lot?"

"No, no. I don't need the TV, Emily. I'm happy to watch the world go by out the window here. And your mother has been spending a lot of time with me." My father was obviously in discomfort and was having a harder time hiding it the longer I was there.

"I'm going to leave you for now," Dr. Iger extended his hand and I shook it again. "I'll see you tomorrow, Emilio. You get some rest."

I followed Dr. Iger into the hallway and peppered him what were definitely too many questions, several of them asked more than once. Dr. Iger mostly repeated information he had already given us, but he did add that the medications my father was on to fight the infection would likely wipe him out, and he would be sleeping a lot and fatigued most of the rest of the time.

"Best not to encourage him to do too much. The more he rests the better chance we have of beating this soon, and then you'll have him back home. Take care now."

Then Dr. Iger was gone. He seemed to genuinely care, but I needed to hear that he knew how to definitely and quickly fix whatever was wrong with my father, and he hadn't offered me that assurance.

chapter 30

We said our goodbyes and Dante and I paid for parking. Once in the car, I grabbed my phone and shot off a quick text to Michelle.

I'm off today. Do you want to do something this aft? I have Dante

Next, we drove to New Dean's. The sign was finally up and the neon popped against the dark building. I was counting on Dean letting Dante pay the staff rate for lunch. Technically, wait staff were only allowed the half-price food deal directly before or after their shifts, and it wasn't transferable to family or friends. My exception to this rule was a perk of my position.

We slid into the staff table booth and I pulled out the iPad kept in my bag for just such situations. The beautiful leather Coach crossbody bag I used to wear in college was now tucked in the back of my closet. Now, I lugged around a big tote I got on sale from Kohl's just after Dante was born. It was definitely a mom purse, but also definitely *not* a diaper bag. Maybe the Coach bag would come out of retirement for my as yet non-existent upcoming date. Having the password was another perk not extended to other wait staff. I connected, opened Netflix, and Dante began happily watched *Paw Patrol* while he sipped his chocolate milk.

I knew better than to bug Mario during a busy time but it was far enough in advance of the real lunch rush to pop my head into the kitchen.

"Mario, you got a minute?"

"A minute. What's up?" Mario still treated me with the same disdain he always had, although the screaming in Greek had died down once Eugene and his family were not around.

"I was wondering if you could maybe text me your sister's number." I wished I knew his sister's name and hoped he had only one sister.

Mario looked at me skeptically.

"Why? What do you want with Sophia?"

"I need to find a babysitter for Dante, but it's tricky because I work strange hours. Zoe told me that, uh, Sophia is a student at Dorsey… I was wondering if she might want to babysit for me sometimes." It was uncomfortable being in Mario's debt, even conversationally. I willed him to either give me the number or tell me to get lost so I could stop talking to him.

"I'll text her your number, how about that? Then if she wants to, she can get in touch with you. But I wouldn't count on it." He turned to the service window and grabbed the order slip Pat had pinned up. The conversation was clearly over and one thing was crossed off my list of things to do today, though I wasn't hopeful.

Dean was sitting down next to Dante, watching the iPad with him. He looked up when I approached.

"Hi, Emily. Dante's been telling me who all these dogs are."

"Pups. They're pups, Dean, not dogs." Dante spoke without taking his eyes off the screen.

"Right." Dean stood up and made room for me to sit beside Dante. "Do you and the pups want some chicken fingers and fries?"

"Yes!" cried Dante, who shared my penchant for fried food even at his young age.

"*Please*," I corrected him.

"Yes, please, Dean."

"Coming right up. You want lunch, Emily?"

"That would be great. Just bring a full order of chicken fingers and I'll share with Dante. And maybe onion rings."

"*Please*, mom. You didn't say please." Dante looked up at me earnestly.

"You're right. Please, Dean."

"Coming right up."

"Oh, and hey, Dean," I looked up from the schedule and smiled, "Thanks for ordering it for me." The outcome would be better if Dean ordered from Mario than if I went back to the kitchen myself.

"No problem."

Zoe brought a Dr. Pepper over to the table and Dante and I ate our lunch. Before we left the restaurant, there was a text from Michelle:

I can meet up this afternoon. Where?

I replied:

Come over around 1:30?

Dante would be down for his afternoon nap by then, as long as he didn't fall asleep in the car on the way home. I checked my watch. It was almost a quarter to one. I would have to keep Dante awake for the twenty minutes it would take to get him home. Then, if I pulled his blinds and lay down with him for a few minutes with *Goodnight Moon* or *Curious George* audio book playing, the odds were pretty good that he would fall asleep.

I was gingerly leaving Dante's room when Michelle let herself in and put the kettle on in the kitchen. I called out a quiet greeting, shoved the Duplo pieces back into their box and grabbed up pieces of train track and the various train engines scattered around the room. Michelle sat down on the couch with a cup of instant coffee and put one on the coffee table for me as well.

"You're almost out of instant. You know that brand is vile, right? Why are you buying crappy coffee all of the sudden?"

"It was on sale and I didn't realize how gross it was. By the time I drank it for a few days I figured I might as well use it up. You kind of get used to it. Put extra sugar. That helps."

"Well, when you have diabetes you'll wish you bought the Nescafe."

"Life is all about trade-offs."

chapter 31

Michelle looked at me with her head tilted and a squint in her right eye.

"You have make-up on. What's up? Do you have a date? Or an 'outing'?" She hadn't let me forget my alternate wording for the evening I spent with Dean.

"No. I decided it was time to make an effort." I filled Michelle in on the kitchen-sink drama with Clara and my mother, and my decision to move forward aggressively on the romance front.

"I think that's amazing. It's totally time. So, who are you going to go out with and where are you going to find him? Your hair is great, by the way. Did you use the new straightener we bought?" I answered in the affirmative to her great delight. "I *told* you that thing would be good." She sipped her coffee, made another exaggerated face and said pointedly, "You should listen to me more often. Now answer the question."

"Question?" She was talking so fast she had lost me.

"*Where* are you going to find someone to date?"

I passed Michelle my iPad and let her peruse the list of ways to meet someone.

"Most of these are not applicable unless you're going prepared to wait until Christmas," she said, perusing the article. "Are you planning to wait that long?"

"No. I'm planning not to wait at all. I want to find someone to go out with right away, before I lose my nerve completely." I retreated to the kitchen and came back with half a bag of Oreos.

"There's no one you already know that you'd like to go out with? Because that would be the quickest, and if you already know the person don't you think it would be more likely to go well?" She paused and stared at me. I pushed the blue bag of cookies towards her.

"No. I don't know anybody. I got together with Tyler when I was eighteen for crying out loud. And all I do now is work and look after Dante. Where do *you* find people to date?"

Michelle had been with a few serious boyfriends over the years, and notably broke up with an ex-college football player about three months before Tyler walked out on me.

"There's a doctor at the practice that I'm kind of into. But I'm not sure it will go anywhere. I've been kind of biding my time."

"How have you not told me this?! Who is he?"

"There's nothing really to tell yet. He's a chiropractor named Brandon. We've been working together for a few months now and I think he's gearing up to ask me out."

"You better tell me the *second* he asks you out. I am now officially living vicariously through you in the romance department." I moved to the counter to click the kettle back on. "But also, your example is not helpful. There's no way I can date anyone from work."

"What about online? Have you thought about online?" Michelle leafed absently through Dante's copy of *Curious George Goes to the Hospital* that had escaped my clean-up efforts.

"Like *Tinder*? Are you kidding? That's so creepy. Plus, I don't want to just hook up with someone. Isn't that what those sites are all about?"

"They're not all creepy. Some are a lot more about matching people based on their personality. Though those tend to cost more money, in my experience."

"You've never met anyone through one of those apps have you?" Surely Michelle would have told me a piece of information like that, but lately a lot of people refrained from talking to me about their love lives, for obvious reasons.

"I didn't actually meet anyone. But before I had a thing for Brandon I was starting to explore the idea. A girl at my office met her husband on Match.com." Michelle pulled an Oreo apart, ate the center and replaced the cookie parts in their column in the packaging.

"I knew this girl in college, her name was Samira, and she was about to get married in this arranged marriage. Her family was pretty modern and she was going to finish college and everything but her parents had arranged the match when she was a baby and the weird thing was she was totally fine with it. At the time, I thought she was crazy – she had to give up all her clothes before she got married. And she had *nice* clothes, too."

"I remember you telling me about that at the time." Michelle had moved on to reading the *In Touch* magazine I had impulse-bought during my grocery shop, and pushed the Oreos towards me and out of her own reach when she sat back on the couch.

"Guess what? She's still married. I see her on Facebook all the time still, and she has these two beautiful children, and a husband, and a college degree. Who's the sucker in that situation? Me, that's who. I wish my parents had set me up with an arranged husband. They couldn't have chosen worse than I did." I bit at my cuticle, then drank my crappy coffee.

"Wow, Emily, what a super interesting story," her tone said otherwise, "but let's focus on the future. We need to find you a date. Download this app." Michelle moved to sit beside me on the couch and showed me an app on her phone called *Bumble.* I touched the app, applied my thumbprint, and waited for the download to be complete.

I swiped through a few screens. "This is the same as *Tinder.*"

"It isn't. This one is different because," she air-quoted, " 'we have sections for finding friends or growing your business.' Which doesn't matter, because the real way it is different is that guys can't contact you. The woman has to make the first move. No gross guys can inbox you."

"Hmmm... I suppose I could give it a look. What picture should I upload?"

"You can go to all sorts of websites to give you advice about what to do in your picture. Men usually have dogs in theirs. Your make-up looks good today, so let's just do it now."

Michelle took several pictures of me with different backgrounds until we got one I didn't hate. It was raining outside and we got a good picture with the rainy window in the background. As soon as the picture uploaded, I set my preferences to 'male' and 'ages 25 – 30,' and started swiping left.

"Don't be hasty. You can't get those swipes back after you get rid of them." She finished her coffee and made a face at me to emphasize her disgust. "But who knows? You might get a coffee date. Or tickets to a Red Wings game. Maybe you go to a party with a loser and meet someone better *at* that party. What have you got to lose, Em? If you want to go on a date, this is a pretty sure-fire way to get one." I grunted in quasi-agreement and shoved my phone in my hoodie pocket for the time being.

"How's your mother? We moved back into my kitchen.

'She's a bit down lately, since James left." She moved to the sink. "I don't like this coffee. And here's what I'm doing with it." Michelle opened the offending box of coffee, dumped all the remaining crystals in the sink and ran the faucet over them until they had washed down the drain. She pointed at me defiantly as I shook my head.

"James left?" I felt a surprise pang of disappointment that I wouldn't be seeing him again soon. His company was so comfortable.

"He took a job in Madison for six months on a trial basis. Something in manufacturing. Managing a manufacturing company's retirement portfolio or something."

"Well, tell him I said hi." Then the thump, thump, thump of Dante's feet came down the hall, signalling the end of nap time. "Hey, Dante! Time to do a pee!" I quickly whisked him off to his miniature potty and Michelle put both our mugs in the sink.

Before Michelle left, the three of us watched an episode of *Bob the Builder.* Once she was gone, Dante and I stayed in front of the TV, where we ate peanut butter and jelly sandwiches for dinner. I picked up *Don't Divorce Your Kids Too* and read a few pages while Dante watched two more episodes of *Bob the Builder.* When the rain stopped, we went for a walk. Dante jumped into puddles with his bright red boots and I took lots of pictures of him. The best ones were posted to Facebook, and I wondered if Amy would see them, while at the same time wishing I didn't care and wondering about her and Tyler's wedding plans. I smiled at the memory of my reaction to the engagement news in the Shawarma Shop. It probably wouldn't be good for Dante to know later in life that his beloved mother had dumped soda on his beloved stepmother. The divorce books would definitely not approve of this behavior in the long term.

Dante got good and dirty on the walk and once inside, I flew him like an airplane directly to the bathroom, and stood him in the tub while I took his clothes and boots off. Dante loved to stay in the bath as long as he was allowed and tonight there was no hurry. If he played in the bath long enough, he would be ready for stories and bed when he got out. He had a million bath toys to play with, including foam letters and nesting cups that Dante used to pour water back and forth. Sometimes they were cups of coffee that we pretend-drank together. Sometimes they were cement mixers or airplanes dropping water on forest fires.

I sat with my back against the bathroom door while Dante chattered away to himself and occasionally splashed water over the side of the tub or made a splash that flew as far as my face. My phone buzzed in the pouch of my hoodie. I took it out and saw a pleasant surprise -

Hi Emily. This is Sophia Mario's sister. He says you are looking for a babysitter.

My fingers flew over the letters immediately -

Yes, mostly for days when I am working. Several times a week. Would you like to meet to talk about it?

A few tense minutes passed while I waited for her answer. I partially drained the bath to carefully add more hot water; Dante had played long enough for the temperature to cool off.

The buzz came back after five minutes -

My classes and apprentice hours are mostly afternoon/evening. I would be interested in meeting.

Over a series of several more texts in which I prayed I didn't sound as desperate as I felt, we agreed that Sophia would come over to talk about the job.

Dante was tucked into bed and sound asleep an hour later. I sat in front of the TV with a fresh bag of all-dressed chips, and a cold can of Diet Dr. Pepper. Reluctant, but also curious, I started to play with at the *Bumble* App on my phone. A Facebook notification popped up telling me four people liked my pictures of Dante and his reflection in a puddle, which sidetracked me while I also half-watched *America's Got Talent.* At ten, I turned off the TV and formally abandoned the dating app for the evening.

I reflected on my list for the day - I had accomplished 'visit my father' and made a good start on 'find a babysitter.' Limited progress had been made on 'find a date.' I brushed my teeth, and decided with just a whiff of satisfaction that the day hadn't been a total write-off.

chapter 32

Two busy but uneventful days flew by. I worked one double shift and gave up another one because there was no one to watch Dante. Would he grow up and remember his mother at work all the time? Possibly.

Before Sophia came over, I used the short time after work trying to make the house look relatively tidy and clean. I piled the last few misplaced things on my side of my bed, ready to be put away later.

When I finished, the house was presentable and the dishes were clean and dry beside the sink. The shoes were lined up in pairs by the door and the pillows were freshly plumped and back on the couch from their various resting places on the floor.

My father was still in the hospital. I hadn't been to see him since my original visit, but I had picked up six of his favorite biscotti from the bakery to take him the next day before work. I reasoned that no news was good news, and remembered Dr. Iger saying Dad needed to rest. It would be hard enough for him to rest with my mother fussing over him; my being there would only tire him out further.

Soon the doorbell rang and I went to answer it, looking around nervously and trying to see my house through the eyes of a person who was just arriving. I worried about who would be on the other side of the door and tried not to be prejudiced by the fact that I loathed this stranger's older brother.

Sophia's appearance began to put me at ease right away. She was wearing an Abercrombie sweatshirt that looked relaxed but not messy. Her purse was a medium-sized Coach tote bag I recognized from the outlet mall where I had purchased a similar bag for half off the clearance price last winter. These were good signs.

I greeted Sophia, noted her appropriately firm handshake, and hung up her sweatshirt. I searched for a resemblance to Mario but other than the dark complexion and wavy hair, there wasn't much of one. Before I could show Sophia in, Dante appeared in the front hall, his head at a slight angle to the right side.

"Dante, this is Sophia. Can you say hi to her?" I watched his face closely, trying to read his reaction to this stranger who would hopefully become an important part of his life.

"Hi, Sophia. You want to see my fort?"

He toddled back into the living room. In the short time it had taken me to let Sophia in, he had put the pillows back on the floor and thrown a blanket between the coffee table and the couch to form a tent. He had several trucks lined up underneath.

"That looks like a pretty cool fort. What's inside?" Sophia sat cross-legged on the floor, making engine noises as she moved one of Dante's trucks up and over his feet.

"Road Block!" he cried, stacking his feet heel to toe so the truck had to stop.

"Beeeeep, beeeep beeeeep," Sophia moved the truck backward. I was impressed by how quickly she had interacted with him, and her easy manner.

"Do you want something to drink, Sophia? Coffee or a soft drink?"

"Do you have a Diet Coke? Otherwise, just a water would be fine." She got up and followed me to the kitchen.

I took two cold cans of soda from the fridge and moved over to the cupboard to get a glass for Sophia.

"That's fine just in the can, don't worry about a glass. Just makes more dishes." Sophia smiled at me and I found myself quickly liking her. She was pretty enough that my instinct was to resent her just a little as she leaned against the counter and sipped her drink.

"Do you have a lot of experience with kids? You seemed to get along with Dante right away." I filled a sippy cup with watered-down apple juice and we moved back into the family room and sat down.

"I have quite a few nieces and nephews. I'm sure Mario told you." She looked around for a coaster, and I passed her a magazine to use, appreciating her regard for the coffee table which was covered in rings from previous, less considerate beverage drinkers.

"Actually he didn't mention that. He doesn't talk about himself very much. Except he did once tell me he drives a Camaro. That's about all I know about him outside of work." It seemed prudent not to mention that the other thing I knew about him was that he was a complete ass.

"He loves that stupid car. It's a nineteen sixty-nine and he bought it from the original owner. Well, from her son actually, after she died. Her husband had it holed up in a storage garage rusting away for about since the eighties. It took Mario three years to get it road worthy." She absently straightened the books and DVD cases on the table as she talked. "He has a Civic too. But as soon as the snow is gone, he only drives the Camaro."

"Wow. I didn't know that."

She tucked her legs up under her, sat back on the couch and continued talking.

"We have two older brothers too. I'm the only girl now. But we had a sister named Val who died in a car accident. With her husband. So my mom is kind of raising her two kids. Percy is three and Penelope is almost five." She registered the shocked sadness on my face. "It's okay. It was two years ago. I mean, it's not okay. It's terrible. It was pretty awful. But having her kids around is a little like having her. Like having a piece of Val still here, I guess. It's helped us heal. So I've been helping out a lot. My dad is more…traditional. He's not so much the raising kids type, you know? Mario is more like him."

"Seems like you have quite a lot of experience with little kids. I'm impressed. And you're going to Dorsey?"

"Yeah, I'm studying Cosmetology. I really like doing hair and make-up. I've wanted to do that ever since I can remember, and I have a great apprentice placement. I'm enjoying it… I'd like to have my own place one day, but right now I just need a part-time job. I used to work at Dunkin' Donuts. God, I gained so much weight." I quickly felt at ease with Sophia because she was so transparent and friendly.

I laughed, "Yeah, food is my weakness too. Food and Dr. Pepper. I think that's mostly why I work at the restaurant. You walk off most of what you eat in that job. You want another Diet Coke?"

"No thanks, I'm good." Sophia had been at the house for a half hour and we had hardly touched on the topic of watching Dante. I got up and pushed a DVD into the player and soon heard the familiar *toot-toot* of Thomas' whistle.

"Let's talk in the kitchen," I suggested, motioning with my head to Dante. "You okay in here, little buddy?"

"Yup!" Dante called, his eyes never leaving the screen. He pulled the roof of his fort onto himself on the couch and wrapped himself up in it.

Back in the kitchen, I chatted to Sophia about my schedule and let her know, nervously, that I was looking for a sitter to look after Dante in the morning or afternoon, a few times a week whenever I was working day shifts. Though we were getting along well, it was too soon to share the information that in the unlikely event that I found a date, she might be asked to work evenings too.

"Is that something you would be interested in? I have to say, you've already hit it off so well with Dante that I'd be comfortable offering you the job right now. On a trial basis," I cautioned myself inwardly to be cautious. She was still Mario's sister, after all, and I'd learned the hard way that people didn't always show their true colors right away.

Sophia hesitated before answering.

"I would be interested...there's just one thing I want to run by you." She paused and inhaled. "The thing is, I sometimes have to take care of my niece and nephew in the daytime too. Like I said before, they're three and four. About Dante's age. And so what I was *hoping*, when Mario told me you needed a sitter, is that I could bring them here with me sometimes. Or maybe other times I'd take Dante to my house and watch all three of them there." She looked at me earnestly. "But if you're not cool with it, I totally understand. I wasn't sure if maybe they could play together, if that might be good for Dante..." Her voice trailed off.

I thought about what she was saying. It was an unanticipated turn of events, and the more I thought more about it, the more it was clearly a bonus. I had been bemoaning the fact that it seemed Dante was going to be an only child, and wishing that he had a brother or sister to play with. Here, out of the blue, was a babysitter with experience *and* two built-in playmates.

Sophia looked like she was getting worried as I stood quietly considering it for several beats. Then I felt a smile spread across my face and my shoulders dropped slightly as the happiness spread over me.

"I think that would be amazing." Sophia was visibly relieved and smiled back. "Assuming it all goes well," I added quickly.

"Of course. A trial basis. I totally agree."

I reached out my hand and Sophia's reached back and shook it. We agreed on an hourly rate that we were both happy with.

"If there's laundry or whatever, just let me know. I'm happy to do it for you. Or any other housework you need help with."

I suppressed an overwhelming urge to hug her.

chapter 33

Sophia followed me back into the family room and we explained to Dante that Sophia was going to look after him from time to time, and introduce him to her niece and nephew. Sitting down beside him on the couch, I picked up my phone and noticed three missed calls from Clara as well as one text on the home screen–

At hospital. Come here if you can. I will watch Dante.

I stood, excused myself, and retreated to the kitchen. I quickly phoned Clara, who told me, in a hushed voice, that Dad had taken 'a sudden turn for the worse.' The antibiotics were not working. Clara was waiting with Mom for the doctor to give them an update. Dad was unconscious. The doctors were keeping him sedated both for pain relief and so he could rest while the antibiotics fought the still-worsening infection.

I assured Clara in a shaky voice that I would be there soon, and hung up.

"Are you okay? Is something wrong?" Sophia approached me hesitantly in the kitchen, looking concerned.

"My father is in the hospital." My throat started to choke up and I motioned for Sophia to follow me into the bedroom so Dante definitely wouldn't hear us.

"He has this thing called sepsis. I don't know how he got it. He just had a broken ankle and it was supposed to be no big deal. But now he's... unconscious..." I sat down on my bed, determined to hold it together and wiped my nose on the sleeve of my sweatshirt.

"You go. Just go to the hospital. I'll stay here and put Dante to bed. Here." Sophia handed me a full handful of Kleenex. I took them and stood up.

"I couldn't ask you to do that. You just came to meet him." I blew my nose with the fresh Kleenex.

"Don't worry about it...Where's his room? In here?" Sophia poked her head into Dante's room. It was a mess, unlike the parts of the house I had tidied for her benefit, but she didn't seem to notice. "Where are his pyjamas? Those?" I nodded. "Does he still wear a diaper at night?"

I nodded again, and realized the only choice was to accept her offer. "A Pull-Up. They're in the bathroom on the shelf with the towels. His toothbrush is in there too. I can't thank you enough for this. I really apologize..." I grabbed my wallet out of my mom purse and shoved it in the pocket of my jacket. "Either my sister Clara or I will come back as soon as we can. I'm not sure how long I'll have to stay."

Sophia sat down on the couch beside Dante and put her arm around his shoulder. He leaned into her, still glued to the TV. I marveled at my good fortune to have found her.

"Dante, Sophia is going to stay with you and put you to bed. Mom's going to work for a little while." I had absolutely no ethical issue lying to Dante any time it made his life easier. "You okay with that?"

He nodded. "Sure, mom."

"You'll go to bed for Sophia? And brush your teeth and everything?"

"Yup. But can we watch more *Thomas*?" He looked up at me.

"You better ask Sophia that. She's in charge now." I forced a smile for him.

"Can we, Sophia?" He peered up at her.

"How about I make you a snack, and we watch one more, and then you go to bed?"

Dante paused. "Okay. Deal." He offered Sophia his left hand, which she solemnly shook.

I kissed Dante's forehead, thanked Sophia again, and left.

My hands were visibly shaking as I shifted the car into reverse, backed it into the street and screeched forward toward the hospital. I had obviously completely misjudged Dad's situation. For crying out loud. It was a *broken ankle*! Why, in this day and age, could the doctors not fix a broken ankle without killing my father in the process? My anger boiled red hot below my skin as I got closer to the hospital and fumed about what the *hell* was the matter with the medical profession.

I circled higher and higher into the parking garage, passing spaces full of cars, and empty spaces labeled *Doctor Pass Parking Only*. Finally, I found a spot on level F-5, parked, and hiked across the pavement to the elevators. I used the cuff of my jacket to turn the germ-riddled door handle, waited for the elevator, descended, not fast enough, to the ground level and walked across the street into the hospital. It was raining again and by the time I was in the hospital lobby my hair was thoroughly damp. I looked longingly at the coffee stand in the lobby but decided I'd better not stop.

Being angry at the doctors, the parking, and the rain had effectively distracted me from how upset I was about Dad. I got to his room where my mother and sister were standing awkwardly. Clara was staring at her phone. Mom stared out the window. Dad was asleep with a peaceful and unconcerned look on his face. He had an oxygen tube in his nose which hadn't been there when I visited last time. Where there had been a cast on his leg, there was now a bandage and his foot was elevated.

"What's going on?" I spoke quietly, aware that the person in the next bed was awake. My mother just looked at me blankly. I was slightly alarmed when she didn't come back with a snide remark about the fact that I hadn't been to visit in two days. It would have been less upsetting to hear her snipe at me than it was to see her with nothing to say.

"We're not sure." Clara's voice sounded as unsure as I felt. "We're waiting for the doctor to come and fill us in. He said he'd be back before nine. That's why I called you."

I glanced at my watch. Eight-fifteen. I was glad I made it to the hospital in time and hoped Dante was tucked into bed.

"How long have you been here?"

"Mom's been here all day. I got here about an hour ago."

"How was your exam?" I glanced over at my mother. She looked stoned. Maybe a doctor had given her something 'for her nerves' as she would say.

"It was okay. Sorry I couldn't babysit this week." She tucked her phone into her pocket and motioned discretely to the door.

"Mom, we're going to get a drink. We'll be five minutes, tops." I took Clara's arm and led her out of the room. "I'm freezing. I need a coffee. You want something?"

"Hot chocolate." We walked in silence into the elevator, descended to the lobby, and stood in the mercifully short line to get our drinks.

"Do you have any idea what's going with Dad? What have they said?" I put my hands over the hot paper cup and felt comforted by the warmth.

"Only what I told you. Mom called me out of the blue an hour and a half ago. Up until then, I assumed everything was going okay."

We arrived back in Dad's room just before Dr. Iger, who pulled the curtain closed around Dad's bed.

"What we have here," he began in a kind and serious voice, "is a case of sepsis that is not responding to antibiotics." He motioned toward the chair in the corner.

"Mrs. Esposito, take a seat please." Mom sat down numbly. Dr. Iger looked at Clara and me. "I need you girls to hear what I'm saying because your mom has been having a hard time processing what's happening to your dad."

Fear wrenched my stomach.

"As I said, your father has a case of sepsis that is not responding to antibiotics. The infection is getting worse. Sepsis is usually not fatal," A renewed wave of nausea gripped me as Dr. Iger continued, "but it is very serious, and it is very important that we eliminate the infection." He looked back down at Mom to make sure she was listening. "In this case, I have consulted with the other doctors on my team and we believe," he paused, "that the best chance your dad has to recover from this is to amputate the area that is harboring the worst of the infection." The following brief silence was like the fallout before my mother's nuclear panic. Then I heard mom's voice, escalating in pitch and volume.

"no… no No No NO NOOOOOO…" she wailed and dissolved into sobbing. Dr. Iger put a kind hand on her shoulder. Clara and I looked at each other and understood that we had to be the adults in the situation.

"Please understand that we have not come to this lightly, Mrs. Esposito. If there was any other way, we wouldn't consider amputation." He looked up at Clara and I. "If we don't amputate the infected tissue, we are afraid that he will soon slip into what we call septic shock, and that *is* very often fatal."

"Okay, Doctor." I heard myself saying. Clara had taken my hand and was squeezing it. "Can you explain a bit more? I mean, what kind of amputation are we talking about?"

"The most prudent course of action would be to amputate your father's leg above the knee." Renewed wails from my mother. "That will eliminate all of the infected tissue and after that, a renewed course of antibiotics should be able to combat what's left of the infection in his system."

Dr. Iger explained that they wanted to do the surgery as soon as possible but they needed consent, from my father, or because my father was unconscious, from my mother. Clara and I convinced Mom to go for a walk with us, under the guise of 'getting a breath of fresh air,' something she put a great deal of stock in. We walked down to the main entrance and walked out into the drizzle. We were quickly overcome by the cigarette smoke from the people smoking directly under the 'No Smoking' sign on the outside of the automatic doors, so we turned back and found chairs in the lobby.

It took Clara and I about half an hour to convince my mother, through her tears and ours, to let the doctors do their job. The three of us went back to Dad's room and asked a nurse to page Dr. Iger, who arrived and told us that our father would enter surgery as soon as possible.

chapter 34

I persuaded Clara to take Mom home and make sure she got into bed and leave me to stay at the hospital overnight.

"Check Mom and Dad's bathroom for anything in a prescription bottle with a name that ends in 'pam.' If you find anything, get her to take one. Or two." I was reasonably sure that my mother had been prescribed an anti-anxiety medication at one time or other and she definitely needed some of it now.

As soon as she got Mom into bed, Clara would go to my house and sleep at my house, relieving Sophia. I filled my sister in about Sophia and my plan as we walked down to the lobby. Before leaving, Clara embraced me longer and more fervently than usual.

"Call me the minute you know anything," Clara said, before she headed into the rain to drive the car from the parking garage to the front of the hospital and pick up our mother.

"I will. Don't worry. Take care of Mom." I paused before admitting grudgingly, "I'm not mad at her anymore." I intended to say it bravely, but my voice wobbled almost imperceptibly.

"God. This is terrible, you do know that?" Clara wiped her nose with a crumpled tissue that she fished out of her jacket.

"I know." I wished I knew a way to make her laugh and break the tension.

Then Clara and Mom were both gone, and I was on my own with my unconscious father who was going to wake up with no leg. I had no clue what to say to him when that happened.

Very shortly, nurses arrived in the room. On the count of three, they moved Dad seamlessly from his bed to a gurney, and then he was gone. One nurse whose nametag red 'Xander' stayed behind and looked kindly at me, explaining the surgery using words like 'ligature,' 'surgical saw,' and 'sutures.' I took very little of it in. The nurse told me about an app I could download, and then pictures and updates of my father's procedure would be sent to me or 'my loved ones' during the operation, which would likely take about four hours if no complications arose.

"Sorry, what? Are you saying you will send me pictures from inside the operating room? Of my father in surgery?" I was so tired that I wondered if this might be an auditory hallucination.

"It's an option loved ones are embracing, for peace of mind. It's a secure process. The images aren't shared with anyone else. You would be assigned a secure code…"

I cut him off.

"Hold on. Who is taking these pictures?"

"Rest assured the pictures are taken by a certified nurse during the procedure. Outsiders are not allowed in the operating room. I'd be happy to walk you through downloading the app. It's very simple." Through my mounting frustration, I noticed that he wasn't bad looking. I checked for a wedding ring. Present and visible.

"I'm going to make this easy for you, *Xander*." I was using a hushed tone but it was becoming less hushed the longer I talked. "The last thing I need is to have pictures of my father's leg being cut off," My fists were clenched and my fingernails were digging into my palms. "What I would like you to do," the volume and pitch of my voice were now escalating beyond my control, "is get him out of that surgery as quickly as possible, and oh, here's a thought," the enduring patience of the scrub-clad man was irritating me further, "why don't you use all the nurses to do the surgery instead of having some of them TAKING PICTURES?" As I almost-shouted the last words that I was now being gently led out of the room by a gentle hand on my elbow. I grabbed my purse.

"I understand completely."

"Do you? Do you actually, Xander? Has your father ever had his leg cut off on a whim when he was fine three days ago?" We arrived at the family waiting room where more than a few people were trying not to stare at the scene that was unfolding.

"Ms. Esposito, your reaction is understandable and not uncommon. We will take excellent care of your father. This," he pressed a piece of paper into my hand, "is his patient number. If you watch that screen, you will be able to see when he has come through surgery into the recovery room and when he has been taken back to his room. Try to get some rest."

Then he was gone, and the people in the waiting room stopped glancing at me clandestinely over their iPads and magazines. I slumped down into the nearest chair and checked the number in my hand, matching it against the screen. My father's number was highlighted in blue, which meant that he was awaiting his surgery. When he was *in* surgery, his color would be changed to yellow. When he was in the recovery area he would be in orange and when he was back in his room it would be green. I figured the color red had probably been strategically excluded to avoid exacerbating the anxiety of the hysterical daughters in the waiting room. I wondered what color it would change it to if he was dead. This irreverent thought, combined with my exhaustion, made me giggle despite myself.

A quick glance at the wall behind my chair revealed that there were no power outlets. On my way out of the waiting room to get a coffee, I had a look around at the other chairs and determined who would have to leave for me to get a spot where I could charge my phone. When I returned to the room, one such spot was available. I plopped myself down, plugged my phone in and closed my eyes, just for a minute.

chapter 35

When I woke up, some of the faces in the waiting room had changed, my phone was fully charged, and my coffee was cold on the table beside me. My phone said one fifty-two. I had been asleep for about three hours. On the screen above, my father's name was now highlighted in yellow. Progress.

"Uh, excuse me," The person beside me seemed to have been waiting for me to wake up.

"Hey," I ventured, still groggy.

"It's just that, I wondered if I can plug my phone in. I didn't want to unplug yours while you were asleep but if yours is charged, would you mind…?"

"Sure. Knock yourself out." I pulled the white charging block out of the wall.

He reached into his coat pocket and I heard him swear under his breath.

"You okay over there?" My brain was slowly coming into focus.

"I forgot my charger. I thought I had it in my pocket."

I hesitated, knowing what my next line was supposed to be in this exchange.

"Did you want to use mine?" I asked dryly.

"Oh God, that's not what I meant. I mean, are you sure you don't mind? My phone's almost dead."

I passed him my charger, and turned to my own phone, ignoring all the little red numbers that glared at me from different apps that required my attention. I sent a text to my mother and Clara. Hopefully, Mom was asleep, but Clara might be awake.

Sorry, I fell asleep. Dad in surgery. All going well.

The part about everything going well was a load of crap. There was no way of knowing it was going well, but also no way of knowing that it *wasn't* going well. I figured it was probably going well. His name was still highlighted in yellow so he wasn't dead.

A text came back from Clara, just to me -

Mom was a mess. I found sleeping pills and gave her two. Told her they were aspirin. Dante is sleeping. Sophia was great. I'm in bed. Talk tmw.

It was a relief knowing that Mom and Clara were taken care of. Now to spend the rest of the night in the hospital waiting room. Getting back to sleep seemed unlikely, and I settled in with my now-charged phone.

I scrolled through Facebook and Instagram restlessly, clicking on a few things and reading enough news headlines to know what was going on in the world.

"Do you mind if I leave my bag here? I just have to go to the restroom. Could you watch it for me?" I asked phone-charger-guy next to me, suddenly glad that I had lent him my charger.

"Sure. But I'm not too sure there are a lot of hospital purse-snatchers on the loose in Michigan right now." He smiled and I looked at him intently...well dressed, decent looking, seemed like he was probably tall but it was difficult to tell when he was slumped in a chair. He had a naked ring finger. I gave him what I hoped looked like a genuine smile, and left in search of the restroom.

I caught sight of myself in the mirror while washing my hands, and was mortified at what crying, rubbing my eyes, and sleeping in a chair had done to my face. I fervently wished I had my purse with me so I could clean up the worst of the damage with a face cleansing cloth or even a diaper wipe. Instead, I did my best with the world's roughest paper towel and water and hoped the skin under my eyes wasn't torn all to hell in the process.

Back in my chair, I thanked the boy-next-door.

"No problem. My name's Liam."

"I'm Emily. Thanks again." I returned to my phone for some diversion.

My eyes settled on the dating app Michelle had practically forced me to install. I hovered over the yellow graphic for a moment before touching it and watching it open. I saw my not-unflattering profile picture, and then a man's face popped up immediately. Which way I was supposed to swipe to get rid of the picture without indicating interest? I tentatively swiped left. It was the correct guess.

A disproportionate number of the men had dogs, just as Michelle predicted, and most of them were Golden Retrievers. A lot of the men were participating in extreme sports. There were many groups of people out having a good time. Weirdly, there were often pictures of these men with other beautiful women, the likes of which I did not want to compete with. After a solid hour of reading and swiping, I screenshotted several comedically notable bios before swiping them away. Most of them were almost too bizarre to be true. Highlighted excerpts included:

Steven, 30, Human Resources manager – I'm a sapiosexual who likes to travel.

I had no idea what that even meant and I didn't imagine I wanted a kind of 'sexual' I hadn't yet heard of. I had enough trouble being a boring old 'heterosexual.'

Ernie, 30, Researcher – I want a woman who looks at me like Kanye looks at Kanye.

Original, if nothing else.

Jason, 27 – I enjoy the beach, bonfires, cuddles, UFC and making you smile.

Creepy. How was he already be making me smile before he met me? It sounded stalker-ish. Also, how to juxtapose UFC with cuddles? Those two things did not seem congruent to me.

Warren, 26 – Divorced. Have two kids who are with me half the time. Non-smoker and I exercise. I save turtles. Star Wars nerd.

I was indifferent to both turtles and Star Wars, but Warren's profile raised a more important point. Would I date a man with kids? And would a man without kids want to date me? My own profile was only a picture with no bio. Reading the profiles of men and how many children they did or didn't have was sobering. A truth dawned on me: if I wanted Dante to have siblings, my future included a family with step and/or half-brothers or sisters. It felt so *complicated*.

With Tyler in my past and Dante in my future, I started to doubt whether romance would ever be possible for me again.

I continued swiping absently through more and less attractive men with more and less bizarre profile pictures and bios when I stopped short and stared at my phone in disbelief.

James.

My eyes blinked in disbelief and I read the bio several times over:

James, 28 - Have not been sprayed by a skunk in over ten years. I hold elevator doors open for people if they show a reasonable degree of urgency. Otherwise, I push the door-close button while maintaining eye contact. I don't hike or dance. I enjoy restaurants and late-night shopping trips.

My heart fluttered. Would I swipe right on this guy if he wasn't James. Maybe. In my discouraged state, a familiar face was tugging on my heartstrings.

Two things about James' bio made me smile. When James got sprayed by that skunk, he was sneaking back into his parents' house after a party. It was late enough to be early morning, and there were always skunks sniffing around that neighbourhood because of the park nearby. James wasn't watching his feet as he crept around the side of the house, and he startled the skunk, which promptly let loose on him. His parents hit the roof, partly because he had snuck out and partly because their entire house and everyone in it smelled like skunk for weeks afterward. The skunk discharged directly under the dining room window. They had to have industrial cleaners come in. Michelle smelled like skunk too.

She was mad for ages but I couldn't remember what revenge she had exacted on James.

James included 'late night shopping trips' in his bio. It seemed like a strange coincidence, considering our recent Target visit. I quickly swiped left on James' profile to put a stop to my internal dialogue. I put my phone down too loudly on the table, and Liam looked over at me.

"You doing okay? Need your cord back?" I glanced down at my phone. Forty-two percent.

"I'm at forty-two percent. How about you?"

"I've got seventy-six. Looks like it's your turn." I laughed at him.

"What are you, some sort of cell phone battery socialist? Everyone has to have the same charge all the time?" I feigned horror.

"If I am, you should have put me right and charged me a fee to use your cord. The cord is your capital after all." He unplugged his phone and passed me the end of the charger.

"But we're both stealing the electricity from the hospital. How does that factor into the political spectrum of overnight phone use?" I plugged my phone in and set it safely on the small table between the two chairs. My father was still highlighted in yellow on the screen. "Who are you waiting for?" I rearranged myself on the chair, tucking my legs up under me in an attempt to get comfortable.

"My mom. She's having a triple bypass. It takes a long time, apparently. Truthfully, I don't know how long, to be honest. But it's been a few hours..." He looked at his watch. "It's been five hours."

"What did the doctor say about how long it was going to take? And what even is a triple bypass? I hear that all the time but I don't actually know what it means." The stress of the previous day made me bolder than usual about talking to this stranger who I would have ordinarily ignored.

"I didn't talk to the doctor. I don't really know what it means either. Presumably, they're bypassing something to do with her heart."

"Wow. I see you did your research. How come you didn't talk to the doctor? Didn't they come out before the operation?"

He shifted in his seat slightly and broke my gaze.

"The thing is," he started, "I don't actually speak to my mother. I haven't spoken to her in three years. Since my dad died. Her neighbor called me and told me about this heart attack, and this surgery and everything. So I came and they sent me up here with this number to watch the screen while she hopefully doesn't die." He exhaled audibly. "If she doesn't die, I'll have to figure out what the hell I'm going to say to her after not talking to her for three years." He looked over to me. "Which she deserved, by the way. She's a nasty piece of work." I thought he was about to go on, but he stopped himself and redirected. "If she does die, then I'm an asshole for not speaking to her for three years and I'll have to plan a funeral for a woman I don't even know."

"That's a lot of information to give a stranger at three in the morning."

"Technically it's only two fifty." He yawned. "Sorry. I'm just so tired. What are you here for?"

"They're sawing my father's leg off. Literally, actually. They use a saw. Isn't that insane?" I maintained a deadpan expression in an attempt at humor. Liam didn't outright laugh, but he did smile a little.

"I'm not sure that's the medical term though? Do they maybe say 'amputation' when they do something like that?"

"They do, but I like 'leg sawed off' better. I think if I keep saying it, it might catch on." I unplugged my phone and handed him the charger. "My mother is a nightmare too if it's any consolation. She was a total bitch to me a couple of weeks ago and I'm not even allowed to be mad at her anymore, according to my sister Clara, because of my dad's surgery. I only got to stay mad for about a week, which is a total rip-off. I would have been mad for months if not for this. I admire your three years. I'm sorry you had to break your streak tonight." I thought fleetingly about Michelle. Maybe no one in their twenties got along with their mother.

"You're right, though. I had a good run. Who knows, I might not break the streak. She might still die. Officially, I'm mad until either she comes out of this surgery, or she dies."

"I'll cross my fingers for you. Don't you have any siblings who aren't mad at her right now? My sister and I take turns."

"Only child. It's a burden."

I hesitated. "You don't have a wife who you could share your matricidal tendencies with?" I'd scoped out his ring finger early, of course, but one could never be too sure, and I was starting to be mildly interested in this quasi-weirdo. Maybe fate had thrust us together. Maybe it was Oprah-brand fate. Preparation meeting opportunity and all that crap. Admittedly this was a strange opportunity, in the hospital at three in the morning, but lately, I wasn't in any real shape to be too picky if this dating thing was ever going to take off.

"Nah. I've never been married. Never really been the marrying type I guess." Not a mark in his favor but I was willing to overlook it. "You?"

"Yeah. I was married. I mean, I'm separated. We're getting divorced. It's kind of a train wreck, to be honest." I hesitated, realizing this was probably the first time I had said all that out loud to a stranger. "And I have a son," I added quickly, not wanting to gloss over Dante for the sake of even potentially getting a date. "He's three. His name is Dante." I offered up a picture of Dante sitting in a puddle on my phone from our recent walk.

My father's name on the screen overhead turned to Orange; he was out of surgery.

"How long do they keep people in the recovery room?" I mused aloud. "My dad's been moved there I guess."

"You're asking the wrong guy. Where did you find the restroom?"

I pointed in the general direction of the restrooms. Once Liam was gone, I rubbed my face with my hands, trying to wake myself up, then stood up and gave my legs a stretch.

chapter 36

Sitting in the overnight waiting room during your father's surgery was not on the internet's list of ways to meet someone. Still, I had spent a couple hours with Liam already and I didn't hate him. He was also taller than I originally hoped, which became apparent when he stood up and walked off to the restrooms, albeit in the wrong direction.

When Liam came back, I was scrolling through Facebook. He sat down and was soon doing the same. It was a surprisingly comfortable, or perhaps just a very fatigued silence. We continued to glance periodically up at the screen on the wall.

After about half an hour, my father's color turned to green. It was three-forty-five. The surgery had taken slightly longer than anticipated and I had no idea what that meant if it was good or bad or indifferent. Now that my father was back in his room, there was a heaviness in my chest, and I knew I had to go and face whatever was going to happen.

"It was nice to meet you, Liam," I said, and reached behind the chair to unplug my charger. I sat down again briefly to wind the cord carefully and put it in my purse.

"You too Emily. And good luck with your quest to replace the word amputation. I bet it will go pretty well for you if you keep at it long enough."

"Good luck to *you*, with your mother-hating streak. Even if she doesn't die, three years is respectable." We smiled wearily at each other. A quick glance around the chair to make sure I wasn't forgetting anything, and it was time to go and face the next problem.

"Actually, Emily," his voice was tentative.

"Yes, Liam?" I was sure I didn't sound as casual as he did, because my heart did a little flip and I shoved my hands in the pocket of my hoodie.

"You want to get a coffee sometime? Or maybe dinner? I promise not to borrow your charge cord. I'd show up with my phone fully charged."

"Aren't you supposed to preface all that with, 'I don't usually do this'?" A smile was playing at the corners of my mouth.

"Oh, no. I do this all the time. Every time my mother has bypass surgery, I chat up the girl beside me and ask her out. It's a calculated plan." Now I was genuinely smiling, and not just because he was delaying my facing the music in my father's hospital room. "In fact," he continued, raising his eyebrows, "for all you know, I don't even *have* a mother in surgery. This could all be a ploy. I might be a serial killer who befriends women in waiting rooms and then kills them in the hospital parking lot."

I grimaced. "That got dark pretty quick."

"Yeah. That might have been overkill. No pun intended." He paused. "But seriously. Dinner? Can I call you?"

I hesitated and then immediately remembered '*put yourself out there.*' Here was my chance. Maybe I could shelve the dating apps, at least for now.

"Well," I started slowly. "My mother doesn't think I should date. That is why I am mad at her. *Was* mad at her." I shook my head. "It doesn't matter. The point is, if we had dinner, you would be helping me piss her off. And that seems very much in keeping with our theme this evening."

"Is that a yes?"

"It's a yes. Dinner would be fun."

We exchanged numbers by text and said goodbye, somewhat awkwardly since hugging seemed premature and shaking hands would have been be weird. I didn't hold out too much hope that he would actually contact me, but giving Liam my number definitely counted as 'making an effort.'

chapter 37

Two weeks went by and there was no real time for anything aside from taking care of Dante, work, and taking care of my parents. Clara was coming to the end of her academic year which was great, because it meant she would soon have more free time, but it also meant that she was in the middle of final exams. I was trying to take the lion's share of the work where Mom and Dad were concerned until she was finished.

My father had a lot of appointments with different doctors and my mother was not up to all the driving. They were in the process of getting an artificial leg, 'my wooden leg,' he cheerfully called it. Dad's surgery had happened so quickly that post-surgery procedures weren't happening in the right order. It was taking a long time to get into a rhythm for his care.

Dad himself was in very good spirits, considering. He was doing a lot of reading about ways to accelerate his recovery, and he found an online support group for people who had lost limbs. He started taking several strange-sounding supplements that he claimed were helping his skin to heal faster. I looked up all the ingredients and decided they weren't doing him any harm.

Mom was not coping as well. Every time I saw her she had just been crying and it was obviously going to take her longer to recover from Dad's surgery than it was taking Dad. I did some online reading of my own and learned that my mother had gone from being cared for by my father to being his caregiver too quickly, especially since it was a role she never thought she would have to play. I fervently hoped she would be able to step up because no way was I ready to become the caregiver of both of them.

The first few days after Dad's surgery were so busy and fraught with emotion that I hardly thought about Liam at all. Several days later it crossed my mind that he hadn't called. I was a little disappointed but told myself it had been a long shot anyway. There were certainly plenty of other things to keep me busy.

The one bright spot during this time was Sophia. She was an absolute gem and I decided to be nice to Mario for the rest of my life, no matter how difficult he was at work. Dante loved Percy and Persephone, he felt right at home with his new friends and Sophia. My house was always tidy when I got home, and Dante's laundry was often washed and put away. I was finally able to let go of the guilt I felt about leaving him to go to work.

Clara was just about halfway between Sophia and me in age. The two of them met a couple of times at my house and they got along great. One night, I came home from the twelve to eight shift and both Clara and Sophia were in the family room eating trail mix and drinking Dr. Pepper.

"Hey Sophia," I called, walking into the family room and looking around for Dante. "Where's the boy?"

"He's gone to bed early. Conked out. We walked to the park before dinner and he ran himself ragged trying to catch those stupid Canada Geese. He went straight from the bath to his bed and was asleep by seven-thirty."

"Nice one. Hi, Sis." Clara was watching *Say Yes To The Dress* with her hand deep in the bag of trail mix, and hardly looked up as I came in. "I saw this one last week," I quipped, "she gets that dress." I sank down in the chair beside the couch and checked the can of Dr. Pepper Clara was drinking, to see if it was cold. It was, and I took a long drink of it.

"No, it must have been another episode. This girl can't afford that dress." Clara took the can back, realized that it was now almost empty, and put it down on the table with a pointed tinny thud.

"Her dad buys it for her in the end. Pass me that trail mix." I grabbed the bag out of her hand and looked down into it. "Did you pick all the chocolate out of this? I hate when you do that."

"You know," ventured Sophia, who had been so quiet I forgot she was there for a moment, "being around you two makes me miss my sister."

Her lip was trembling as she blinked rapidly, but a tear still fell from her eye and she wiped it away on the sleeve of her sweatshirt. We both moved to where Sophia was sitting at the far end of the couch. I put my arm around her shoulders and squeezed her. I felt protective of her, even after the short time we had known her because she was so important to Dante, and she was so wonderful with him.

Clara and I listened to Sophia talk about how hard it was bringing up her sister's children without her. She clearly loved her niece and nephew dearly and never complained. At nineteen, she was understandably overwhelmed as she tried to figure out her place in bringing them up, trying desperately to do the right thing by them and her sister.

"Sophia, if it makes you feel any better, I *never* know what I'm doing with Dante."

She watched me hopefully. Her eyes were wary.

Clara and I reassured Sophia for about half an hour. She seemed comforted by the time she got up to leave.

"You know, I'm probably just tired. I've been burning the candle at both ends lately." She looked up at me, apologetic. "Not that I mind the time with Dante. That's not what I meant at all. I love this job."

"You need a good night's sleep. Wouldn't it be nice to be able to pass out like Dante at the end of the day?" My arms wrapped her in a quick hug, tight enough so she would know I meant it. "You know what? The three of us could use a night out. We should make that happen soon." It struck me that until recently I had been hoping for a very different kind of night out with Liam.

Clara's face was drawn. She had lost weight, probably from the stress of the last few weeks. Stress had the opposite effect on me - I was eating a lot of fries at the waitress station lately and the occasional plate of onion rings as well. A couple of times Dean had raised an eyebrow at me, but he was aware of my current circumstances and didn't say anything.

Clara and Sophia left at nine forty-five, but it already felt like midnight. I quickly tidied away the snacks and empty soda cans from the living room, cracked open the door to Dante's bedroom to watch him sleep, and pulled a pair of clean pyjamas for me from the pile on the bed. The next morning, I would drop Dante off at Tyler and Amy's. He would stay with his father while I worked a couple of double shifts and went to two appointments with my dad. I had purchased a small yellow spiral-bound notebook that Dad took to all his appointments. This way, whoever was with Dad could write down what the doctors said. Neither my mother nor my father had any real recollection of the details of the first appointment they went to after the surgery, and we were left guessing what the doctor said.

I lay in bed thinking about Sophia trying to raise her sister's children, and shuddered at the thought of losing Clara. Sophia seemed so young to have experienced such a drastic loss, and she seemed to be dealing with it unbelievably well. In contrast, I still wasn't dealing with the loss of Tyler very well at all. I still had the occasional crying spell when no one was around, and I had teared up in Michelle's presence a couple of times.

I fell asleep, wondering what to do for Sophia to cheer her up, and how to support Clara's fragile state of mind.

chapter 38

As arranged, I dropped Dante off at his father's the following morning at eight. Days, when Dante was with Tyler passed quickly because I had become adept at keeping myself occupied. Work was often busy and just as often uneventful. The weather was finally turning warmer but because it was only April, the milder temperatures couldn't be trusted to last just yet. Not infrequently, there was snow, either in the air or on the ground on Michelle's birthday at the end of April. It was unwise to be hopeful that it was Spring before that day came and went. My own birthday was at the beginning of June, and as well as being my birthday, it was a celebration that Winter was finally over and beach weather was in sight. This June would be my first birthday without Tyler. As an adult without a husband, I wasn't sure whose job it was to plan the celebrations for my birthday. I hoped someone would at least buy me a cake.

Things with Dad had become, if not easier, more routine. Several times, my finger hovered over but did not touch the dating app on my phone. I was unconvinced that there were any good men out there, and was even less convinced that I would find one who would actually want to go out with me. The original urgency borne of my anger at my mother had fizzled. It was anyone's guess when I would be ready to make another attempt.

I was pushing my father down the hall in a wheelchair to the hospital elevators after an appointment when I saw a missed call from Liam. In spite of myself, a wave of anxious energy rose up in my chest. Was I excited to talk to him or just relieved he hadn't blown me off? Pushing the button inside the elevator, a smile crept over my face.

I pushed my phone back into my purse and told myself not to be so eager. I willed myself to hold on to the almost-giddiness flooding my brain and body for as long as possible before calling or texting Liam back. There was a chance that he wasn't into me anyway, that he had pocket-dialed me, or worse. It was a long shot that he would call me to tell me he wasn't interested after weeks of radio silence, but the idea of a possible letdown, combined with terror at the idea of further rejection made me put off calling him back.

That fear of rejection prompted me to let an entire day go by before I contacted Liam. Many times, over the next twenty-four hours, I contemplated calling or texting. I was edging toward being rude by not returning the call, but he had waited over two weeks to call me, so a day's delay didn't seem unreasonable.

When I got home from work the next day, I called Michelle and blurted out my news.

"Remember that guy I met at the hospital? Liam?" I worried she was about to tell me it was a bad idea to call him back but pushed forward.

"When your dad had surgery?"

"Yeah. What I didn't tell you at the time was that he asked me if he could call me and I said yes. But then he didn't call, and I thought he had blown me off."

"But now he *has* called," Michelle finished the thought for me.

"Yes. He called yesterday."

"What did he say?" Her interest was piqued. She sounded excited.

"I didn't answer."

"What?" She nearly shrieked. "How long have you been talking about being serious about finding a date? *Weeks* already. And now you meet this guy out of the blue? Call him back. What is the matter with you?"

I breathed a sigh of relief. If Michelle had thought it was a terrible idea, it would have been harder to go through with it. "You're sure? You don't think he'll turn out to be some kind of criminal or pervert?"

"Emily, anyone could be a criminal, or a pervert. I doubt many people introduce themselves like that. You tend to find that out later, after you've invested a lot of time." Michelle's tone was dry.

"He didn't seem like a criminal. I think I'm going to call him back…I might go out with him." I squared my shoulders and spoke with more confidence. "Yes. I will *definitely* go out with him. He's probably going to be the great love of my life."

"For crying out loud, Emily. Just go on one date. You always try to do everything at once, you know that? Just go out for dinner with this Liam. Go paintballing, or take a macramé class. Whatever."

I laughed. "I don't think macramé will be an option. Or paintball. I'll call him right after I hang up."

"And Emily?" Michelle continued, just as I was walking into my room to see what I could wear on the date I didn't yet have.

"Yeah?"

"I know that you called me so I would convince you to go out with this guy."

"I totally did not!" This was a lie.

"You totally did too. And if he *does* turn out to be a mass-murderer, I'm not taking the blame for that. You get mass-murdered at the Longhorn Steakhouse, that's your problem."

"I got it. I'm hanging up. I've got to call him before I lose my nerve."

I hung up and was instantly anxious again. I surveyed the huge pile of clean laundry on my bed and decided it was necessary to fold it before calling Liam.

With the laundry put away and my sheets shoved into the washing machine, I paused over trivial details like how much they had recently improved the scent of the Tide Pods, and how I really needed to donate some of my clothes to the St. Vincent de Paul society because my t-shirt drawer was overflowing. Finally, sitting down on the couch with a Dr. Pepper, gripping my phone, I touched Liam's name under 'missed calls.'

I held the phone to up my ear and listened to the ringing. One, two, three rings. And then, the eventuality I had not planned for: the answering machine. I had only about five seconds to decide whether to leave a message. In the end, I left the world's lamest-sounding recording.

"Hi, uh, Liam. This is Emily. Emily from the hospital? Anyway, I saw you called yesterday and, uh, sorry it's taken me so long to get back to you. But, uh, I'm just, I guess, calling you back. So yeah. Okay then. I guess I'll talk to you soon? Or maybe not. Okay then. Bye."

I hung up and buried my face in my hands. How could I be such a moron? I had likely ruined any chance of a date with Liam by sounding like a punch-drunk sixteen-year-old at junior prom in that voicemail. I headed to the laundry room to put my sheets in the dryer and felt my phone buzz in my pocket. I looked down to see a text, incredibly, from Liam -

Saw you called. In a meeting. Will call you later. Hope you're doing well. ☺

I stared down at the phone, not believing my luck, and considered texting back -

Don't check your voicemail. I sound like an idiot.

Of course, this was not a real option, so I had to just hope Liam would call back despite the voicemail. I sat down on the sofa, sipped my now less-cold soda, wished I had picked up potato chips at the store, and reached for the remote control. My intention was to read one of the parenting books on the coffee table. Instead, I got up, trudged to Dante's room, stripped the sheets off of his bed and put them in the washing machine, along with the bath mat and all the dirty towels from his and my bedroom floors. I jammed a second Tide Pod under all the towels and set the cycle for an extra hot rinse so no blue slime would be left in the water return reservoir at the bottom of the machine.

A short time later my bed was made, and Dante's bedding was in the dryer with the towels. The kitchen was tidied up and wiped down. All of this was to distract myself from longing for the phone to ring. What kind of meeting was Liam in? I knew nothing about this man, other than his mother had a bad heart. He could be an investment banker, a stockbroker, a big shot movie producer… the list of careers got less and less realistic. I tossed the dishcloth and tea towels into the laundry hamper, pulled fresh ones from the drawer, and felt the satisfaction of the house finally clean and tidy around me.

After an hour of kind-of reading *Don't Divorce Yourself Too*, while flipping between HGTV and TLC, another text came from Liam -

I'm not great on the phone. Want to meet for coffee? Maybe tonight?

It was only eleven in the morning, although I had been awake and keeping busy for what seemed like days. I made a few quick calculations. I was working twelve to eight, so if I showered right away, dried and straightened my hair and applied an appropriate amount of make-up, I'd still make it to work for twelve. If I packed an outfit to change into after work, I could meet Liam by eight-thirty, as long as no one came in and ordered a steak dinner at seven forty-five.

In the bathroom, I brushed my teeth for exactly two minutes so as not to seem too desperate when I texted Liam back -

I could meet you at 8:30. Would that work?

He texted back almost immediately -

Sure. Tim Horton's? 8:30?

It was a promising sign that he hadn't suggested Starbucks. It was farther away, and I considered it pretentious. My preference was Dunkin Donuts, but I was okay with Tim Horton's.

Sounds good. See you then.

chapter 39

I hit send on the text to Liam, turned on the water in the shower and kept my hand under it until it heated up. Abandoning all the day's efforts to be tidy, my clothes hit and stayed on the floor. I pulled a still-warm towel out of the dryer. Using clothes or towels straight out of the dryer before going through the steps of folding them and putting them away made me happy. I set the clean towel on the bathroom sink, kicked the clothes on the floor out of the way and got into the shower.

I scrubbed myself with the only body wash in the shower that didn't have *Bob the Builder* or *Thomas the Tank Engine* on it and banged the bottle of conditioner upside down on my hand, forcing out enough to finger comb through my hair. After towelling myself off, I quickly grabbed leggings, a sweater and my Uggs out of the closet for my meet-up with Liam, and hastily applied make-up. Sophia had been giving me a few make-up tips, and promised to take me to buy a few things that she felt would 'highlight my best features.' From most people, this manner of unsolicited advice would have been bitchy and annoying. When Sophia said it, it was genuine and sweet, and made me look forward to the makeup shopping trip.

Satisfied with the make-up job I'd accomplished, in a limited amount of time, I double-checked my reflection in the mirror, tossed my make-up bag in my purse and spritzed myself with my favorite scent from Bath and Body Works. Mentally, I resolved to get some grown-up perfume, then locked the door behind me, and stepped out into the cloudy, cold weather. The sky was threatening rain.

Waiting tables soon took over my thoughts and even stopped me from panicking for short periods of time. Zoe looked at me suspiciously after the lunch rush died down.

"That's the second plate of fries you've scarfed down already today. What's your deal?"

"I'm not the only one eating them. There are three of us working. We're sharing them." I knew I sounded nervous.

"You *are* the only one, actually. Vivian has given up carbs and I ate before I started work." She walked away with the coffee pot, topping up the small white porcelain mugs throughout the restaurant.

I considered the half-empty plate of fries sitting beside the soup bowls, placed my hand over them to check their temperature, and decided they were cold enough to throw away. I usually wasn't above eating cold fries, and I shot Zoe a pointed stare and while tipping them into the garbage by the kitchen. She just shrugged. Zoe didn't care what I did but she didn't judge me either. It was a strange social trade-off.

Later, when the restaurant was quiet, we took our fifteen-minute break at the same time. Having held it in for most of the shift, I was now unable to stop myself from gushing about my coffee date with Liam. "I'm having coffee with someone tonight. I met him at the hospital when my dad was in surgery."

Zoe peered over the top of *USA Today* at me.

"Your dad had surgery? When was that?" She seemed mildly interested, which was about as good as it got with her.

"Zoe. Seriously? I was off for two days and you worked my shifts. Don't you remember that? A few weeks ago?" Was she merely unconcerned or was it possible she had low-level selective amnesia?

"Oh right. I remember the shifts. Mandy called in sick to that breakfast. It was insane. Dean had to wait a few tables."

"Right." Conversations with Zoe were sometimes downright painful. "What I'm *trying* to tell you is that I met a guy in the waiting room of the hospital and I'm having coffee with him tonight." I waited and hoped she would mirror my enthusiasm.

"That's nice." She folded the paper, then went out the back door for a cigarette.

I gave up, refilled my Dr. Pepper and spent the rest of my break playing on my phone, not sure why I even bothered trying to ever have a conversation with Zoe.

Dinner was so slow that Zoe left at seven. I spent the hour between seven and eight cleaning up, repeatedly checking my reflection in the glass of the pie cabinet, talking to Dean, and tweaking the schedule.

At seven fifty-five, my phone buzzed where it lay on the stainless-steel worktop of the waitress station. I looked down, certain it was Liam canceling. Instead, the display showed Tyler's name -

Emily, I'm ill. I need you to take Dante. Amy will drop him at the restaurant.

Immediately I felt sick myself, with anger. Once again, I had to solve Tyler's problem. He didn't even ask. Just told me he was dropping Dante off. What could I say? Saying no would make me a selfish, bad mother.

In addition to being angry that Tyler couldn't handle parenting, I was angry that my coffee with Liam, which I had been looking forward to, was off. I was also angry at myself for wanting to meet up with essentially a total stranger instead of taking care of my son. I willed myself to calm down before picking up the phone to reply. Deliberately, I took a fresh cloth and started at the far end of the restaurant, wiping down already-clean tables with vinegar, cleaning the tops of the napkin dispenser and the sugar, salt, and pepper for good measure.

Only slightly calmed by my self-imposed distraction, I picked up the phone and texted a single word back to Tyler –

Fine

Then I touched my conversation with Liam and texted quickly before I lost my nerve or questioned what I would say–

Sorry, have to cancel. Change of plans. I have my son this evening. Reschedule?

The little grey dots in the bottom corner flashed and indicated he was texting back -

No problem. Bring him with?

I paused and then glanced down at the time. It was two minutes after eight. Amy would already be outside with Dante. She had probably already been outside when Tyler texted me. If Tyler was really even sick. It was just as likely that they wanted to go out for a romantic evening and needed me to take Dante.

I decided to go for it. If Liam and I ever got serious, Dante would be part of the equation. I might as well weed Liam out now if they didn't get along. I headed to the bathroom to change out of my uniform and touch up my makeup -

Sounds good. See you at 8:30.

I almost texted *thanks for understanding* but thought better of it.

chapter 40

Amy and Dante were waiting in her car outside of New Dean's. The weather had turned and there was drizzle in the air. I smiled civilly at Amy but said nothing to her as I opened the door, grabbed Dante's bag from the floor of the back seat and took him by the hand. He was thrilled to see me and raised his arms in the air, which meant he wanted to be picked up. Almost before his hands were over his head I swung him up and on my hip for the dozen steps between Amy's car and mine. I hugged him tight and breathed him in before buckling him into his car seat in the back.

On the way, I told Dante about the plans.

"Buddy, we're going to go to Tim Horton's."

"All right! Can we get Timbits?" The tiny donut holes were one of his favorite treats. I liked them because they were so small that it was easier to portion out how much sugar he was eating.

"Sure. But listen. I want to tell you something." I watched him in the rearview mirror to make sure he was paying attention. "We're meeting a friend of mine there."

"Okay. Is it James? McDonald's James?"

I was surprised that he remembered.

"No, His name is Liam."

"Okay." Dante was unfazed in the way that only a three-year-old can be.

We rode on in comfortable silence. I was excited to meet up with Liam and happy that he wanted to include Dante. I also felt the familiar pang of sadness and frustration that came with carving this new life out for myself. There were no rules and no role models for this. My parents were ambivalent at best about my new situation. At worst, my mother was openly hostile and judgemental, both of my choices, and things that were not my choice. I shook my head to clear my mind of my parents, squishing both my mother and father down into the mason jar in my mind like the book said, and then mentally shoved the mason jar into the glove compartment of the car.

Dante and I pushed open the door of Tim Horton's. As the smell of coffee and donuts washed over me, I looked around for Liam. We were early, even after driving around for a few minutes to kill some time.

Liam was in a booth in the corner, near the electric fireplace. He raised a hand slightly. I put on my waitress smile, gripped Dante's hand and we headed over to where he was sitting.

"Hi, Liam." I didn't know whether I should extend my hand, hug him or maybe give him a high five. Instead, I used my son to get out of the situation. Hashtag bad mother. "Dante, this is my friend Liam."

"Hey Liam," Liam extended a fist to Dante, and Dante fist-bumped it with his small hand. I smiled.

"Dante, have a seat. I'll get you a hot chocolate."

"No, no. You sit down. I'll get the hot chocolate. What can I get you, Emily?" It gave me a few butterflies in my stomach to hear him say my name.

"Coffee for me, please. But Dante's going to want a box of Timbits. Honestly, I can get them. His hot chocolate needs to have milk in it. I'll come up with you."

Liam was bemused.

"It's okay. I got it. You want chocolate Timbits or the ones with the jelly filling?" He addressed Dante directly and I liked that.

"Chocolate." He looked up at me. "Can I have four Timbits, mom?"

"You can have three. That's enough for this time of the night. You'll never get to sleep otherwise." He should have been in bed already.

"Three chocolate Timbits, a cooled-off hot chocolate, a coffee for you and a decaf for me. Got it." Liam winked at Liam and turned to walk to the counter.

"Actually," he might as well get to know me now, "I'd like an apple fritter too please."

"No problem." He went to the counter and Dante and I sat on our own. I hung Dante's coat on the corner of the booth, immediately smelling Amy's fabric softener on his t-shirt as soon as his coat was removed.

Liam returned with the drinks and my donut, and I connected to the Wi-Fi and Dante quickly started watching Netflix.

Our conversation was amicable, and we soon recovered the easy banter from the hospital waiting room, and I felt bold enough to ask the question I had been wondering.

"Why did you wait two weeks to call me? Were you trying to make me like you more? Or did you have a few other women you were working through before you got to me?" I was joking but also curious to hear the answer.

"I would have called sooner," Liam sipped his coffee and absent-mindedly folded the paper bag my donut had come in, "but my mom died. She made it through the surgery and then died the next day."

I was shocked and my hand flew to cover my mouth.

"Oh my God. I'm so sorry. How's everything going? Are you okay? How are you coping?"

"Yeah," he sighed. "It's been harder than I thought it would be, given that we weren't close, as you might remember."

"I remember. Still, it must have come as a shock."

"Honestly, it wasn't the shock that was a problem. I'm an only child and my dad died about ten years ago so I had to make all the arrangements on my own. What struck me was how many different things there were to do when someone dies. I had to arrange the funeral, which was awkward as hell. Then I had to list my mom's house, which was full of thirty years of her stuff and a lot of my stuff too, so I hired an auctioneer to come in and empty it out, which should be done tomorrow. Then I'll have to go back in and clean out what he didn't want before the cleaners come in to make it look presentable. Then I'll get the house listed, and the market is strong at the moment. My agent says she should be able to sell it, and likely it will take weeks, not months."

I was shocked by Liam's news, and taken aback by how much he had just told me in just a few sentences.

"I'm really sorry, Liam. And sorry for giving you a hard time about not calling."

He shrugged. "You couldn't have known. Like I told you before, my mom and I weren't close."

I looked over at Dante, whose eyes were drooping slightly as he held my phone.

Liam noticed.

"Listen, Emily, do you want to go out on a real date? Not that I don't like coffee and donuts. Maybe not as much as you and Dante..." he smiled.

"I like just about all food, actually," I grinned. "This is a fundamental fact about me. Food is love. It makes working in a restaurant very satisfying." I reached for Dante's coat. "Hey, what do you do? For work, I mean. I haven't even asked you. And yes, to the date. I would like to go on a real date with you." A genuine smile spread across my face.

"I'm a teacher. First grade." Liam smiled at Dante. "That's how I know how to cool down hot chocolate. And fist bump."

"I'm impressed. I didn't know that there were, I mean..."

"Men, who teach first grade?" Liam's smile was broad. "There aren't a lot of us, but I love it. And then of course, the real reason I'm a teacher..."

I looked at him quizzically.

"Weekends and summers off." He laughed while he held up my coat for me.

"Well, I only waitress for the free onion rings and Dr. Pepper."

We paused inside the door before venturing outside to our cars.

"About our date. What do you think about next Saturday? I promise to call you this time. I don't have another mother who could die."

"I'd like that. Saturday it is. Without Dante this time. I appreciate you coming out to meet him tonight, but I'd like a dinner without him. I'm sure that makes me a horrible mother..." I trailed off.

"Only if it makes me a horrible human to be happy you said that." I smiled again, this time meeting Liam's eyes.

"Wonderful. We're both horrible people. I like that as a starting place."

"Bye Liam," called Dante. "Thanks for the Timbits." They fist bumped again.

Then we were in the car driving home. When we arrived, I unbuckled a sleeping Dante from his car seat and woke him up just enough to take his jacket off, make him go pee, and put a pull-up on him. When he was tucked into bed, I texted Sophia that Tyler was sick. She texted back that if I dropped Dante off at her house in the morning on my way to work, she'd be happy to watch him there.

I then sent a group text to Clara, Michelle, and Sophia –

Going on a date with Liam next Saturday night.

Immediately my phone pinged three times.

From Michelle –

You need to go shopping.

From Clara –

I have a mailer from Kohls for 30% off.

From Sophia –

I will do your hair and makeup

I sent them back the sleep emoji and the thumbs up emoji and went to my bedroom. In my fit of domesticity that morning I had cleared all the clean laundry from the bed and made it up with the clean sheets. Without the divide in the middle, the whole thing looked like my bed to me for the first time. It looked good.

chapter 41

Tyler's man-flu lasted for four days, which cost me two extra days' babysitting, even with Clara pitching in to watch Dante when Sophia was unavailable.

My father's recovery felt to me like it was progressing slowly, but the doctors said that was to be expected. Both my parents had aged significantly in the month since my father's amputation. Mom and Dad's house was noticeably dirty, even in the absence of Dante's usual mess. The baseboards were dusty and the windowsills seemed perennially grimy. Although they were well able to afford a cleaning lady, my mother's Italian pride kept her from admitting that she needed help of any kind, other than what was ordered by a doctor. The nurse who came to change my father's dressing offered to connect my parents with community supports. Clara encouraged the nurse to leave a stack of pamphlets behind with the information. The pamphlets were in the recycling box the next time I stopped by.

My life still felt overwhelming most of the time. I wasn't sure it was wise to add a date, or a potential relationship to everything else I was dealing with on a daily basis.

We tried unsuccessfully to find a time when Clara, Michelle, Sophia and I could all go shopping together. The best we came up with was a time when Michelle and Sophia were available, but when Clara would have to go to a doctor's appointment with our parents.

The trip had to wait until Dante was back with Tyler, because everyone who would normally watch him would be necessary to the operation, and shopping *with* Dante was cruel and unnecessary.

I picked Michelle up first. "Where do you want to go?" Michelle had wanted to do a fashion rescue mission operation on me for a while, and was eager to get started.

"I don't know," I honked aggressively at a white pick-up truck that hesitated when the light turned green.

"Feeling on edge?" Michelle raised an eyebrow at me and changed the radio station, swatting my hand away when I tried to switch it back to my preferred country music.

"I don't know… I guess. I haven't really bought myself anything new, you know, since…"

"Since Tyler left with 'that bitch Amy Ballantyne?' It's okay, you can say it. Grace-Ann's not here. Just because I think we should be friends with her doesn't mean I disagree with you about Amy. Amy is a bitch on wheels. She was a bitch before she ran off with Tyler."

"Yes to all those things. I haven't bought anything since… that time, and I agree with your assessment of Amy. I'm trying to worry about her less, but does bear repeating every once in a while, if only for the sake of solidarity." My hand moved once again to change the station and was swatted away once again by Michelle.

"Watch the road. Quit messing with the radio."

We approached Sophia's house. "I don't even know what kind of clothes I'm looking for. What are you supposed to wear on a first date?" I pulled into Sophia's drive and tapped the horn. Sophia ran out of her house and hurried down the driveway to the car. She slid into the back seat and closed the door.

"Hello, ladies. What are we talking about?"

Looking behind me, I backed out of her driveway.

"What to wear on a first date," replied Michelle. "Sophia," she continued without skipping a beat, "do you want to listen to country music?"

"Ick. No. Why would you ask that?" She made a face.

"Just wondering" Then to me, "two to one. Don't try to change it again."

Michelle had a way of bossing me that was generally comforting. It was nice to have someone else make a decision for me, however small.

"What did you wear on your date with Dean?" Sophia asked from the backseat.

"I don't even remember. Besides, it wasn't really a date." I sighed. "That restaurant was amazing though."

"Let's hope that this time, you've found a man who is more memorable than the restaurant he takes you to." Michelle quipped dryly. "Why are you turning here?"

"I'm going to Walgreens. We need makeup."

"Negative," called Sophia from the back seat. "Get back on the road. We're going to Sephora. I'm not sending you out into the world wearing drugstore makeup."

"Sophia, I can't really afford Sephora. Are you sure you can't make do with Maybe it's Maybelline?" Despite my protests, I turned the car around as she directed, and signaled to get back on the road.

"What you cannot afford," said Michelle, who was clearly happy to have found an ally in Sophia, "is to show up to this date looking like crap. This might be the first date with the man of your dreams. Or it might be the last guy who asks you out. This could be it for you. Treat this occasion with respect."

Sophia was hooting in the back seat.

"Thanks a bunch, you jerk!" I slapped Michelle's thigh with my right hand and turned the steering wheel with my left.

"The truth will set you free, my friend," Michelle was laughing now, and I couldn't hold back a small giggle.

"And Sephora. Sephora will set you free too." Sophia patted me on my shoulder. "And you'll look amazing."

We arrived at the entrance to JC Penny, the store with the closest Sephora counter.

"But I'm not buying clothes here. I'm finding something at Kohl's. Michelle has a mailer for thirty percent off. That's non-negotiable." We started the search for a parking spot, driving up and down the rows.

"I can live with that. Sophia? You good with that?"

"Yup. Park there. Right there!" Sophia patted my shoulder again, forcefully, and I pulled the steering wheel sharply to the left to slide into a space three spots from the front. "By the time I'm done with your face and your hair, it's not going to matter what you wear. You can wear a velvet tracksuit and he won't even notice."

"Great," I muttered as we approached the mall. "I'll be 'Leisure Suit Larry' in drag. That sounds alluring. I'll be sure to get a second date dressed like that."

"That's progress," Sophia remarked. "That's the first time I've ever heard you talk about a second date." She pulled me by the elbow away from the brightly colored body washes and toward the Bobbi Brown counter.

"No, no, no." I insisted. "Not Bobbi Brown. That is completely out of my price range. That's final."

Sophia sighed. "Okay. I can work with that. Let's get you sorted out."

Forty-five minutes and two hundred dollars later, I was equipped with the solid beginnings of a pretty good make-up bag, Michelle tried to put my mind at ease by reminding me that I had spent no money on myself since Tyler left. Sophia added that she had seen my current makeup situation and I desperately needed these products, which would 'practically last forever.'

"Next time we'll update your brushes." She quipped. "I've seen those too."

Despite the borderline-extravagant Sephora trip, I felt no guilt taking Michelle and Sophia out for lunch. I rationalized that one couldn't put a price on friendship, and we had a discount code for Kohl's which would save us loads of money on the clothes.

At Kohl's, both my friends refused to let me buy a new sweater and leggings and accused me of never wearing anything else.

"But I *like* sweaters and leggings. And I look good in them." I whined.

"No. You look like a comfy mom. This is not the time for a comfy mom outfit. Trust the people here who are *not* moms." I cast an injured look at Michelle. "Don't get me wrong. You're a great mom. That's probably why you always dress like one. But this is the time to dress like..."

"Like a woman!" called Sophia, and threw her hands in the air.

This was the atmosphere of the trip. Lots of laughs and a few hard truths. Before we left Kohl's, I chose a ruffled top and a pair of skinny jeans. Both pieces were on sale, further reduced by Michelle's thirty percent, and not 'mom clothes.' For good measure, I picked up two t-shirts and a pair of jogging pants for Dante.

Now that the shopping trip was in the bag, my thoughts were of little else but my impending date with Liam. I spent hours dusting, cleaning and tidying everything in my house to distract myself, and took long walks outside with Dante, pushing his stroller stubbornly through puddles for the sake of getting some exercise and killing some time. Even though my new book was called, *Fun Moms Need to Have Fun!* I struggled to push away a certain measure of guilt that I was spending time away from my son to go on a date, and resolved to double my efforts to spend as much quality time as possible with Dante before then.

chapter 42

Liam was scheduled to pick me up at seven p.m. on Saturday. Sophia showed up at five. Although I was unsure that my face or hair needed two hours' worth of work, she insisted. As soon as Sophia arrived, she pressed a 'brightening mask' into my hands and told me to wash my face and apply it. Meanwhile, she started making macaroni and cheese for Dante. She let him dump the cheese powder in and he made a mess. This always stressed me out, but Sophia took it completely in stride and cleaned up the fluorescent powder as he stirred in more butter than I usually used.

"Go!" Sophia commanded as I watched the Kraft Dinner fiasco unfold. "I know how to make macaroni. Go and wash your face and get that mask on. Time's a wasting."

I gave in to her expertise, and followed the bossy instructions. When I came back with the mask on, there was a bowl of orange macaroni waiting for me. Dante had happily tucked into his.

"Sophia makes the best Kraft Dinner, mom," commented Dante with his mouth full.

"I see that." It was proving difficult to eat without also ingesting the face mask.

"I'm not being funny," Sophia stated calmly, "but you should have taken that mask off before you started eating."

I rolled my eyes dramatically.

"Thanks for the advice. Super helpful. That explains why my dinner tastes like Rose Oil."

"Go wash it off and I'll make you something else. There's pizza in the fridge. Is that edible still?"

I thought about it. "It's from Thursday. Should be okay."

"Eat it before I start your makeup. You're not eating anything after that. I'm not even sure you should eat in the restaurant. I've seen you eat."

Shaking my head, I walked back to my bathroom to remove the mask and checked the instructions on the package, afraid of Sophia's reaction if I did it wrong. My new make-up bag was on the vanity. I had taken out all the makeup that was more than a year old, packed it into a plastic bag, and thrown it out at work, so I couldn't change my mind and pull any of it out of the garbage at home. The quantity of my make-up was a lot less than before, but the quality had increased dramatically.

I cradled the sleek black mascara tube and the pretty pink 'lipglass' in my hand and touched them lovingly, feeling guilty about owning such beautiful things. Probably

I was putting too much effort into this date. A nagging desperation played at the corners of my mind. Michelle had said it jokingly but it could well be true: Liam might be the last guy who would ask me out. This might be my last chance. Once all my new products were in my beautiful sparkly new makeup bag, I grabbed my straightening iron and returned to the kitchen to let Sophia work her magic.

By six-forty, Sophia had performed a miracle on my average face and transformed it into the realm of definitely above-average, which sparked a glow inside me. My hair was flat and glossy and I was rocking my new outfit. Somewhere on Facebook I read that the skin regenerates itself every twenty-seven days, which meant the outside of my face was new and un-besmirched by Tyler's touch or presence. All the clothes on me were new, including socks and underwear – decidedly not sexy underwear, but new and freshly washed. The only regrettable exceptions to my apparel renaissance were my boots and my jacket. No way could I justify spending that kind of money on superstition. Instead, I had taken extra-fine-grain sandpaper that was kicking around in the garage and sanded the bottom of my boots down ever so slightly so at least the bottoms were fresh. That would have to do. My suede jacket got a rub down with a clothes brush. Being borderline neurotic and detail-focussed was a lot of work, but the mental gymnastics had helped me get through the day of anticipation. I figured there was lots of time to be normal later in life.

All that remained was to wait for Liam. I perched on the edge of the armchair, my hands nervously ran through my hair.

“Stop it.” Sophia’s reaction was automatic. “I swear I’ll get that straightening iron out again and start over, and Liam will have to wait for you in the driveway.” She said all this without looking away from the pups on the screen. Dante was comfortably settled into the crook of her arm.

I clicked the button on the side of my phone on and off to illuminate the time. A few seconds after it changed from six fifty-nine to seven o’clock, the doorbell rang. Dante jumped up, ran to the door and pulled at the doorknob, which he was unable to turn with his chubby little hands.

chapter 43

The door opened and Liam stood on the step wearing his goofy smile. Almost instantly, my shoulders dropped and my stomach felt less flippy.

I watched him with hypersensitive scrutiny to see if Liam noticed my improved face and hair but if he did, he didn't give it away. After greeting me, Liam's attention turned to Dante. They started with the required fist bump, and then from behind his back, Liam produced a present. The paper wrapping paper was distinct and came from the local independently-owned toy store. Impressive.

"This is for you, Dante. Thanks for letting your mom come out with me tonight." Dante grabbed the gift eagerly and started unwrapping it.

"What do you say, Dante?" I asked pointedly, but not before he was ripping the paper from the toy.

"Thank you, Liam," he chirped mechanically, then threw the paper on the floor and held up his prize.

"Mom, look! It's Chase! It's Chase's fire engine!" he ran off into the family room. "Sophia, look at this! It's an engine!"

I bent down to pick up the discarded paper and scrunch it into a ball.

"Thank you. You didn't have to do that. He loves that show."

"I know," replied Liam, "I remember him watching it at the coffee shop." He picked up a stray piece of wrapping paper that I missed and handed it to me. "A lot of my kids at school watch it too."

Sophia turned up in the doorway to the family room.

"Hi. I'm Sophia." She extended her hand and Liam shook it. "You guys have fun. Everything is under control here." She turned back toward Dante who was making his new fire engine drive over every surface in the room, up over couches and the table and even over the top of the television. "Dante, come say bye to your mom."

"Bye, mom!" he shouted, not looking up.

Liam held my coat out for me and then we left together. Sophia gave my arm a quick squeeze and whispered, "Good luck!" into my ear.

I was so nervous when we got outside that I headed reflexively over to my own car.

Liam paused. "Did you want to drive?" he asked me, bemused.

"Oh jeez. Sorry. Force of habit." I walked over to his car which was considerably, bigger, newer and nicer one than mine. He opened the door for me, and I mentally awarded him points for gallantry.

Once Liam started driving, I ventured to ask, "Where are we going? What exciting adventures do you have planned?" Instantly it seemed like a stupid thing to say. My anxiety about the evening was still running high.

"I've heard you say you like food," Liam, grinned, "more than once, actually, so I did some research and I thought we would go to a few different places for one course each." He had tried. It would have been more work to find several restaurants than to find one. "I found a bar that has good apps, a mom and pop place that does good comfort food, and a late-night bakery that specializes in cupcakes."

"Wow. I'm impressed." I was suddenly and fervently thankful for Sophia's make-up wizardry. Liam was revealing himself to be a better and better catch.

We drove a few miles and gradually, the conversation became more relaxed. There were still some punctuating pauses, but even these were becoming less stressful. We drove, talking on and off, for about fifteen minutes until we were beyond the city limits of St. Clair Shores, and heading toward Detroit.

"How far away are you taking me?" He had given away very little about where we were going and I was intrigued. I was also very hungry, having not eaten much of my warmed-up pizza at home, what with the brightening mask taste that was stuck in my mouth. I had also been hesitant to eat too much pizza in the hopes that the fare wherever Liam was taking me would be a lot better than warmed up pizza. As an avid eater, I was a pretty good judge of when to max out on current food offerings and when to hold out for something better. Appetite is a finite resource.

"It's a little place called The Silver Monkey. Supposed to be sort of a throw-back to a Honky Tonk. There's no music on tonight until a lot later, but they have a lot of deep-fried appetizers on the menu so I thought we'd start there." He glanced over briefly, watching for my reaction.

"Now you're talking. Deep-fried is my middle name. And I am *starving*." A look over at Liam revealed that he was clearly amused with my enthusiasm.

"The sky's the limit. If you want, I'll ask them to bring the extra fryer oil right to the table in a bucket for you."

"I know you're joking, but the quality of the oil is a serious factor in a place like this. If you have Fish and Chips, say, from a restaurant where they haven't changed the oil, you can really taste the difference. Clean oil is important." I was completely serious and therefore deadpan, and Liam laughed.

"Emily, I've misjudged you. You're a food critic as well as a donut connoisseur." He pulled into the parking lot of a neon-lit restaurant surrounded by mostly industrial buildings. "I hope you'll be pleased with our first stop of the evening." He got out, walked around the back of the car and opened my door for me.

We walked into a space that felt surprisingly cozy and inviting. The hostess showed us to a table and gave us large laminated menus. The waiter looked a little rough around the edges, but was very efficient. He took our drink orders without writing them down and returned quickly with a soda water for Liam and a glass of pinot for me. Liam insisted I order wine, even though he was not drinking because he was driving. I hoped the glass would take the edge off my nerves.

We ordered deep-fried oysters and a basket of deep-fried chicken livers.

"And also deep-fried pickles," I added quickly as the waiter was taking our menus. He nodded and disappeared.

"Did you want me also to ask for a sample of that oil after all? You're clearly serious about the deep-fried portion of the evening." Liam raised his glass of soda water and touched it to my wine glass. "To deep-fried foods and the women who love them."

"I'll drink to that," My glass of wine was already half empty, and my stomach was still completely empty. I put the wine down and picked up my water, sipping it through the straw and giggling a little.

"What's funny?" Liam asked.

"Nothing. Um, I don't, um, I don't drink wine that often. It makes me giddy."

"A cheap drunk! Why didn't you tell me? I could have been plying you with alcohol all this time."

"Yup," I said. I misjudged how much water was left in my glass, and the straw made a slurping noise. "Here's your chance." My tone was turning flirty, and it was only partly because of the pinot.

"Another glass of white for the lady please," Liam said as the waiter passed by.

Being in Liam's presence was increasingly easy, and the alcohol was helping things along.

"How is the sale of your mom's house going?" I asked, dipping one of the clams in aioli sauce. I felt less and less self-conscious about my thorough enjoyment of the food, and the evening itself.

"It sold already. For over the asking price. My agent says the market is red hot right now and I'm lucky my mom didn't die two years ago when the market was slower." A burst of laughter escaped my mouth and Liam raised his eyebrows. "The guy's not much of a people person but he gets the job done."

"I'm sure it will be good to have it put behind you. The house, I mean, not your mother. When does it close?" Were my plumped-up lashes fluttering at him as I spoke? Maybe a little.

"End of June. Just after the school year. I had to negotiate a longer closing date because I need to get all of the auction stuff sorted out, but also I need more time with it, to get closure. I grew up in that house," he was suddenly less lighthearted, "I need to make peace with some stuff in there."

There was a moment of silence, which was broken by my phone vibrating on the table. A text from Sophia -

Dante says can you call him to say goodnight?

"Liam, I'm just going to step out and call Dante to say goodnight. I'll be right back." I was careful again not to apologize for talking to Dante.

Dante was perfectly capable of going to bed for Sophia – he did it all the time. Sophia just wanted to know how everything was going and she was very happy with my report. I walked back to the table smiling, aware that at that moment, Sophia would be texting Michelle, who would then text Clara.

chapter 44

Liam and I worked our way through all the deep-fried food on the table. My giggling and flirting increased slightly. My judgment might have been off because of the wine, but it sure seemed like Liam was flirting with me too. Empirically, it was going well. In fact, it was going very well. I began to wonder how the evening might end and set off a happy flurry of butterflies flapping their wings in my chest.

It was becoming increasingly obvious to me as we ate that there was no way I could stomach an additional main course at a subsequent restaurant. The plates of clams, livers, and pickles were enormous and my stomach wouldn't take much more. The conversation ventured through other restaurants we both liked, the weather, and our predictions about when it would finally warm up for good.

We settled into a game of 'what is your favorite?' Curious how much his artistic preferences would affect my opinion of him, I took a lead in the conversation and peppered him with good-natured questions. The waiter offered a third glass of wine but I waved him off. Two was more than enough to eliminate my conversational inhibitions.

"Favorite board game?"

"Chess. I was in the chess club at school." Liam seemed pleased with himself.

"Chess is boring. Next question. Your turn."

"Ouch! Favorite novel?" He paused almost imperceptibly. "And I swear, if you say *Fifty Shades of Grey*, I'm leaving and you can walk home."

"Oh, thanks a *lot*. That's not quite my style. I would have to say, *Confessions of a Shopaholic*...And *Trainspotting*."

He made a face. "The first one is only marginally better than *Grey*. I thought *Trainspotting* was a movie."

"It was a book first. I didn't like the movie, actually. Your turn. Favorite book?"

He thought for a moment.

"I'm going to have to have to go with *The Very Hungry Caterpillar*. With a close second being *Love You Forever*."

"I'll let you get away with that answer because your affinity for children worked out well for my son today." The waiter put the bill on the table and my hand darted out to grab it, but Liam got to it first. "Favorite movie?" My eyes watched his as he thought.

"That is a tough one because I love movies." Liam tucked his credit card into the top of the folder and put it back on the table.

"Me too," I interrupted.

"I'm going to pick three." Liam held up three fingers.

"No, you have to pick *one*!" The bill was whisked away amid my protests.

"You picked two books, and that set a precedent. Now I'm going to pick three movies."

"Are you a first-grade teacher or a personal injury lawyer?" I poked his arm playfully, aware that the poke broke the touch barrier.

"I'm full of surprises. But that is not the question at hand. So..." he paused and made an exaggerated concentrating face, "my top three movies, in no particular order, are," My index fingers beat a drumroll on the table for effect, "*Rosemary's Baby*, *Psycho*, and *The Dark Knight*."

I stared at him.

"You can't be serious. Those movies are the *worst!* I'm surprised you didn't add *The Exorcist*!" I was partly genuinely shocked, but also enjoying making a show of looking shocked.

"You're right. I forgot *The Exorcist*. I love dark movies. What can I say? It's a nice contrast to *The Very Hungry Caterpillar*. What about you? What are your favorite movies?" Liam folded his hands under his chin and waited for my response.

"They're pretty different from yours. As I am a *normal person*." The ice in the bottom of my water glass shook noisily as I stabbed at it with the straw.

"I've seen no evidence of that so far, but continue."

"Okay then. My three favorite movies are *Forrest Gump*, *Gattaca*, and *Good Will Hunting*." He smirked. "And you know what? Those are *great* movies. *Forrest Gump* won five academy awards including Best Picture. And *Good Will Hunting* won two. And *Gattaca* was nominated for one." I stuck out my chin for emphasis. "So you can see that my movies are actual films. Not like that slasher crap you named."

"First of all," Liam pointed at me, "Those are not slasher films. Slasher is something else entirely. We can discuss film genres later if you like. And I will have you know…"

"Is this 'second of all,' then?"

"Yes. This is second of all. Second of all, *The Exorcist* won two academy awards, and *Rosemary's Baby* won one as well, I'm pretty sure. For Best Actress."

Liam helped me on with my coat, then put his arm through mine as we headed to the door.

"I'll look that up in the car. I doubt it." His arm felt good and I squeezed it slightly with my other hand. "I should tell you I don't really want to have a main course. And it is already nine-thirty. What would you say to going right to dessert and coffee?"

"I would say that's the only logical thing you've said since we sat down."

The brightly lit bakery Liam had chosen was a five-minute drive away, and a stark contrast to the Honky-Tonk. We ordered three cupcakes to share.

"I'm getting this. You paid for dinner." Liam started to protest but my hand pushed his wallet away. "I insist. What do you want to drink?"

Liam perused the overhead chalkboard menu.

"Cappuccino. Fat-free."

I sighed audibly. "I'm sorry, I can't let you do that."

"What do you mean?" His face showed genuine surprise.

"Cappuccino is a morning drink. And you shouldn't use skim milk in a cappuccino, or in a latte. You need the fat in the scalded milk for flavor. And sweetness." I addressed the teenager behind the counter. "Tell him I'm right."

She looked at me skeptically. "Honestly, I just work here part-time. I don't know that much about coffee. And people order fat-free cappuccinos all the time... did you want one of those, or...?" She glanced at the line forming behind me.

My hand rested on Liam's shoulder.

"Don't listen to her. I'm in charge of dessert." I addressed the girl whose name tag said 'Shirley.' "We'll have two twelve ounce full-fat lattes please, Shirley. In cups for here please. And please scald the cups if you don't mind." Shirley stared at me and I gave her my sweetest smile. "I'd really appreciate it."

"Can I have cinnamon on mine please?" Liam ventured, partly to Shirley but mostly to me.

"No. Forget that Shirley." To Liam, "That ruins it. You can't appreciate the cupcakes if you put cinnamon in your latte. You have a lot to learn about dessert."

"Clearly," he muttered, taking the tray with the cupcakes to a corner booth. I slid into the booth while Liam lined up at the counter to wait for the lattes.

I grabbed my phone out of my purse and frantically sent a group text to the three women who were waiting for an update -

Going well. Eating cupcakes and drinking coffee.

I tucked my phone away before any replies bounced back.

When Liam came back to the booth, he slid in next to me instead of sitting across. Our knees were touching. We spent the next half hour fighting over the cupcakes with our forks and sipping our lattes. Once the plates and cups were empty it felt silly to stay in the booth. The effects of the wine had worn off, but the sugar and caffeine gave me a warm, cozy glow. When we stepped out into the parking lot, Liam grabbed my hand. It was snowing. There was no way the snow would stick when it hit the wet ground and any other time it would have annoyed me beyond belief, but tonight was different. I let go of Liam's hand and called out, "Look! I'm a sugar plum fairy!" twirling around the parking lot, catching snowflakes on my tongue.

By the time we were both in the car, my hair was wet and a quick look into the passenger side mirror revealed that Sophia's perfect make-up job was just a memory. It amazed me how little I cared.

On the drive back to my house, the nervous energy in my gut started spinning again. The flirting was going very well. I very much wanted to have some kind of physical interaction with Liam but I had no idea how that might happen.

"Uh, Liam, don't drive right home. I mean, don't drive to my house straight away."

"You can't possibly still be hungry. Although I guess I could get you a package of Twinkies from the convenience store, and maybe a Big Gulp." The oncoming headlights illuminated his smiling face, and we rode for a moment in silence as I tried in vain to think of a witty comeback.

"Or were you thinking," he ventured, smiling, "of something more like make-out point?" A laugh burst out of me.

"Make-out point? Are you kidding me? How old are you, sixteen?" My case of the giggles was starting up again.

"I'm twenty-eight, actually. But I'm not above a little making out."

The next hour was full of the kind of excitement I hadn't felt in forever. A lot longer than since Tyler left. Liam drove to the outer reaches of the Walmart parking lot, where we spent about forty-five minutes talking and also making out. How long had it been since I had done that?

The sound of an incoming email illuminated my phone, and I realized it was quarter after twelve.

"Liam, uh, we have to go. I mean, I have to go. I told Sophia I wouldn't be late." The familiar mom guilt was creeping back in. It had been a blessing to have escaped from it almost completely for the evening.

We drove back to my house in amicable silence, Liam's hand over mine on my thigh. I was tired and happy. He walked me to my door and kissed me one more time.

"I'd like to see you again."

I looked up at him and squeezed his hand.

"Me too."

"I'll call you."

And then he was gone.

chapter 45

I paused on the step with my hand on the door handle. I had just gone on a real, actual date with a man who seemed to actually like me. And I definitely liked him. This could be it -this could be the beginning of the rest of my life. My mind's eye conjured up what our children would look like, until Sophia carefully edged open the door.

"Emily? Are you coming in? You're going to get soaked... Oh. You're already soaked. Come in for goodness' sake!"

I towelled off my hair and put on my comfiest pyjamas. Sophia and I hashed over the events of the evening, before she hugged me furiously, put on her coat and left.

My mood was so good that the next day I ran the vacuum for my parents when I visited my father. Their TV had moved to the main living room and my mother had given up denying that she watched *Young and the Restless.*

"Your father likes my program, Emily," she said as she colored with Dante at the kitchen table. "It distracts him from his situation." She still wasn't good at talking about Dad's surgery or the amputation, or any of the upcoming implications. We made careful, non-Dad conversation and Mom let me know stiffly that she appreciated seeing Dante. The previous confrontation in the kitchen was not brought up. She didn't know about, or at least didn't ask about my date with Liam, and I didn't offer any information. This was how my family was. We just didn't talk about things we didn't want to acknowledge, and they either faded away or blew up and turned into different problems.

Dante was my sidekick, running errands for the rest of Sunday. I said 'yes' to pretty much everything he asked for in every store and didn't care that every parent book would say that was a bad idea. Michelle and Clara both called, to receive their happy report on the events of the previous evening. Dante and I ate grilled cheese and carrot sticks in front of the TV for dinner, and I let him spend as long as he wanted in the tub, reheating the water twice while I sat with my back to the bathroom door, scrolling through Facebook on my phone.

With minimal sleuthing, Liam's profile popped up, but sending him a friend request was definitely a bad idea. It was one thing making out with him, another linking myself to him on the internet for all time, and unfriending him would be awkward if things didn't go well. I limited myself to scrolling through his limited public profile and checking to see if we had any mutual friends.

Dante went to bed with minimal fuss after his long play in the bath, and I was folding the second load of laundry of the evening when a text from Liam popped up on my phone. I had been trying not to wait for it all day and my heart did a little flip when I read it -

Can you meet me tomorrow?

Wow. That seemed quick, even given the amazing time we had my fingers flew over the keyboard -

Sure.

Right away Liam came back -

Just need to chat.

Maybe he wanted to plan the next date? Maybe he wanted to ask me to go away for a weekend! Almost giddy, I texted him again -

I work 12 – 8. How about 8:15?

There was a pause of several minutes, during which I didn't dare put my phone down and back to the folding. Finally, all of three minutes later, Liam's name flashed up on the home screen of my phone. I pressed my thumb to the button to unlock the screen and read the text.

Tim Horton's? Can you come without Dante?

Hmmm. That had potential. I texted back -

Sure but I'm not making out with you in Tim Horton's

There was a long pause. Five minutes inched by.

Lol. See you then.

Why exactly had he used Lol? Nothing about this seemed funny to me...

My mood had changed to doubtful based on a few dozen characters of text. The happiness of the day lingered in my memory but try as I might, I couldn't get back to the contentment of the memory of our near-perfect date last night. What could have gone wrong between then and now? Probably nothing. Likely I was overreacting, I thought, as I folded towels and tiny Spiderman underwear.

I was being ridiculous, and focused on being happy that Liam wanted to see me so soon.

Michelle phoned a few minutes later, and we talked it through every way possible. In the end, we agreed that the only thing to do was focus on how well the date had gone, and how 'into me' Liam must be. But even though Michelle did her best to convince me, I couldn't shake off my fear that something not-very-good was up.

I dropped Dante off at Tyler's house just before noon the next day. At work, I was jumpy and possibly short, mostly with the other waitresses but clearly also with customers, because my tips were light throughout my shift even though I won the coin toss for the best section. My thoughts vacillated between unbridled optimism and abject dread. Sometimes I was convinced that Liam was going to tell me he had fallen completely in love with me, and my biggest problem would be holding him at bay. Other times I was sure he had re-evaluated our evening and decided I was too eager, or too needy, or too food-obsessed, and he was going to cut me loose.

Questions plagued me from all sides. Why did he want to meet specifically at Tim Horton's again? Why text when he said he was going to call? Why did he want me to come without Dante? All of these might have happy answers. Or not. The hours dragged by all day. At seven o'clock I started counting the minutes.

I arrived at the coffee shop at five after eight and waited in my car so I wouldn't be early. At eight-sixteen, I headed in. One shaky hand clutched my purse, while the other beeped my car to lock it. I took deep breaths and forced my feet towards the coffee shop. Pushing through the heavy door, I wasn't even comforted by the smell of coffee and pastry. My stomach had been in knots all day.

Liam sat at a table for two. There was a coffee in a dark brown paper cup sitting at my place, as well as an apple fritter peeking out from inside a paper bag. He looked up and saw me come in. I flashed him the best smile I could muster. He stood up and hugged me stiffly at the table. It wasn't the hug of someone who had initiated a make-out session with me in the Walmart parking lot less than forty-eight hours before. I hugged him back, hesitantly, and sat down.

Liam sat down too and stared at me earnestly.

I waited for him to say something, anything, that would give me a clue about what was happening. After an eternity, but actually only seconds after we sat down, I blurted out – "What's going on? Why did you need to meet me? And why here? And why without Dante?" My voice was considerably less casual than I was aiming for. People sitting nearby tried not to notice.

"Emily," he started. He folded his hands. "I really like you. And I enjoyed our date on Saturday." I looked at him incredulously. "Honestly, I did. It was fun. And you're great."

"But?" My disappointment, even though I didn't know yet what was going on, threatened to break out in full force.

"There's no but. At least not how you mean... I like you a lot. I really did have fun."

"I had fun too. And that was just the day before yesterday. What's changed? Obviously, something is wrong, or you've changed your mind about me." There was a ripple of anger now in my disappointment.

"I got a job."

"I thought you already had a job, teaching first grade."

"I do. But when my mother died, I applied to a bunch of International Schools. There's nothing to hold me back in the States with her gone and I felt like it would be an adventure. I don't know if you remember when you called me a while back and I was in a meeting. It was an interview at a job fair." I could not believe this was happening. "The job fair didn't go that well. I had a couple of interviews but I didn't hear back from any of them, and I didn't think anything would come of it."

"But something did," I said softly.

"Yeah. I got a call yesterday, offering me a job in Lima. In Peru." He paused. "I took the job. It's something I've wanted to do for a long time. I'm truly sorry about the timing. If I wasn't going away, I would definitely want to see you again. We could still see each other again if you're up for it. I don't leave until August."

"No." I was thankful for the resolve not to say yes. The anger helped. "I don't blame you for going. Really. I had a great time too, but there's no point seeing each other again. Honestly, I don't think there's much point to us even talking again. I'm hugely disappointed and I'm going to leave before I start crying." I put the apple fritter back into its little paper bag. "I'll take this for later if you don't mind." I stood and Liam did as well. He stuck out his hand awkwardly and we shook for a beat longer than a necessary.

"Emily. I am sorry."

"You said that already. I'm sorry too. But it was only one date. You don't owe me an explanation or an apology." I smiled, a little. "Have fun in Lima. I'm sure it will be a blast." He let go of my hand and I turned around and walked away. As I walked through the door I realized my donut was still on the table.

chapter 46

I managed to get to the car before the real crying started. Blinking back tears, I texted Michelle before pulling out of the parking lot -

Liam is moving to Peru. All bets are off. All dates are off. WTF?

Immediately she texted her response -

I'm coming over. Do you have Dr Pepper? Want me to bring?

Michelle was the best. And her offer of Dr. Pepper was the perfect thing to say.

Bring diet. Maybe he's leaving because I'm too fat.

The familiar self-pity began to settle in. She texted back -

Don't be an idiot. I'll be there in 20.

As soon as I got home, I slumped down on the couch in the dark. The sadness took me right back to Tyler leaving. I told myself this was ridiculous, that I had known Liam for about five minutes. Still, the sting of rejection cut deep.

Liam had jabbed a sharp stick into an almost-healed wound. I cried and cried until Michelle let herself in and sat beside me in the living room. She handed me a box of tissues, and sat quietly, listening as my sniffles slowed to a stop.

Michelle and I had gone through good times and bad together since we were little kids. Now, she listened to me and didn't interrupt, careful not to put her arm around me until she was sure it wouldn't start me crying again. About ten minutes after she sat down, Michelle retrieved the two Diet Dr. Pepper cans with wet paper towels wrapped around them that she put into the freezer on her way in. Another ten minutes after that, I finished telling her my story and asked for her opinion.

"Do you really want to know what I think? Because maybe it's too soon to be direct with you about it."

"I know what it means to ask for your opinion. Let me have it." I crossed my legs under me on the couch.

"Liam sounds like he's a nice guy and you had a good time. However," she continued, "This grief and sadness you're going through is more about Tyler than it is about Liam. You hardly knew the guy." I had asked for her opinion, now I had to listen to it. "You had a great time the other night and I'm super happy for you. Because it means you can have a good time again. This isn't as much about Liam as it is just about you finally being able to have some fun."

"But he was so great..." my bottom lip quivered again.

"I know. He was also the first guy you've gone out with in what, seven years? It's great that you had a good time. I'm very glad you didn't go out with an asshole on your first date because that would have been catastrophic. I fear you would have run away and joined a convent if you had gone out with an asshole."

"What about Dante? I don't think he could join a convent with me." A half-smile played on my lips.

"He could clean their chimneys. Nuns love little kids. But that's not the point. The point is," she plumped up the couch cushions as she talked, "that you went out with a nice guy, and you had fun. And that means you could do it again. You *should* do it again."

Before I could voice my protest, Michelle continued. "Here's what I think, in three parts. Number one, you're upset about Liam because you're still upset about Tyler. Number two, you've proven that you're capable of going out on a date and having fun. You might not like number three, but here it is. You need to go out on another date. Right away. Seriously. Like, this week or next week. Otherwise, you're going to make Liam into way more of a big deal than he was and he'll start to have legend status in your rejection-addled brain. Get back on the horse. That's it. That's my opinion." She raised her eyebrows and pointed at me. "And I'm right."

Not long after that, Michelle went home and I headed to bed, knowing she was probably right because she was almost *always* right. That didn't make it any easier, and it didn't stop me from crying myself to sleep for the first night in a long time.

chapter 47

The next morning, I was pissed off at Tyler for dumping me for Amy Ballantyne. I was angry at Liam for taking off to South America, and extremely angry at myself for falling for him so hard. Michelle's advice played in my head, especially her third point. I needed to go on another date, and there was comfort in the fact that this was at least one thing I could control.

On my break at work, I took another look at the dating app that I'd almost deleted a dozen times. I updated my profile, added a bio that sounded a little flirty, and started swiping. I set a goal for myself to swipe right three times before the end of the day, and to set up one date for this weekend. I would be discerning but not picky. And more importantly, I was getting back on the horse. Proverbially. Although a guy who owned a horse had a certain appeal. Note to self – swipe right if he has a horse.

Alone at home after work, I shampooed the smell of grease out of my hair, sat on the couch in my pyjamas and opened a fresh bag of Cheetos. When I opened the freezer to get a carton of ice cream, I saw a third can of Dr. Pepper that Michelle had left inside that had since exploded. I closed the freezer door and left that problem for later. I was on a mission.

My fingers touched the yellow app and started searching for someone swipe-worthy. I soon discovered that once I swiped left, there was no going back to that profile without a premium account. I'd swiped left on James a few weeks back. Was there a statute of limitations on deleting someone? Maybe his profile would pop back up. Would I swipe right if I found him again?

Within five minutes I paid for the upgrade that would let me un-swipe left, then realized it still only let me move back to the immediately preceding suitor. The system was clearly designed to make me bite the bullet, not take a look at everyone available and decide between them. What if I swiped people away and then they were better than who was left? I told myself to lower my expectations. This was about getting a date, not getting married.

As if it had a mind of its own, my index finger started swiping right.

The first man I swiped was Greg, 26. Greg's first picture was of him holding a monkey on a beach, looking quite muscly. In another one, he was dressed in full hockey goalie attire at an ice rink. The third picture was the obligatory 'suit and tie at my best friend's wedding' shot. Greg's profile read:

Fun Facts about me:

Adventurous in the outdoors and in the kitchen.

A part-time resident of San Diego.

One time I almost bought six school buses.

Accepting applications for a plus one at a wedding in Bolivia.

Greg seemed pretty good-looking. I liked the part about the kitchen, and his bio seemed like he put some effort into it. My own bio had turned out nowhere decidedly unexciting. I had no real desire to go to Bolivia but decided that would be a problem for future Emily.

The second swipe right was Warren, 27, who was a nurse. His profile pictures were clean-cut and not too athletic. In one picture he was walking a Golden Retriever. It was a popular choice of breed the among the many dog-holding men. I had no idea where these guys were getting these dogs. There was no way men were as collectively into dogs as these pictures made them out to be. Warren's other pictures included one of him scuba diving. His profile had borderline too many emojis, but the text was okay and funny:

Would prefer face-to-face conversation, to help me help you realize I'm not a murder-death-killer.

I'm a nerd, recently accepted it.

I value altruistic behavior and informed decision making.

Dog dad.

Bonus points if you can set up a date over message.

Then there were emojis of a dog, a cooked shrimp, a cup of coffee, the world, and a thunderstorm. Setting up a date over message suited me fine because I was in a hurry, although his offer to award me 'bonus points' was a little on the condescending side.

It became clear to me that I had a type. I definitely was not into facial hair, or men under six feet, or men who were scrawny... This eliminated a lot of men between twenty-five and thirty in my geographical area, which I had limited to within fifteen miles.

Just as exhaustion was setting in and I was ready to settle for two right swipes instead of three, I saw Johnson, 24, a preppy-looking fellow who was over six feet tall and worked in Real Estate. There was a picture of him standing with a flag on the top of a mountain, maybe Everest, which got my attention. There was also a shot of him in what appeared to be an industrial kitchen, with a white apron and a chef's hat. This had potential, and there were no dogs. It was enough to think about taking on a man. It probably wasn't necessary to add a dog as well. Johnson's bio read:

Not too sure what I'm doing.

I'm someone who likes to cook and eat but not necessarily in that order.

I like to try new things but nothing too dangerous.

In my spare time I stage houses.

What the hell, I thought, and swiped right. Johnson was into food, and that couldn't be bad. He also seemed to be into mountain climbing, which I could do without. I reminded myself that the goal was to get a date, not mate for life.

It was eleven o'clock and I had the breakfast shift the next day. When I stood up, an avalanche of Cheetos crumbs tumbled off my lap, and when I wiped my hands on my pyjamas the orange mess spread there too. Ever so fleetingly I considered cleaning it all up but thought better of it, carefully peeled my pyjama bottoms off inside-out and threw them in the washing machine.

Focussing so ardently on finding a new date had distracted me for the evening, but when I got into bed and shut my eyes the sadness crept back in. I fell asleep wondering how many more failed attempts I would have to endure before finding someone to be with, or giving up completely.

Two of the three swipes messaged me the next morning. I put my phone securely away during my shift to avoid the temptation to look at it every five seconds. The excitement I felt about the prospect of a man actually liking my profile enough to get in touch was a boost, and Liam seemed all but forgotten. This lent credence to Michelle's point that it wasn't really about Liam. I would have to see if I could avoid admitting she was right.

When I sat down with a toasted BLT at the staff table after my shift, I glanced at the restaurant's schedule quickly to make sure all the shifts were covered, and directed my attention to my phone. Unfortunately, Dean joined me for lunch and I was forced to make polite conversation with him while he ate his toasted clubhouse sandwich. Going out with Dean made possible my foray back into the dating world. Besides being thankful to him for taking me out for a fun evening, I was glad for his friendship at work.

Finally, Dean finished eating and ambled back to his perch behind the cash register. He picked up my plate with his and deposited them into the tub for dirty dishes. I clearly wasn't going to get anywhere with my swiping until I left the restaurant, so I grabbed my bag, shoved my phone into my coat pocket, and waved to Dean on my way out.

chapter 48

On the way to the car, I called Clara. No answer. Then I tried Michelle, who answered, laughing, and obviously in the middle of another conversation.

"Hi Em. I'm just with James."

"James? I thought he was in Madison for six months." Had it been that long? I counted on my fingers.

"He didn't like the work, so he came back. We're just about to get lunch. You want to come with?" I wanted to say yes, even though I had just eaten three eggs over easy with sausage and home fries.

"Uh, where are you going? I ate already. Maybe I can join you for a coffee after?"

"Bob Evans." The sound of the blinker meant that they were already in the car.

"Okay. I'll meet you there in about thirty-five minutes. Don't have dessert without me." It would take me that long to get home, shower and get back out to Bob Evans.

"Emily, you do realize not everyone has dessert with every meal," Michelle said dryly.

"Then don't have coffee without me. I'll be there as soon as I can."

"Aren't you within five minutes of here? What's going to take you thirty-five minutes?" She sounded suspicious.

"I have to dash home first. I'll be there soon. I'm driving. Gotta go." I wasn't actually driving yet, but wanted to terminate the conversation before Michelle realized that I was going home to have a shower and change…just to look presentable after a shift. Nothing to do with seeing James.

In just under thirty minutes, I was changed not into my date clothes, but still into one of my less 'mom-like' ensembles. More makeup than normal, but not a Sophia amount.

Michelle's car was parked near the entrance of Bob Evans. A small part of me worried that they would leave before I got there, but it was a small, paranoia part. Michelle would never leave without texting me first.

My hands were ever so slightly shaky, and I was keenly aware of my carefully chosen outfit, and the fact that my makeup was more on-point than usual. I told myself to stop being ridiculous. Michelle was my oldest friend and James was her goofy older brother, nothing more. I chalked my churning insides up to all the adrenaline coursing through my veins in the last few days.

As soon as I sat down at the table, the waitress appeared.

"Do you want those coffees now, hun?" She addressed us with a smile. Her uniform was pristine and neatly starched, and I wanted to ask her how she managed to keep it like that. She disappeared and came back with four coffees and a small bowl of cream and sugar. I hoped the caffeine would calm me down.

Soon it felt like old times. We were laughing and lightheartedly teasing one another. Then Michelle touched on a subject I wished she had left unsaid.

"Emily went on a date last weekend." As soon as she said it she clearly wished she hadn't. "Oh sorry. I don't know why I said that." She looked at James and made a face. "It ended badly."

I decided that saying something would be less awkward than saying nothing.

"He's moving to Peru." I was surprised by how little it bothered me to talk about it. "I'm not that upset anymore. You were right, in the end." Michelle gave me two thumbs up, obviously very pleased with herself.

"I usually am." She sipped her coffee. "Are you going to take my advice about getting back into the dating scene right away?" I trained my eyes on the table, not wanting to meet James' gaze.

"I am actually. I decided to use the internet." I mentioned the name of the dating app and glanced furtively at James to see if he would give anything away. His face was unchanged as he stirred cream into his coffee and picked up the check. Maybe he had created that profile a long time ago and had forgotten about it, though that seemed unlikely.

"It's weird. There's a lot of swiping, but then there's no un-swiping." I was trying to decide how much of my plans to divulge with James present when Dante appeared out of the corner of my eye. I turned my head and saw him running into the restaurant with Tyler and Amy. Michelle saw them at the same time and glanced over at me nervously.

"It's okay," I reassured Michelle. "I'm not going to dump hot coffee on her." Just then Dante ran over to me.

"Hi, Mom!" His hug made seeing Tyler and Amy better. "You want to come and eat with Dad and Amy?" I squeezed him a little tighter.

"No thanks, Dante. I already ate with Michelle and James. Can you say hi to them?"

"Hi Michelle, Hi James." He high-fived them both.

Before I could say anything else, Amy was at the table, taking Dante's hand.

"Come on, Dante. Let's go get you some lunch."

I raised my head to fake-smile at Amy, but before I saw her face my eyes passed over her middle. Almost level with my face was her belly. She was clearly pregnant.

Michelle's hand was instantly over mine, holding it tight. My eyes pushed on upward until they met hers. Amy was smiling like a Cheshire Cat.

"Hi Emily...James, Michelle. Nice to see you all." She turned on her heel and walked over to their table.

"Emily..." Michelle's tone was concerned, and had a hint of warning in it.

I gritted my teeth and resolved not to make a scene, mostly so Dante wouldn't see me upset or have a memory of me losing it on his stepmother in public.

"Did you know?" I asked Michelle in a low, steely voice.

"Of course not!" She squeezed my hand again. I glanced over at James, who looked a little lost.

"I'm going to count to five and then walk out calmly." My head was spinning.

"I'll come with you in your car. James, you drive mine home." She pushed her keys across the table to her brother.

I stood up slowly, walked at what was hopefully a normal person's pace with a normal person's look on my face. I held that face until I was in the car with Michelle beside me in the passenger seat.

"Do you want me to drive?" She ventured quietly.

"Can you even drive a stick?"

"Actually, no. But I felt like I should ask. Do you want me to go back in and get James to drive us?"

"No, because I am going to hold it together until we get out of this parking lot. I don't want to see James because that will make things worse."

"Okay." Michelle was doing me the favor of looking straight ahead, avoiding eye contact. The car shifted into reverse and stalled. I closed my eyes and reassured myself that there was no way Tyler could have seen that from where he was sitting in Bob Evans, then steadied myself and tried again. Soon we were on the road. Red, hot angry tears sprang to my eyes and I knew there was a very real chance that soon I wouldn't be able to see well enough to drive. I signaled and pulled into the parking lot of Burger King.

"Are you hungry?" asked Michelle. I can go in and get you something to eat…"

"No, I just had to get off the road..." Then my face was in my hands. When they got wet and covered in makeup, I wiped them on my leggings. Michelle put her arm around me. She listened while I lamented and yelled and screamed and swore. She found a stack of old napkins from McDonald's in the glove compartment, and handed them to me to blow my nose. After about ten minutes, I started up the car again.

"I'm coming home with you." She stated. "Hold on." She picked up her phone, called work, and told them she had a family emergency. "You should do the same when you get home."

"I already worked today," I pointed out in a shaky voice.

"Then take tomorrow off. This is the real deal when it comes to kicks in the teeth. I can't believe she's pregnant. And that was a very crap way for you to find out. I'm really sorry that happened to you."

My hands gripped the steering wheel. "Don't. Not until we get home." I sniffed and wiped my nose on the cuff of my sweatshirt. "I can hardly see as it is."

"I wonder if that's a technical driving charge. What would they call it? Impaired driving? Driving under the influence of tear-impaired eyes? Driving under the influence of having just seen…"

"That *bitch* Amy Ballantyne." We said it together as I pulled into my driveway.

"My house is a mess," I said as the key turned in the lock.

"When has that ever mattered?" Michelle followed me in.

"I need to wash my face." The tears were over and it was time for damage control.

"Okay. I'll be out here when you're done. Take your time, Em." I nodded. "You know," she said, "It's going to be okay. Don't get me wrong. This massively sucks. I'm not going to try to tell you otherwise this time. But you'll get through it." I grunted something close to agreement. "Go wash your face. You'll feel better."

chapter 49

As I scrubbed my face too hard and got water all over the vanity, frustration and grief and anger screamed in my head – *I was the one who was supposed to get pregnant. I was the one who wanted to have a baby.* I wanted to be the one to give Dante siblings. And now Amy would be the one to hold his little sister or brother instead of me. I hated her. I hated Tyler. I hated them so much.

When I got back to the living room, stubbornly railing against tears, Michelle had tidied up and done the dishes. The washing machine was running. A marathon of *Dr. Pimple Popper* on TLC was in progress.

I plopped down on the couch and texted Dean that I was ill and wouldn't be at work tomorrow. Two more texts had the shift covered by another waitress. That bought me a full day before Dante came home and I had to face a world where Amy Ballantyne was pregnant and I was alone.

Michelle and I settled into an easy silence, sipping soda, and being intermittently disgusted by the procedures on the screen. There was nothing resembling a meal in my house that I actually wanted to eat, so we ate Lucky Charms on the couch. The conversation was mostly me saying in a flat voice, "I can't fucking believe she is pregnant."

Then Michelle would answer with, "I know. It sucks, big time."

Eventually, *Pimple Popper* turned into *Sister Wives*, and that set me off ranting.

"This weirdo can find four wives and I can't even find a date? What the hell kind of world are we living in?"

"I know. It sucks."

"Honestly, Michelle, I'm going to quit trying. It's all total bullshit."

"That is *exactly* the wrong attitude. You should try harder now. Let me see these guys you swiped on. When did they message you?"

"This morning I guess. I'm not a hundred per cent sure." I pulled up the profiles for Michelle. "Honestly I don't know if I can even be bothered to message them back."

"You only have twenty-four hours from when they message you, Em. Come on. Let's do it. I'll help you. The fact that Amy is pregnant is the worst, for sure, but it doesn't change anything for you, in the here and now. You still need to find a date. Maybe someone who will get *you* pregnant!"

I made a gagging noise. "Give me a break."

We had a look at the guys who had messaged me. Warren the dog dad on Mount Everest, and Greg, who was 'adventurous in the kitchen.'

After much deliberation, we decided on Greg. Mostly Michelle decided on Greg and I just went along with it to shut her up. There were about twelve hours left to reach out to Warren if Greg immediately fell through.

Completely unsure of how to proceed, I messaged Greg, trying to sound non-threatening and vaguely flirty.

He got back to me surprisingly quickly, and before Michelle left, Greg had asked me out to see a movie in the mall that coming Friday, preceded by dinner at the Mexican restaurant next door. The Chinese restaurant in the mall was my preference, but it was not the time to split hairs.

By the time all of this transpired, it was after ten.

"You should go," I nudged Michelle with my toe on the couch. "You've been here forever. I feel like all you do is help me get through bad stuff lately."

"Don't be stupid. You've done the same for me...but I will go, I think." She hesitated and looked at me intently. "If you're sure you're all right."

"I'm sure." I followed her to the door and we hugged. "Thanks again. For everything. Not just tonight. You've been so great lately. And please apologize to James. I totally ruined your lunch date."

"No, you didn't. Amy did. In fact, Tyler ruined it when he knocked her up. Blame Tyler wherever possible." She hugged me one last time and then she was gone. I locked the door, resumed my position on the couch, and passively watched TLC while searching for books on Amazon about dealing with your ex-husband's fiancée's pregnancy. At midnight the marathon changed to *Say Yes to the Dress* and my stomach lurched at the very sight of the lovely Randy, so I turned the TV off and went to bed.

I told myself sternly that the only way to outwardly deal with this new surreal and horrific reality was to at all times appear happy and well-adjusted, even though I had already begun to obsess about sticking it to both Tyler and Amy. I googled 'ex-husband revenge,' and found a candle that started out smelling like apple pie and changed to 'a dirty fart' halfway through the burning time. I bookmarked the page.

Thankfully, dear Dante was too young to watch me behave like such a bitch, and it was only for him that I didn't enact any of the revenge porn in my head. Fleetingly, I imagined a world in which Tyler left Amy for someone else...but that wouldn't be good for Dante either. I hoped for Amy's sake she didn't send Dante back to me in a t-shirt that said, "I'm the Big Brother," or something equally nauseating because I would have no choice but to send it back, cut into tiny pieces and shoved in an envelope stuffed with glitter.

Instead, I would be a grown-up. When Dante started talking about the baby, I would be happy for him, and help him choose a present for his new sister or brother. But I wasn't giving up the googling or the fantasizing. This seemed to me to be a reasonable balance between the angel on my right shoulder and the devil on my left.

chapter 50

I spent the all of next day 'keeping busy.' I read, watched *The Office*, ate a lot of potato chips, and decided to focus on getting ready for my upcoming date with Greg. We texted back and forth sporadically. I was careful to wait a decent amount of time between messages. Greg worked in hospitality, which was a plus, although he was light on details. I straight-up asked him about the school buses in his profile, figuring that the point of flaunting such a bizarre fact was so that everyone would ask about it. He told me that the school buses were to have been converted to food trucks for a business venture he and a friend was putting together. At the last minute, Greg got cold feet and thought better of buying, because he stood to lose a hundred and fifty thousand dollars if the business failed. The point of that exchange was obviously to let me know that he could have dropped six figures on school buses if he'd wanted to.

"Well, whoop-de-do for you," I said out loud as I sniffed the clothes that had been in the washer all night and decided they were still fine to go into the dryer.

By noon, all the laundry was done and I had made a batch of Dante's favorite brownies to welcome him home. I thought about making chocolate chip cookies but they were far more labor intensive. Brownies took ten minutes to put together and then just had to be thrown in the oven. As long as I set the timer and took them out in time, I would be Dante's hero, at least in the short term. I decided to drop half the batch off to Michelle.

Soon, the brownies were on the top of the stove and the mixing bowls were clean and put away neatly in the cupboard. Tragedy made me very efficient. I knew that Amy being pregnant wasn't strictly a tragedy, but it felt like one. I called Clara and asked her to go shopping with me for something new to wear on my date.

"Wear to what? Didn't we just do that? Are you going out with Liam again?" It had been only a couple of days since I talked to her but she was several major life events behind.

"I guess I haven't talked to you in a couple of days. It's gone so fast. Liam took a job in Peru

"What? When did you find that out?" Clara was semi-whispering into the phone so I knew my mother was within earshot.

"On Monday. Apparently, he got the job on Sunday. But I'm pretty much over that, actually. Michelle had some good advice on that one." I put the phone on speaker, double-checked that the oven was off and put on my coat.

"Something else happened. I found out that Amy is pregnant."

"WHAT?" All attempts at being quiet had been abandoned by Clara. "What you do mean, pregnant?"

"There's only one meaning that I know of," I replied, outside now and turning the key to lock the door. "I'm coming over now. There's more news but I'll tell you in person. Also, I do want you to come shopping with me, please."

"Sure. Whatever. How are you not freaking out?"

"I did freak out for about a day. Wait, do you mean freaking out about Liam or about Amy?"

"Either. Both."

"I'll be right over. Don't tell Mom I'm coming."

I pulled into my parents' house less concerned about their opinion than any other time I could remember.

Inside, I took off my shoes and sat down on a kitchen chair. Immediately my mother asked, "Where's Dante?"

"He's with his father. Who has, incidentally, knocked up Amy Ballantyne." My father lowered the newspaper.

"That's such crude language, Emily," my mother tutted.

"That's your response, Mom? Seriously? I give you what is probably the worst news of my recent life and rather than be supportive…"

"Emily…" Clara said in a low voice.

"No, I'm sorry, Clara. I don't care." I turned back to my mother. "Rather than be supportive, you decided to criticize my choice of words. Do you have any idea how difficult this is for me? Do you even care?"

My mother looked at me with pursed lips.

"Emily, of course, we care. You mother is shocked. That's all." My father tried to assume his role as peace-keeper but I wasn't having it.

"You know what, Mom, I came over here to try to figure out a way you could see Dante more often because Dad is doing better and I'm sure you've missed him."

My mother still said nothing.

"But instead, you know what I'm going to do? I'm going to give you several hard truths, *mother*."

"Be careful, Emily," Clara warned again, but I was in full swing.

"Here are a few things I want you to know. First, your house is dirty. You need to get a cleaning lady." Clara was staring at me with eyes as big as donuts. "In fact, this house is probably too much for you to take care of, in general. Who's going to do the gardens this summer? Not Dad and certainly not you. You'll have to pay someone to keep them up for you."

My mother's lips had all but disappeared into her face.

"Here's a news flash, Mom. Tyler left. He left me for Amy Ballantyne. Like it or not, that woman, who believe me, I hate more than you can fathom, is part of our lives now. Because she is Dante's stepmother. And also, just for good measure, she is pregnant."

"When did this all happen?!" My mother finally interjected.

I continued, ignoring her. "And as much as you would like to believe otherwise, *none of that is my fault.* I did my best. He left. That's the end of it."

"We never thought it was your fault, Emily." From my father, who sounded defeated. I almost stopped my tirade for his sake.

"What you also might not like, is I'm dating again. And I really don't care what you think. You can like it or not like it. If you don't want to see me, then you won't be seeing Dante. And here's another little nugget of information for you," something new occurred to me as I was speaking. "Dante has a new set of grandparents now. So if I were you, I'd try to make sure he knows who you are and doesn't get to like them better." The last part was off-side and I knew it.

"Are you finished?" my mother sounded genuinely hurt and looked teary.

"Sure. Now you can go ahead and play the victim, Mom. It's what you do best. While you're doing that, I'll be shopping with Clara. And then picking up Dante. On Friday I'll be out on a date. So you let me know when you're ready to drop all this crap and I'll see you then. Bye, Dad."

I grabbed my purse and put my shoes back on, while Clara bent down and hugged Dad and Mom respectively before following me out.

In the car, Clara and I were silent for several minutes.

"Was I a bitch just then?"

"Uh, yeah. You were most definitely a bitch."

"Damn."

A few more minutes of silence.

"But she has been extremely awful to you. You should hear what she says when you're not around." Clara clearly regretted saying this right away.

"What? What has she said?" New bile rose in my throat.

"Mostly the same stuff she's said to you. Honestly, it's not worth going over. I'd say you're definitely even now. In fact," Clara popped a piece of gum out of its foil wrapper and into her mouth. Then she offered me a piece, "You probably did us a favor. They do have to move out of that house and at least now you've brought it up."

I accepted the piece of gum from her and then accidentally dropped it in between the console and the driver's seat. I held out my hand to Clara, "Can I have another piece please?"

"Sorry. Last one." She took the partly chewed piece out of her own mouth. "Want mine?"

"No thanks." It was silly enough to lighten the mood.

"So what the heck happened with Liam?"

I brought Clara up to speed on what happened with Liam, how I found out Amy was pregnant, and my plans to set up a date for the weekend. Once we were at Kohls, I showed her the screenshotted profiles with the pictures of each, and the chat with Greg.

"Hmmm. You've been busy. Your life is a lot more interesting than mine all of the sudden, that's for sure."

"I've got some catching up to do. The date with Liam was so amazing, and then I was gutted when it all turned to shit. But Michelle was right – most of that sadness was still about Tyler. I'm sick of being sad about Tyler. So even if this dating thing doesn't work out right away, I've got to try to move forward. I want another shot. Seeing Amy pregnant made me imagine the three of them are a family. And I want a family like that too – I don't want to be old and dependent on Dante."

"You're getting way ahead of yourself." Clara grabbed a top I had picked out for myself out of my hands and put it back on the rack.

"I know. But I just want to be back in the running. Does that make sense?"

"Sure. That's what we all want. At least it's what I want. I think it might be harder for you because you already thought you had all of it once." Clara continued to sort her way through the racks of clothes.

"I thought I had it all figured out. And now everything's gone." We headed to the bank of change rooms. "But I'm getting better at this. Maybe Amy getting pregnant did me a favor."

"I wouldn't go that far. Take these in there. And not this one." She grabbed back a red number that I had thought looked very comfortable.

"Why am I surrounded by such bossy people?" I asked, walking into the dressing room.

"Because you need to be bossed!" Clara called behind me.

chapter 51

The rest of the week passed quickly. I spent as much time as possible with Dante, and then dropped him off at his father's on Friday morning before I drove to work. Dante didn't mention the baby, and I decided not to bring it up before he did. I was surprised he hadn't put it together, because from the look of Amy, it didn't seem like much of a secret. Maybe he knew but didn't think it was a big deal.

Sophia wasn't watching Dante on Friday night, but she insisted on coming over anyway to supervise the preparations. She admired the new top Clara had insisted I buy. We chatted as she did my makeup.

"You're getting better at sitting still for this."

"You might have set a dangerous precedent helping me before I go out. I could have dozens of first dates ahead of me before I find someone more permanent."

"I have a good feeling about tonight."

"Really? Based on what?" I tried to hold my eyes still as she blended shadow. Until a few weeks ago I hadn't even known what blending eyeshadow was.

"I don't know... I just think this guy might be the one."

"And I think you're just being overly optimistic." I opened my eyes and admired her work in my hand-held mirror.

"Would you rather I was all doom and gloom? If blowing smoke up your ass gets you in the right mood for success, that's what I'm going to do every time."

Sophia left early enough to be gone before Greg showed up. I thanked her profusely and wished there was a way to help her out the way she had helped me, both with Dante and with my hair and make-up, which had really never looked so good, if I did say so myself.

Greg pulled into the driveway. I watched out the window where he couldn't see me, wondering if he would come to the door. He didn't. Instead, he texted –

I am outside. ☺

Perhaps he thought the smile emoji would make it more polite not to come to the door. It was a small thing to nitpick, and I had resolved not to compare him to Liam, reminding myself that not many first dates went as well as that one. The goal tonight was to go on a date, not find a life partner.

I walked out to the car and Greg got out to shake my hand.

"Emily. Nice to meet you. This is a nice neighborhood."

I shook his hand back and thought that it was a strange comment. Maybe he was nervous too.

We got into the car and began talking, kind of awkwardly. "Have you been doing this long, the online dating?" Greg asked me.

I wasn't sure it was a good idea to tell him that he was my first meet-up. I decided not tell a lie, or the whole truth.

"Well I'm still kind of just dabbling in it. I've been single for a while now. I was married and I have a son." I had decided earlier that I was going to mention Dante as early as possible. If he wasn't cool with that, I didn't want to waste my time. Dante was mentioned in my profile but I wanted to make sure.

"You seem pretty young to have already been married." He knew my age from my profile, but his attempt to make complimentary conversation was noted.

"Yup. I was young when we got married." I left it at that.

"What do you do for work, when you're not buying school buses?" Information from his profile seemed like a good starting point for conversation.

"I'm in hospitality. Right now, I'm the head chef at a Casino."

"Wow. How did you get a Friday night off?" He smiled, "I work in a restaurant. I'm a waitress. I'm the head waitress actually." As soon as the words were out of my mouth, I knew how lame it sounded. "Anyway, it's hard to get a weekend evening off there so I can't imagine what it's like at a Casino. Do you like the work?" The words were coming out too fast.

"Getting a Friday night off can be tricky, but there are also perks to being the head chef. And yes, I like the work. I like the busyness of it. It's never boring."

"Me too. That's what I like about waitressing I mean. It's always something different." I paused and when he didn't fill the silence added, "And the food. I love food. I'm pretty sure that's the real reason I'm a waitress."

"I love food too but when I'm cooking I don't eat too much. I never sit down and by the end of service, I'm sick of the sight of my own cooking."

"That sounds like a good problem to have," I replied. "I'll pretty much eat anything that can't move away fast enough. If you deep-fried it, I'd probably eat an old cowboy boot."

He laughed. "You don't look like you have a problem with overeating." It was the first flirty thing he had said and I felt myself blush under my carefully applied foundation.

"I guess I walk around a lot when I'm waitressing." His compliment, while ham-handed, felt good.

The conversation continued to go reasonably well. The uncomfortableness was disappearing a little. I didn't sense any real 'spark,' but it wasn't a disaster. We had to wait for a table at Hermanos Caliente. I was watching the time because I didn't want to miss the movie.

"Have you eaten here before?" It was difficult to make conversation in the loud vestibule of the restaurant.

"No. I've been to the Chinese place around the corner, but not here." I motioned to Greg that we should take our buzzer out into the mall.

We moved beyond the door just as the alien-looking device started vibrating and flashing. I held my breath, hoping Greg wouldn't make an obvious joke about the vibrating. Thankfully he did not.

We were ushered to a table in a space that was almost as loud as the waiting area. There were a lot of dishes I had never heard of on the menu. The waitress took our drink orders. I decided to play it safe with soda water. Greg ordered an exotic looking Mexican beer.

"You want to split nachos? They're amazing here." I was thankful for his suggestion because the menu was freaking me out a little. I didn't realize how little I knew about Mexican food.

"That sounds good. Which ones do you usually get?"

"I like the 'King's Crown.'"

I read over the description – 'Crisp corn tortilla chips covered with salsa roja, piled high with frijoles, ground beef, tomatoes, onions, mixed peppers, jalapenos, melted cheese, topped with guacamole and sour cream.' I didn't know what half of those things even were.

"Sure. Sounds great. Thanks." The menu was pricier than I anticipated but there was time to figure that out later. With any luck, he would pay and I could insist on paying for the movie tickets and the popcorn.

Dinner was nothing special. We didn't seem to have a love connection but it was pleasant enough. The nachos were *very* spicy. I felt the heat rise up the back of my neck. Greg didn't seem fazed at all.

"Are they too hot for you?" he asked. I was drinking my soda water as quickly as my throat would swallow. Thankfully the glass was replaced before it was empty. "More sour cream, please," Greg smiled at the waitress and she was soon back with two more way-too-small containers of sour cream. I started dipping my chips into it more liberally, realizing that I had for sure overdone it in the first few minutes with the hot peppers.

"No, no. It's fine," I all but inhaled more soda water. "It's a nice change. I don't eat Mexican too often."

"Obviously." Greg laughed and I felt myself joining in, despite my burning mouth. He was funny.

I paused to drink again. "I like trying new food. What was it your profile said? 'Brave in the kitchen?' "

"Something like that. But you should be careful if you're not used to that much heat. They're actually hotter than usual tonight."

"I'll be fine. I'm a seasoned eater. I might cut back on the peppers though."

"Good idea."

It was on the tip of my tongue to say, 'Next time we should try the Chinese place,' but I wasn't yet sure whether there would be a next time, or whether I wanted there to be.

chapter 52

Greg had bought the movie tickets online, and we made the movie with a few minutes to spare. I insisted on buying popcorn and soda, but when I opened my purse to pay, I was surprised, no, horrified, to realize that my wallet was not in my purse.

"Oh my God. This is crazy. I, uh, I don't have my wallet. I took it out today to pay for something online. I guess I didn't put it back in my purse." I didn't know where to look.

Greg seemed more bemused than annoyed… but still a little annoyed.

"Don't worry about it, Emily. I got it." He was gentlemanly and I convinced myself that maybe it was going to be okay.

We found our seats and the trailers started. Tyler wouldn't sit through a whole movie, and Dante was still too young to go, so this was my first visit to a cinema in several years. I was impressed with the improvements, especially the reclining seats. Usually I waited to watch big blockbusters after they were released to DVD, at home when Dante was in bed and Tyler was 'working late.' I shook my head in my comfy seat and wondered what Tyler had actually been doing while I was sitting at home watching the last *Mission Impossible* film.

The trailers had given way to the opening credits when I felt something not quite right in my stomach. It was gurgling and moving around in ways that were not good. I chalked it up to the nachos and my nerves and decided to ignore it.

Ten minutes later my stomach was at it again. A sideways glance at Greg revealed that he was engrossed in the movie. He showed no signs of hearing my stomach. The safest course of action was to excuse myself and go to the ladies' room. It was a good thing I made that decision, because by the time I sat down, what must have been the entire contents of my stomach exploded noisily out of me into the toilet. I gritted my teeth and tried to be thankful I wasn't vomiting, which would have been worse. The episode passed, but not before I had stayed in the restroom for a good five minutes. I waited for another three to make sure it was safe to leave and left the stall, hoping no one who had been within earshot of my episode was still around. Thankfully, the rest of the stalls were empty and I washed my hands in peace. Now to face Greg.

I made my way back into the theater and excused myself to the six people between our seats and the aisle. I leaned into Greg and whispered, "Sorry. My sister had a little crisis. Had to talk her down." He mumbled something back, and we both returned to watching the movie.

It did not take long for my intestines to let me know that this chapter of my evening was not over. Again, I hoped it would pass, and again I had to excuse myself, this time grabbing my purse and taking it with me. I moved gingerly and hastily past the six people who had already excused me twice, and practically ran into the restroom.

There followed a full ten minutes of agony. How could such a ridiculous thing be happening to me? I was swearing off Mexican food forever. There was no way to go back into the theater. I couldn't face Greg, who must think I was either the rudest or craziest person he had ever met. Furthermore, my stomach was not going to make it through the rest of the movie. I was going to be lucky just to make it home. I pulled out my phone to call a cab and remembered that I didn't have my wallet.

Several plans ran through my mind, including having a good cry right there in the theatre bathroom stall, but I'd already been in there long enough that a manager was soon going to come and ask me if I was all right. If that happened I was planning to flush myself down the toilet and be done with it. Goodbye cruel, spicy world.

I weighed up my actual options. I could go back in, try to last out the movie and go home as planned with Greg. But there was every probability that I would be forced to leave again, and there was the matter of explaining my absence for the past fifteen going on twenty minutes. I could try to walk home, but that seemed even stupider than trying to stay. It would take me a good hour and there was no way my intestines would last that long without ready access to facilities. The only thing left was to try to get a ride home. For the briefest of moments, I considered explaining the situation to Greg and asking him to drive me home. Then I took out my phone and texted Michelle, Clara, and Sophia, spelling out the story of how I came to be a hostage in the ladies' room at the movie theater.

Michelle – *Been drinking. Try James. He's at home.*

Clara – *Out with friends. Didn't drive. Maybe dad?*

Sophia – *Sorry Em. Watching P&P*

My finger hovered over Grace-Ann's name on the screen, but anything she knew would immediately be relayed to Amy and therefore Tyler. The last thing I needed was those two laughing at me. Desperate, I texted Zoe. No answer came back after a minute and I retexted. Then, just –

No

My options were becoming limited. I was not, not, *not* going to involve my parents. That left just James. Shit. Cautiously my thumbs tapped out a text to James –

Hey there James. It's Emily. I'm in a funny situation. I maybe have some food poisoning and I'm stuck in the movie theater at the mall with no car. Lol. Any chance you could maybe drive me home? Michelle suggested asking you.

My eyes squeezed together as I took a deep breath and hit send.

Almost immediately I saw that he was typing his reply.

Hi Emily. Of course. What door should I pick you up at?

I almost cried, this time with relief. And embarrassment, obviously.

The cinema doors, please.

And his instant reply –

Be there in 15 ☺.

That was one problem taken care of. Now to get out of here without Greg seeing me leave. I composed a text to Greg and decided not to hit send until James' car pulled up. I didn't need Greg trying to rescue me... although he hadn't even come out to check on me. Leaving him in the movie theater was rude, for sure but maybe someday it would also be kind of hilarious. It would be a great story down the road if I didn't die of embarrassment first.

After five minutes, I walked to the exterior doors of the mall, hypersensitive to the activity in my stomach. It seemed calm - this was promising.

James pulled up, and I hit send on the text to Greg. He didn't respond.

James got out and opened the door for me.

"You okay?" he looked concerned and waited for me to sit down before he closed the door.

"Yeah," I replied as he pulled away. "But James, I'm really sorry, I just can't talk about it now. I mean, I can't talk at all. My stomach is still reeling."

"No problem. I brought you a puke bowl. Just in case." At my feet sat a mixing bowl that James must have liberated from his mother's kitchen. I was relieved that he assumed my stomach problem was puking, and touched by his thoughtfulness. Without thinking, I reached over, squeezed his hand, and then immediately felt absolutely mortified. James said nothing and just drove.

Finally at home, I rummaged around in my bathroom and found some Pepto Bismol that was only slightly past its best before date. I opened it, gave it a sniff and figured it was worth a shot, and drank it straight out of the bright pink bottle.

I decided to lie down on the bathroom floor, just for a few minutes, and dozed off. I woke up to the sound of my phone buzzing, picked it up and looked at the screen. It was just past midnight. My stomach felt calm. The phone stopped buzzing just as I decided it was safe to answer. There was a missed a call from Michelle, as well as calls from Clara and Sophia. When they got no answer, all three texted asking if I was alright.

More notably, James texted about half an hour after he dropped me off –

Let me know if you need anything else. Hope you're doing okay. You can use my puke bowl anytime!

chapter 53

After rousing myself from the cold tiles, my brain scrolled through the usual playlist - *Why did Tyler leave me? Why is Amy pregnant? Why is Liam moving to Peru? Why can't I have a normal date?* The only good news was my stomach had definitely settled down. I rooted through the cupboard for some stale saltines and ginger ale, hoping the bubbles would calm my stomach.

Half an hour after eating, things felt a little better inside. I was still exhausted, but no longer felt like I was going to puke. I decided to sit and soak in the bath. Tyler's mother had given me bath stuff for Christmas a couple of years ago. Shoved way back under the sink sat the small, bright pink box from Lush, full of products just for the bath. The gift had annoyed me, partly because everything Tyler's mother did annoyed me, and partly because I didn't take baths. I drooled over the lovely things at Lush that were too expensive to justify on our budget. But there was nothing in the box I would probably ever use. Until tonight.

The scent when the box was opened was magnificent. I breathed it in and consulted the guide page that detailed each product. I picked out a pink and white swirled bath bar. The legend in the box called it 'The Comforter.' Perfect. The directions were to crumble a fifth to a quarter of the bar for lots of scent and bubbles. I used half, just for good measure. I started the water, generously crumbled in the chalky loveliness, then set off to get my pyjamas so they would be ready to slip into after the bath. I got distracted shoving saltines in my face in the kitchen, and when I returned to the bathroom, the tub was full of bubbles that had risen far above the sides of the tub and were threatening to cascade onto the floor. Many things that would have made me crazy a few months ago seemed like less of a big deal lately. I moved my pyjamas to a higher perch on the sink, quickly checked to make sure the actual hot water hadn't made it over the side of the tub, and stepped in. Lowering my body into the bubbles pushed the water to a dangerous level and the bubbles spilled even more copiously out to cover the tiles and the bathmat.

"Oh well," I said out loud to no one. "I guess I don't need to wash the floor."

I turned the tap off, slipped way down into the water and closed my eyes. The last week had gone by at breakneck speed and I didn't want to live like that anymore, at least for the foreseeable future.

With my eyes still shut, I made a list of factors that had contributed to my situation:

1. Tyler leaving. Obviously. Not much I could do about that. And it was long enough ago that it didn't really even count.

2. My father's surgery, and the disastrous conversation with my mother. I would have to try to make that right at some point. But not tonight. And not before she apologized. Just thinking about it started my anger up again.

3. The date with Liam and his subsequent decision to take a job in the Peruvian jungle. Who could have seen that coming?

4. Amy, pregnant. Ugh.

5. And now, a date with Greg that ended with diarrhea in the movie theater. How very charming.

What would all the self-help books say? *Look at the positive.* I decided to make the opposite list - five good things that had happened recently:

1. Work had improved. My new position was definitely a good thing.

2. Dante was adjusting well to his new reality. He seemed to be coping and happy. That was good.

3. Sophia was an absolute godsend and was making it possible for the first two things on the list to be true.

4. I had good friends. Both Michelle and Clara had come through in absolute spades lately.

The happy list needed one more item to make it even with the crappy list. My brain was made blurry by drowsiness and the hot water. I scanned through the past few days, looking for one more happy event to round out the list. There was the moment tonight when I grabbed James' hand in the car, it had been so intimate and at the same time so *comfortable*. He hadn't reacted to it at all, probably because I had asked him not to talk to me, and he was afraid I might puke in his car. A drowsy smile played over my face. James was the real deal.

My eyes popped open as soon as the thought was complete. James was the real deal. James. Good old James, Michelle's older brother from high school. Good old James who had twice now rescued me in the last six months when no one else would. James who schlepped through Target with me. Oh my God. He was there all along. And hadn't Clara said something about me going out with James? Something like that. Damn. I should have swiped on James instead of Greg. Suddenly it was very clear to me. I liked James. Not just liked... *Liked.* I spent five minutes playing it over it in the rapidly cooling bath and my mind came up James every time. A fresh wave of sadness and anger broke over me. Why couldn't I get anything right?

With my big toe, I flipped the drain up to let the water out of the tub, and hoisted myself out of the bath, grateful again that my reaction to the nasty nachos had passed. Wrapped in a towel, I checked my phone. No message from Greg. Fair enough. It was a pretty rude thing I did to him. He would probably never take me to Bolivia as his plus one now, but oh well. I settled down into the covers on my bed, still wrapped in the towel, my pyjamas forgotten in the bathroom.

I fell asleep and dreamed that James and I were in the Mexican restaurant at the mall. We were sitting in the same booth I had shared with Greg. Just as I was about to eat my first nacho, James held up his hands and levitated the plate out of sight. With the same magic powers, he floated down a Big Mac, a big plate of onion rings and a two-liter bottle of Dr. Pepper with an enormous straw sticking out of the top.

In the morning, I woke up late, got out of bed and slipped on the wet bathroom floor, hitting my knee on the bathtub and swearing loudly. I was almost late for my shift and it hurt to walk. Things were not heading in a good direction.

On the way to work, I deleted the dating icon on the screen of my phone, again. I told myself it was for good this time. Absolutely nothing good had come from the stupid thing. It didn't help that James was on the same dating app, and by now he had probably found and hooked up with someone else. James was handsome, and funny, and had an amazing career. He was a great catch. And I had screwed it up and missed my chance.

chapter 54

Over the following few days, my friends must have noticed my low-level rage but didn't comment. Instead, they remarked that I was becoming a recluse and made efforts to get me out of the house. Michelle offered to take me to a movie or shopping. I laughed outright at Clara when she suggested a night dancing at the bars, and she shot me back an injured look.

Zoe was light on sympathy, as usual.

"What is your problem lately?" We were clearing tables together after the lunch rush.

"Nothing. What's yours?" I didn't look at her. She was annoying me, although to be fair, everything was annoying me.

"That's what I'm talking about. You're usually nicer." Her tone was distrustful with a side order of admiration.

"Zoe, just do your job and keep your comments to yourself. You've said it before. We're not friends. We just work together." I regretted my words and my tone immediately but I wasn't backing down. Anger was proving to be a powerful motivator for me. I was still pissed off at Zoe for not helping me out when I texted her from the cinema without even offering an explanation. She was lucky she even had this job. It was me who fought to hire her back when she quit, I reminded myself. She should show a little more gratitude.

We didn't speak for the rest of the shift. Or the rest of the week. I told myself I didn't care.

My anger dulled as time went on, but not my sadness. I had completely blown it, first with the dating game, and more importantly, with James. I focused on the things within my control: being a good mom, a good friend, and a good waitress. Being a good daughter was on the back shelf. My current simmering rage would not stand me very well in a conversation with my mother. I dropped Dante off one day a week to spend a couple of hours with her and my dad. That was all she was getting.

Sophia was the first person to get me out of the house during my self-imposed funk. She used Dante to further her cause, and I was fully aware she was doing it. She asked Dante if he wanted to go to Soft Play Day, an indoor playground with lots of space to ride tricycles, and a foam maze-obstacle course. She told him, in front of me, that she would take him with Percy and Persephone if he 'and his mom' wanted to go.

"Mom, want to go to Soft Day Play with Soph and Pete and 'Sephonie?" He always got the name of the place wrong, and couldn't quite get his mouth around Persephone's name. "Sophia says we can go tomorrow. Can we? Can we mom?"

Sophia smiled at me mock-innocently.

"You're just trying to get me out of the house." I accused. Still it was sweet to see how excited Dante was about the event.

"So?" Sophia was cheerfully defiant.

"So I don't like emotional blackmail. Why didn't you just ask me?"

"You would have said no. Plus," she put on her coat and hugged Dante goodbye, "It's going to rain tomorrow, you have the day off, and it will be good for you." She stood in the doorframe. "Meet me there at ten. I'll buy you a coffee."

"You know they don't let you bring coffee into that place. They're like drill sergeants about it."

"Emily, I swear I will smuggle an entire Keurig machine in there in a suitcase and set it up in the bathroom if it will get you out of this house."

"You got yourself a deal." She started out the door and I swung Dante up onto my hip. "And Soph..."

"Yes?" She turned around.

"Thanks. I know I've been...difficult lately."

"Oh really? I didn't notice." She winked exaggeratedly at Dante and beeped her key fob to unlock the car. I closed the door and hugged Dante tighter.

We arrived at Soft Play Day just after it opened. I made it very clear to Dante that I would not be climbing to go into the play structure, because my knee was still killing me from bumping it in the bathroom. Once the three smaller members of the party had run off, Sophia hesitantly began expounding a narrative she had clearly co-created with Michelle and Clara.

"Emily?" I looked up absently from my cup of terrible three-dollar coffee that I had been forced to buy from the counter at Soft Play Day. It should have been called Soft Play Rip-Off.

"Yes?"

"Can I talk to you about something?"

"Oh God. You're not quitting, are you?" Adrenaline shot through my veins. "Is it money? I can pay you more. Not a lot more, but we can make it work. Please don't quit. I don't think I can take it, honestly."

"No, no." Sophia put her hand comfortingly on my knee. "Nothing like that. It's just that, well… Emily, are you okay? Like I mean, *really* are you okay? Because I'm kind of worried about you." She looked at me tenderly. "Michelle and Clara too." I hated the thought of them conspiring, it was impossible to be angry that they cared so much.

"I know," I focussed my eyes on the floor. "It's been so brutal lately. I just feel like I've screwed everything up, you know? I screwed up my marriage and now I've screwed up this whole dating thing. I just don't want to screw up work or Dante. He's all I have left." My voice wavered.

"You have us, you know. We're rooting for you."

"I know you are. I'm lucky to have you. All three of you." Dante ran up to me and jumped into my lap squealing with laughter. "But stop ganging up on me!...I can look out for myself, you know." I smiled a little, genuinely touched by their concern.

"We're looking out for you too." She squeezed my knee again.

"Are you coming on to me here? Is that what this is about? I put my hand on her shoulder and feigned a very sincere face. "Because I should tell you, I don't know if you've noticed, but I'm sort of into guys."

She snorted a laugh. "Maybe you'd have more luck with women. It doesn't seem like you're doing too great on the guy front."

We both laughed. Because we were laughing, the three children hanging onto us started laughing too.

"Who wants ice cream??" I called, throwing my hands in the air.

"Emily! What about lunch first?" Sophia feigned a serious face.

"Ice cream for lunch!" I called loudly. This was received very well by the children, and we were soon at Dairy Queen, throwing caution to the wind.

"You only did this because *you* wanted ice cream for lunch." Sophia accused.

"Sophia. Remember being worried about me? This is making me happy. You should be praising my efforts at self-care." I pushed the spoon down into my Skor Blizzard. "And you can tell your two partners in crime that I am fine, they should stop worrying about me, and I will even go to Michelle's stupid birthday party. Which I said no to. But now I am saying yes." I crunched Skor pieces between my teeth, "But I am *not* bringing a plus one."

"Excellent. Michelle and Sophia bet me I wouldn't get you to agree to that. I just won ten bucks."

I decided to interpret their ridiculous wager as a good sign.

chapter 55

On the day of her birthday party, Michelle texted me that Grace-Ann was going to be there, but that she would keep her away from me and I shouldn't be anxious. Little did she know that I wasn't nervous about seeing Grace-Ann. I was nervous to see James. Despite my efforts to push them aside and mask them with anger, my feelings for him were coming to a head.

Asking Sophia for help with my make-up would be a red flag to the three of them that something was up. Ditto for asking Clara to come shopping with me for a new outfit. So I had to make do with my own clothes, and my own makeup skills.

Dante would be at Tyler's until the morning after the party. Anything I said or did all evening would likely be relayed directly to Amy and Tyler by Grace-Ann via text. I told myself this was the reason I cared so much about my appearance. I arrived half an hour late, for not wanting to look too eager. Michelle hugged me and I was soon mostly at ease among her family and lots of our mutual friends. There were about thirty people at the party. I set my present, a lamp Michelle had admired at an antique market, on the table. It's not easy to wrap a lamp. She knew right away what it was and thanked me enthusiastically.

I didn't see James, and casually asked if he was coming.

"He's going to be late. He's at a job interview. A Wall Street type of thing."

"You mean, a job *like* Wall Street or a job actually *on* Wall Street?"

"I'm not sure. Maybe on Wall Street? It's in New York. He was saying it's a super good deal and they're going to set him up in an apartment. Blah blah blah. I didn't really listen that closely. Do you have a drink?" She picked up a wine glass off the buffet and filled it with sparkling wine.

"Just one. I drove." I took it and we clinked glasses.

"To your birthday," I said.

"To happy endings," Michelle said at the same time.

"I'm not sure I believe in those," I muttered under my breath as I circulated and drank my prosecco.

I wandered around the party and talked to mostly people I hadn't seen in a long time. My waitress smile was firmly in place and I discussed my life as though it were fantastic, which everyone else was probably doing too. It was painful how happy everyone else looked on Facebook compared to how I felt most of the time. I refilled my glass and continued drinking. Two glasses would be okay. I was planning on staying for at least three hours or so. That would be fine. By the third glass I was a lot happier and had decided to keep drinking and call a cab home. I put my purse, which I had been carrying around for some reason, in Michelle's room.

When I came back, I practically collided with James. It was like he had just teleported into the space immediately in front of me with absolutely no warning. My glass hit his chest and spilled out onto his sweater.

"Oh no. I'm sorry, James. Let me help you." I looked around awkwardly for something to clean up the spill.

"It's okay, Emily. Don't worry about it. How are you doing? Better I hope?" His eyes had a twinkle in them and my insides melted a little. The almost-three glasses of sparkling wine were giving me quite a lot of Dutch courage and I laughed in what was meant to be a coy or flirty way but, sounded closer to maniacal.

"Let me get you another drink and we can catch up." James took my empty glass and brought it back full.

"I heard you had a job interview today," The effects of the wine were in full force. It had been a long time since I was this tipsy.

"Yeah. They offered me the job, actually." My heart sank.

"Oh really?" I hoped my face was not giving me away.

"I'm not sure about it." He stared off to the side. "I'm not sure if I want to live in New York." He looked directly at me. "What do you think?"

I hesitated.

"I guess you have to weigh up the pros and cons." I sipped my wine too fast, trying to calm my nerves. "Is it a good job?"

"It's an amazing job. It's everything I've been hoping for professionally." He continued to gaze at me intensely and I squirmed a little inside.

"Sounds like you should take it then, I guess. It's not like you have anything tying you to here, you know, no wife or kids or anything. Do you have a girlfriend?" I was aiming for nonchalant but aware, even in the moment, that I sounded at best goofy and at worst like a complete flake.

"I don't, as it happens," he paused, still looking at me. "Emily...there's something I need to talk to you about. I've been thinking about you a lot and before I make this decision..." His eyes softened. I looked down at my glass. It was empty too quickly.

"Hold on, James. I just need another glass of prosecco. I'll be right back."

Instead of going back to James, I filled my glass and moved to a group of people as far away from him as possible. As if from outside my body, I was watching myself screw things up with James. Again. It had all seemed to be too late, and now he was offering me another chance to have the conversation I so desperately wanted to have, and I was at the other end of the party, avoiding him. I knocked back another glass of fizzy poison. What was that? Four? Five? Suddenly everything felt woozy. I wasn't used to drinking that much and suddenly decided to go into Michelle's room to sit down for a moment to collect my thoughts.

I intended to just put my head down on Michelle's bed for a few minutes, but instead fell fast asleep. A very startled Michelle woke me up when she came into her room to retrieve a coat about an hour later.

"Emily! What are you doing here? We all thought you'd left!"

I blinked. My head felt fuzzy.

"I guess I fell asleep. I was a little bit tipsy." I shook my head, trying to wake up.

"You were more than a little bit tipsy...Come on." She gave me a hand and helped me to my feet. I walked out into the seemingly blinding light of what was left of the party. There were three or four people left, including Grace-Ann and James. Mostly people from high school, the old faithfuls.

James shot me a surprised smile. "I thought you left."

"Emily, maybe take a trip to the powder room?" Grace-Ann's smile was genuine, and not even a little snarky. What I saw in the mirror made me very relieved she had not taken a picture. My hair was a disaster and my makeup looked like The Walking Dead. I cleaned it up as best I could and went back to face the rest of the party.

"I thought I'd go with the Heath Ledger look this evening, everyone. What do you think?" I gave a little twirl.

"I'd say the hair is more like *Something About Mary*," quipped Michelle. There were various other suggestions, all funny, and good-natured laughter. I sat down, among friends, and joined in reminiscing about high school and before. It was comfortable. Partly because of the lingering effects of the alcohol, I felt a happy camaraderie for the first time in a long time.

I avoided James' eyes during the conversation, unable to face him, and worried I had messed things up for good. This might be my last chance tonight, especially if he was moving to New York. Then it would definitely be too late.

Most people were leaving, and James offered to drive me home.

"Oh, James, you don't have to do that..." I decided to at least pretend to protest.

"I insist. It's no trouble. You're in no shape to drive, that's for sure."

He was definitely right about that. I had put back another glass of prosecco since rejoining the party and my head was very fuzzy. I was terrified of the conversation we were about to have, but even more scared that we wouldn't have the conversation.

Once we were in the car, the silence strangled me. I had to tell him that I wanted to talk to him.

James pulled up to my house.

"There you go, Emily. Thanks for coming tonight. I know Michelle really appreciates it. You mean a lot to her, you know." This time it was his hand covering mine on the console. "And to me." He looked at me. I didn't pull my hand away. This was it.

"James, do you want to come in and, uh, talk? I'm sorry I ran away from you at the party. I was scared." My voice was barely above a whisper.

"I'd like that." His voice was soft too. In the short walk from the car to the door, every emotion from the last six months flooded through me in rapid succession. I thought I might pass out.

I opened the door, turned on the lights, and showed James into the living room.

"Can I get you a drink? I have water or apple juice...various diet sodas."

"No thanks. I'm okay. Emily. Sit down." I sat in the chair opposite where he was perched on the sofa. "No, sit here with me. Please. I want to talk to you."

I moved to sit beside him. He took both my hands in his.

"Look at me, Emily. I need you to hear what I'm saying." It was torture but my eyes met his, and I felt more vulnerable than I could remember. "Emily, I don't know if you know this. I've had feelings for you for a long time." I turned my head away and he gently moved my chin back with his finger. "A *long* time. Since high school."

"What? What do you mean since high school? I never knew that." I was confused. The conversation was not going where it was supposed to go. He had thrown me for a loop.

"No one knew... well, except Michelle actually." I was shocked.

"What?! She never said..."

"I swore her to secrecy. She caught me once, writing a letter I was going to send you in the mail. And she convinced me not to send it. Promised that if I didn't, she would keep the secret." My head was spinning. "It was when you were with Tyler. In the beginning. Michelle thought it would just make you angry. She's been rooting for me all along, you know..." he trailed off. I sat in dazed silence.

"I've had these feelings for you, as I said, for a long time. And when you married Tyler, well, it broke my heart, Emily. It devastated me in fact. When you had Dante...I had always hoped that *we* would have a family. You and I.

And then I saw you have a family with Tyler...so I left. That's why I took a job in Atlanta. I couldn't bear to watch it. I hoped that if I moved far enough away, I'd meet someone else and forget about you."

"And did you? Meet someone else?" My voice was small and timid.

"I met a few people, yeah. But no one who I cared about as much as you. I tried, you know. To forget you. I even made a profile on a dating app. But nothing really stuck."

"I know about that, actually." I grinned at him sheepishly. "The dating app. I saw it. 'Haven't been sprayed by a skunk for ten years...'" My fingers mocked him with air quotes. "I was on that app too."

James looked at me, intrigued. "I didn't see you on there."

"I swiped you left, like, the first day I joined... I guess at that point I wasn't thinking about you like that. You were just James, you know, Michelle's brother. I guess I friend-zoned you pretty hard in high school."

"I've been well aware of that for a long time, I assure you." His eyes sparkled at me. "So to finish the story, when I heard you and Tyler were finished, I came home. I had to give it one more try. And then nothing was happening, and you were dating other people. I got this job offer today and...I decided to give it one more shot tonight, to let you know how I felt, and if you didn't want to be with me, I would go to New York."

"That's why they were trying so hard to get me to the party," I said softly.

"Yes. Michelle knew about my plan. She thought it was a good one. She thought if she could get you to the party then I would have a chance to talk to you there. When you asked about a girlfriend, I thought that was the right time."

"And then I ran away from you." Suddenly I was very sober. My hands gripped his. "But I'm here now."

Awkwardly, and in the bumpiest way possible, James leaned forward and kissed me. I waited for the fairy-tale feeling but mostly just felt terrified.

"James, the stakes are very high for me here. I have to think of Dante. I don't know if this is such a good idea."

"Emily, I *have* thought about Dante. I have worried I might not like him. I was scared to take him to McDonald's that day because I was afraid he wouldn't like *me*."

"He did like you." I smiled. "But mostly because you took him to McDonald's."

"I will take him to McDonald's every day for the rest of my life. That's a promise." James was earnest. I laughed.

"You can take him to McDonald's once a week," I started, "But he has to get the book instead of the toy in the Happy Meal."

"Done. McDonald's no more than once a week. Book in the happy meal. Got it."

"But *me*... you have to take me out to a real restaurant once a week. And not a greasy spoon either...but I do love greasy spoons, actually. So I guess *sometimes* a greasy spoon. And I get to pick the restaurants, except sometimes you have to surprise me with something better than what I thought of."

"Have you finished?" asked James. "Should I get a piece of paper, or maybe contact a notary public to draw this up?"

"Oh no. I'm only beginning my list of demands. I'm very high-maintenance. Are you sure you're up for this?"

"Very." James moved in to kiss me again and this time it worked. There was more kissing. Then there was kissing in the hallway. And then, in the bedroom, the laundry was pushed onto the floor with reckless abandon and the two of us were kissing, and then tangled up, and then kissing again. Afterward, for the first time in forever, loneliness wasn't the last thing I felt when I drifted off to sleep.

chapter 56

The smell of bacon cooking woke me up the next morning. I took me several seconds to remember what had happened the night before. I stumbled out into the kitchen, cinching my robe around my waist on the way.

"Hey," my voice was croaky with sleep. "What time is it?"

My eyes blinked several times, surprised to see James at the stove, and Dante at the kitchen table. I was suddenly fully awake.

"Dante! When did you get there?" I looked in alarm at James who was relaxed as he flipped pancakes.

"Tyler dropped him off half an hour ago. He said you were supposed to pick him up? I told him you were in the shower. We're getting along just fine though, aren't we Dante?"

"Yup! James put chocolate chips in the pancakes."

"James," I walked to the table and wrapped Dante in a bear hug, "is just trying to win you over, little man. How about we go to Target later? James knows where the DVD's are." I winked at Dante, and he did an exaggerated wink back, closing both his eyes instead of one.

"Sounds good to me." James must have been up for a while. He was showered and dressed, albeit in the same clothes from last night but he looked presentable. Actually, he looked great.

I took a deep breath that wasn't a sigh. This felt like it might be okay. It might actually be good. Maybe things were finally turning around. All the mistakes I made with Tyler had come together and given me one amazing result – Dante. Now, all the mistakes I had made since Tyler left had led to one more good thing – James. Maybe I hadn't completely messed things up after all. I cracked open a Dr. Pepper.

"Are you kidding? For breakfast?" said James. "There's juice, you know."

"Put that on the list of my demands. Dr. Pepper whenever requested."

"You got it." James hugged me and Dante came and jumped onto my leg. I closed my eyes, shoved all the ways this could go wrong into a mason jar, and focused on all the ways it felt right.

chapter 57

The only Magnolia tree on the block had already bloomed and lost its flowers in a thunderstorm. The swimsuits were on full display at Target and Kohl's, and the ice cream trucks were tentatively emerging on the street by the park.

We invited James' family and my family along with Sophia with Percy and Persephone, to my birthday party. After Michelle's birthday, I brokered a tentative peace with my mother, mediated by James, who Mom had always liked and admired. Her anger about my choice to date was mitigated by *who* I was dating, and she told Clara, in confidence, that she had always preferred James to Tyler anyway.

Michelle was forgiven for keeping James' secret all those years. "I cannot believe you kept that from me for all those years. What if you had told me earlier and James and I could have been together all this time?"

"That is utter bullshit and you know it. You would never have been into him in high school. He was a geeky math guy and you were only interested in dumb jocks like Tyler. If he had sent that letter he wrote, it would have been the end of any chance you two had." She looked at me and pointed in her usual way, "I was right. Admit it."

"Yes! I admit it. You were right. Again." I hugged her again, tighter.

At the party, once everyone had eaten and was in good spirits, James touched his glass lightly with his dessert spoon.

"Everyone, Emily and I have something to tell you." An expectant hush fell over the room.

"I'm selling this house." I saw my father put his hand on my mother's knee just as she opened her mouth to say something, and her mouth closed silently. "Tyler has given me a few more months to pay him out. I'm going to list in July and try for a closing date at the end of August."

Dante had been sworn to secrecy until this moment and could hold it in no more.

"And then we're getting married!" he cried in his three-year-old squeal.

"Yes. We're getting married." James asserted happily, meeting my eyes. My father's hand tightened on my mother's knee, and her lips disappeared.

"Congratulations!!" Michelle cried immediately, and suddenly the room was full of hugs and happy tears.

After the announcement, there were cards, and gifts of books and coffee mugs and candles. James put a large gift-wrapped package from behind the couch into my hands. It was heavy and squishy. I tore back the paper and gasped.

"The Royal Star," I whispered. It was the quilt, the exact quilt I had admired at the craft fair with Michelle in the fall.

"Do you like it?" James sounded anxious.

"Like it? It's amazing. How did you know? Where did you ever find it again?" I burst into tears and hugged James.

When I had composed myself, Michelle said, "The lady gave me the card, remember? And then I wrote down the one you liked on the back. I had a hunch it might come in handy." I rushed over and hugged her too, through more tears, hers and mine.

"Mom, why are you crying?" Dante stopped playing with his friends and looked over, concerned.

"Honey, sometimes grown-ups cry when they are happy."

"Grown-ups are weird," we heard Percy tell Persephone in an exaggerated whisper.

I hugged the quilt to myself and opened it up to show everyone the pattern. As I unfolded it, an envelope with my name scrawled on it fell out onto the floor. James smiled at me, his own eyes a little teary.

"Is this what I think it is?" I asked James in wonder.

"I kept it all these years. I always hoped I'd be able to give it to you. But don't read it now. Save it for later."

"I like that. I like the idea of later." I put my arms around his neck and whispered into his ear. "As long as later means I'll be with you."

the end

about the author

Elizabeth Allison lives in London, Canada with her husband, their four teenagers, two Golden Retrievers, and an indifferent cat. She has been an educator for 25 years and currently serves as an Elementary School Principal. Elizabeth drinks a lot of coffee and eats a lot of cupcakes. She enjoys planning Disney vacations and beating her brothers at poker. *Emily's New Everything* is her second novel, the first to be published with Black Rose Writing.

note from the author

Word-of-mouth is crucial for any author to succeed. If you enjoyed *Emily's New Everything*, please leave a review online—anywhere you are able. Even if it's just a sentence or two. It would make all the difference and would be very much appreciated.

Thanks!
Elizabeth Allison

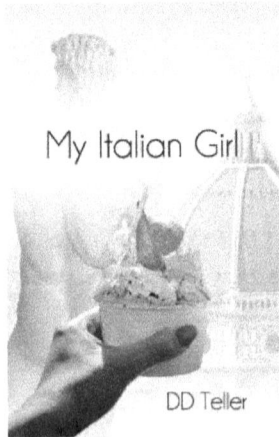